DEAD DROP

Julia McAllister Mysteries
Book Four

Marilyn Todd

SAPERE
BOOKS

DEAD DROP

Published by Sapere Books.

20 Windermere Drive, Leeds, England, LS17 7UZ,
United Kingdom

saperebooks.com

ISBN: 978-1-80055-435-1

For Susi and Eva-Maria.
The roots of our friendship run deep.
Almost down to their natural colour...

CHAPTER 1

On the bridge across from Oakbourne canal, Julia McAllister paused. Behind her lay the narrow, cobbled streets and fine half-timbered houses that comprised the genteel side of the town. In front rose the mass of factories, refineries, gas works and mills that comprised the other half. A dark world, shrouded not just by the fug coughing out of the chimneys, stinking the air with soot and sulphur, but by misery, poverty, and pain.

Julia rubbed her pounding temples. Four weeks ago, approaching a moneylender had seemed a good idea. Four weeks ago, she hadn't imagined the extortionate interest rate would spiral out of hand —

Julia had run out of luck. Her photography studio was no longer keeping her afloat. At first, when her employer, friend, mentor, and owner of Whitmore Photographic Studio had died, Julia had managed to keep up a pretence. She placed advertisements in the *Oakbourne Chronicle*, modernised the equipment, enhanced the backdrops, and installed a telephone at hideous expense.

All of which counted for nothing. As far as the good folk of Oakbourne were concerned, Sam Whitmore would make an appointment then fail to turn up, leaving his hapless assistant to muddle through the best that she could. Never mind that her work was good.

When it came to excuses, her creativity knew no bounds. Her employer was suffering from gout / influenza / a bellyache / migraines. He was recovering in the Sanitorium. He'd slipped a disc. Broken his leg. Was visiting his invalid mother in

Edinburgh / his grandmother in York / his uncle in Wales, or burying his father / his aunt / his sister / his son, take your pick. In fact, the poor man suffered more trials and tribulations after death than he ever experienced in life, but the upshot was the same. This once-esteemed photographer had become unreliable. People took their custom elsewhere.

Sam Whitmore had taken Julia in at the lowest point in her life, becoming not just her mentor, but father-figure, confidante and friend. He listened without judgement, gave love without condition, and then, right when Julia thought his generosity couldn't stretch any further, bequeathed her the business when he died. The photographic studio downstairs that still bore his name — but that was the problem, wasn't it? For all the advances in women's suffrage, this was still a man's world.

Putting china dogs in the studio window had turned the tables for a while. Skye terriers and sheepdogs had proved especially popular, catching the kids' eyes and luring their mothers inside. This snared a few christenings, the odd wedding and a couple of portraits — but nowhere near enough to keep the wolfhound from the door.

Just when she was at her wits' end, though, she was offered a contract to supply nude photographs. Setting up a secret studio across town, it was an easy switch from run-of-the-mill poses to flip books, where you thumb through at speed so it looked like the girls were teasing off their clothes in real time. Lust became the lynchpin of Julia's independence. It paid the bills, allowed her to take photographs for pleasure, indulge in adding artistic touches to her portraits, and, more importantly, save enough money to capture Niagara Falls in full flow, the Pyramids at sunrise and the Grand Canyon at sunset.

Until her models were picked off one by one, and she found herself framed for their murders.

Even though she convinced the authorities that she had no involvement in the "French postcard" business, to the point where the police now paid her to take scene of crime photos, the investigation led to the operation being shut down. It also cost Julia her savings, every last farthing, and, without an income, soon everyone from the butcher and the baker to the candlestick maker was threatening to call in the bailiffs.

Julia's focus shifted to the waterway below — a ribbon of locks and winches, depots and barges, populated by watery nomads who had their own dress code and culture. The lives of the bargees were tough and their livelihoods were precarious, but they had the one thing Julia would give her right arm for at the moment — their freedom.

With a deep breath, she pushed back her shoulders, and headed into the stench.

'Meess McAllister.' The smile from the man surrounded by crates, pulleys and chains was as false as his words. 'I am sorry to kip you waiting.'

Some said his parents were refugees from Sebastopol. Others said he came from Moscow, some claimed Odessa, a few even suggested Siberia, and, depending on who you spoke to, he'd been in England for ten years, twenty years, forty if his parents had truly escaped the Crimea.

'Not at all, Mr. Kuznetsov.' Julia deliberately kept her eyes off the blood on the warehouse floor. 'I passed the interval in most pleasant conversation with your colleague here.'

One eyebrow rose lazily. 'Then you had more success than moss visitors,' the Russian drawled. 'Malik iss more — how do you say? The quiet type.'

Julia felt a lot of words suited Malik better. Thug topping the list. 'I confess, most of the chitchat in the yard was on my part.' She forced a girlish giggle. 'You know how we women love to talk.'

Or in this case, override the sounds of fists connecting with noses and ribs. There were drag marks on the floor, too, where they'd scraped the poor sod away. Had he shopped his boss to the police? Dipped his fingers in the till? Suppose it was a borrower who'd welched on his debt…?

Kuznetsov crossed his fat arms over his chest. 'You haff my money?'

'Tomorrow.' Keep it light. Don't let him see fear. 'That's what I came to tell you.'

'You are aware off the consequences off failure?'

'You take my studio.'

'And?'

'I work for you.'

'Exactly.' He smoothed his lapels and walked to the door, more factory owner than ruthless loan shark. 'Until tomorrow, Meess McAllister. In the meantime, Malik will explain the nature of the work you will be undertaking, eef the first instalment fails to materialise.'

Julia screwed her handkerchief into a twist. *How in God's name had it come to this?* 'Get your greasy hand off me!' She tried to pull away, but Malik's grip on her breast clamped tighter.

'There's an 'ouse down the docks, where men like posh bits like you.'

'Take. Your. Hand. Off. Me.'

'Or what, luv?' He grabbed her other breast and squeezed both until she cried out. 'Tomorrow,' he whispered. 'Don't be late, 'cause one way or another, you'll be makin' a payment.'

CHAPTER 2

Julia was still shaking long after she'd run home, ripped off her clothes and burned them. Long after she'd thrown up three times and scrubbed her skin raw. Long after she'd stood at her bedroom window all night, and was now watching the sun rise behind the little Saxon church of St. Oswald.

Worry won't take away the pain of tomorrow, JJ. It merely drains today of its strength.

The wisdom of a man who'd been five years in his grave echoed in Julia's memory. Good old Sam. No matter what life threw at him, he took the rough with the smooth, rolled with the punches, and came up smelling of roses. All *she* could smell was the dust and blood in Kuznetsov's warehouse, and Malik's beery breath on her face.

Her eyes stung, and the rays on the church steeple blurred. In the street below, a small girl in a ragged shawl was selling four bunches of watercress for a penny. Costermongers hauling green-painted barrows with trademark red wheels peddled everything from pollack to peas, while the organ grinder cranked the same tune over and over.

Ding!

Before the shop bell finished tinkling, Julia was running downstairs, smoothing her hair and her skirts. *Please let this be the morning paper! Please let the advertisement be running!*

'Miss McAllister?'

Sadly, paper boys don't swan around in fine tailoring or speak with cultured, clipped accents. They don't narrow their eyes, purse their lips, or have backs stiffer than pokers. And most of them grow out of the job long before they reach fifty. Still. If it helped a Pekingese find a new shelf…

'Mrs.' Julia's surname was fake anyway, so she might as well make it respectable. 'What can I do for you this lovely spring morning?'

'I'm hoping you can help me.'

'I know I can.' Julia had not met a man yet who didn't need help choosing presents — and never mind a tall and distinguished one, with the neatest clipped grey beard this side of the Andes. The silk lapels on that tailored frockcoat said Maltese Terrier as well as a Pekingese, and possibly a Schnauzer as well.

'I believe you undertake certain photographic commissions for the Boot Street constabulary?'

So much for Crufts. 'I do.' Admittedly, the profit margins were lower than the calls for her services, most murders being clear-cut, without the need to preserve evidence. But when calls did come, it was a bloody sight more interesting than Borzois and poodles.

'Then perhaps you might be able to tell me about the body they found on the railway this morning.'

What body? 'Ah, well, that's the thing, Mr —?'

'Vance.' He held out a finely gloved hand. 'Titus Vance.'

'I'm not allowed to discuss my cases.' If there was one lesson she'd learned since taking over from Sam, maintaining an image was everything.

'Of course, of course.' His dark eyes flickered from portrait to portrait on the walls. 'I wouldn't dream of putting you in a difficult position, only —' His eyes paused on a wedding where, thanks to Julia's judicious use of angles and light, it was impossible to tell the bride was six months pregnant. 'It's my son.'

'Your son's dead? Mr. Vance, I'm so sorry —'

'Ah, no, you misunderstand me. My fault, entirely, I should have explained myself better.' He dug into his pocket and brought out a photograph. 'This is my boy, and he —' Vance broke off to compose himself. Julia waited. 'He has not been home for three days. Naturally, I've enquired of his friends, at the hospital, and his place of work. I've shown his picture round the railway station, the bus stops, the library, the bank, the shops, in fact everywhere I can think of, but to put it bluntly, Mrs. McAllister, my son has, quite simply, vanished into thin air. The instant I heard about the body on the London line, I rushed to the police station, but the desk sergeant refused to give out any information. I can't begin to tell you how deeply that response alarmed me, and I thought … perhaps … well … you have connections. If, by some chance, you recorded the scene —?'

'I didn't. I'm sorry.'

His mouth shifted sideways. 'It's the uncertainty and … dare I say, the fear. I can't eat. I can't sleep. I know it sounds foolish, but the sheer helplessness —'

'There's nothing foolish about loving your son, or worrying about what might have befallen him, Mr. Vance.'

'You're very kind.' He almost smiled. 'Which is why I have a terribly big favour to ask.' He passed her the photo with a shaking hand. 'I realise it's a grave imposition, but if you could show this to the officers at Boot Street, perhaps even the mortuary attendant, I can at least rule out that the victim isn't my son.'

'Consider it done.' Limbo was a torment far worse than grief. In limbo, the imagination runs wild, and the pictures it draws are not pretty.

'Thank you. Thank you so much, you don't know what this means to me. The police see this picture, and think *three days is nothing for a man of thirty-three not to come home*, but —' He smoothed his striped silk tie. 'They don't know the circumstances. You recall the train crash at Hampton Wick?'

'Vaguely.' She'd never heard of it.

'Nine years ago, why would you remember? But for my son and myself, it could be last week, because that broken axle broke our hearts, too. My wife and daughter-in-law were both killed in the derailment. Afterwards, my son moved back into the family home, and while some might say we lead terribly staid lives, routine dulls the pain. Every day without fail, we take breakfast together, we take lunch together, we take supper together, so you can believe me when I tell you he would not go absent without at least leaving a note.'

Julia's heart twisted. 'Then you've come to the right place, Mr. Vance. I am personally acquainted with Detective Inspector Collingwood at Boot Street; in fact, I'll go round straight away. Once I've passed on the facts, I'm sure he'll give your case top priority.'

No one knew heartache and loss more than John Collingwood. If anyone could give Vance an outcome, it was him.

The instant Vance left, any fine intentions of dashing to Boot Street popped with the delivery of the *Chronicle*. A travelling circus was in town and they had placed an advertisement looking for rooms for their girls. Within ten seconds, Julia was pinning on her hat and giving a racehorse a run for its money.

The exotic tent rose up from the Common. Navigating a minefield of ropes, poles and boards, Julia couldn't help noticing the swarm of matrons, housewives, servants and governesses who had found an excuse to deviate from routine. By coincidence, most of those excuses were hauling on poles, their corded muscles testing the strength of their soft cotton shirts.

'Excuse me.' Julia's heart was pounding as she pushed through the crush of bombazine, straw boaters and leg o'mutton sleeves, and not from this wretched corset that clearly doubled as a boa constrictor. 'Coming through.'

'Oi, Miss!'

Typical. No sooner had she broken through the petticoat army than she was mobbed by a gang of grimy urchins, none of them older than eight.

'Is there really ponies 'ere like the ones in Lord George Sanger's show? The ones that tell fortunes by reading alphabet cards? Me dad swears he saw a wolf boy, half-human, half-beast, biting the heads off live frogs. Wasn't pulling my leg, was he, Miss?'

Julia glanced at the posters nailed to what seemed like every tree round the Common, and pasted on virtually every lamp post and wall in the town.

BUFFALO BUCK'S MILD WEST SPECTACULAR!

Genuine re-enactments of
the Klondike Mould Rush,
the Deadwood Stooge,
and Custard's Last Stand.

Should she tell them she wasn't part of the troupe? 'Your father's mistaken.' She paused and watched disappointment cloud their bulging, star-struck eyes. 'It was live hedgehogs.'

'Cor!'

'Even better!'

'Me dad's seen eagles in a gold cage what recites the Psalms, too. An' a real Cherokee squaw, wot catches cannonballs in her hands like John Holtum.'

Julia prayed to God the child's father would never be called to court as a witness.

'What about cannibal pygmies?' another boy piped up. 'Lord George has them, too.'

'Don't suppose you boyos could help me?' The Welsh lilt belonged to a young woman in a soft, broad-rimmed cowboy hat. With a fringed leather skirt that fell just past her knees, she was attracting more than her fair share of scowls from the women, whistles from the men and, now, open-mouthed stares from the boys. 'I need volunteers to pass round these flyers.' The leaflets were out of her hand before you could blink. 'Saw your camera,' she told Julia. 'Thought a rescue might be in order.'

Julia's Box Brownie camera was of little use when it came to portraits, but it smoothed the way to many an introduction, and was the perfect prop to underline her profession. 'You thought right.' She held out her hand. 'Julia McAllister.'

'Annie Oaktree.'

'I should have guessed!'

The big, brown eyes under the hat were smiling and kind. 'Buck wasn't expecting you reporter types till this afternoon, but if you go on inside, I'll find 'im and tell 'im you're here.'

'Thank you.' Lies by omission were becoming a habit this morning. Then again, when weren't lies a habit these days?

Threading her way towards the tent, Julia imagined the impresario to be tall and stocky, with a handlebar moustache fronting a loud, booming voice, coupled with a propensity for strong liquor and even stronger women. Showmen were rarely shy and retiring types — least of all those staging a show that boasted live appearances from Kwyatt Burp, Doc Vacation and Crazy Hearse. But whether he was short and bald, or ancient and wizened, Buffalo Buck was either going to turn Mount Everest into a gentle sloping hill — or have Julia praying Kuznetsov's men weren't watching the station when she made a run for it.

Inside the pavilion, which somehow seemed to have quadrupled in size, more men were hard at it, lugging in rows of bench seating, bracketing stanchions together, and unfurling backdrops of red Utah deserts and Wild West saloons. With the show opening tomorrow, it was hardly surprising that dress rehearsals were already underway. On Julia's left, a girl in an outrageously tight, white spangled outfit was stepping into an upright cabinet, while a handsome riverboat gambler, with glossy dark locks and flowing black frock coat, opened and closed the front to prove that this was just an ordinary door. On Julia's right, a man with Jack-the-lad dimpled cheeks and oversized holsters on his hips, juggled what, from this distance, appeared to be six Chelsea buns.

She really must get her eyes tested.

Meanwhile the magician's assistant was pushing her tangle of red curls through a cut-out in the door, squeezing her right hand through another hole at hip height. Bursting into a song that couldn't be heard for the hammering, she waggled her fingers to prove that yes, it really was her.

Across the way, the gunfighter fumbled his juggling act, and could you blame him, when the canvas wall next to him was still flapping? Julia turned back to the riverboat gambler, eyes popping from their sockets when he pushed the central section of the cabinet sideways, creating a gap where the mid-section of his assistant's body had been. Julia blinked. The girl's head was still poking through the cut-out in the top. No mistaking those frizzy locks! She was singing, moving her eyebrows and rolling her eyes, yet the hand in the box that was now out to the side was waving like crazy.

'Clever, isn't it?' piped up a pretty blonde, encased in a mass of red feathers and frills, and a skirt even shorter than Annie Oaktree's.

'They can't have modified the back of the cabinet, to make it look as though there's a space in the middle.' Julia squinted. 'Or the gambler couldn't pass his hand through the gap where his assistant's navel should be. And it isn't a mechanical hand, or the fingers couldn't curl and wiggle.' Holy smoke, now he was sticking his head between the top and bottom boxes to prove there was nothing between them except air. 'How does he do that?'

'Are you from the newspaper?' the saloon girl asked.

'No.'

'In that case — promise you won't tell a soul?'

'Cross my heart.'

'Only Dodge and I would lose our jobs, if Buck found out I'd been giving state secrets away.'

'Dodge?'

'Dodger. My husband.' She pointed to the juggler. 'The bunslinger.'

Julia laughed. 'Of course. The Hot Cross Kid. I've seen it on the flyers.'

The reason music halls were exploding in popularity — there were over three hundred in London alone — was because humour crossed every age, social divide and, it had to be said, persuasion. In the bawdy thrall of cross-dressing comedians, high-kicking showgirls, magicians, illusionists and, yes, clairvoyant ponies, toffs and clerks rubbed elbows with packers and smelters, eating, drinking and laughing together at long plank tables, happy to put their worries behind them, if only for a few short hours. Julia could see why. In the space of just a few short minutes, she'd been so mesmerised by jugglers and illusionists that she, too, had almost forgotten why she was here.

But only almost.

'Hey, Honky-Tonk!' The bunslinger put two fingers in his mouth and let out a whistle. 'Do us a favour and get your lardy arse over here, will ya? My rhythm's gone to pot from that bleedin' racket outside.'

'Delighted, old bean.' The lardy arse in question was up a stepladder, holding the backdrop in place. As it happened, he was a dead-ringer for the Prince of Wales when he was younger, with his long, oval face, kind eyes and pointed beard, but more pertinently, he made the average lawn rake look chubby. 'Just as soon as the Grand Canyon stops slipping.'

'Uh-oh. Don't think that's going to be for a while,' the blonde whispered to Julia. 'If you'll excuse me, I'll go and set the rhythm for Dodge.'

'You play that contraption?' Julia pointed at the upright piano.

'Gosh, no. But I'm very good at clapping! I say, you haven't seen my fan, have you? I could have sworn I left it on the props box.'

'Would that be it?'

'Honestly, I'll forget my own face one of these days!'

As she skipped off, light as one of her own feathers, Julia's attention returned to the riverboat gambler. With a *whoosh!*, he clicked the central section back into place, at which point the redhead wriggled her face and hand back inside, then stepped out, her showgirl smile as wide as a house.

'I see you've met Avalon,' a voice drawled in her ear. 'I honestly couldn't imagine this show without her.'

This was it, then. Win or lose. Do or die. All or nothing…

Heart pounding, she turned, and sod carefully rehearsed conversations. One look at the showman, and Julia did something she'd never done in her life.

She fainted.

CHAPTER 3

Degas, Renoir, Monet and Manet were all famous for painting true-to-life scenes that captured mood, rather than detail. The movement, which started twenty years earlier, when Julia was a small child, became known as Impressionism, and quickly grew in popularity. Ten years later, though, a new band of artists emerged, with the likes of Gauguin, Rousseau and Cézanne rejecting naturalistic depictions in favour of vivid colours and distorted, geometric shapes. But not even Van Gogh's *Sunflowers* were as surreal as Julia coming round under a red and white sky, staring into the face of a dead man.

'I'm not sure you've quite got the hang of this showbusiness lark,' the ghost was saying. 'It's me who's supposed to make the dramatic entrances.'

'I'm not sure you've got the hang of this encounters with the gentler sex lark. Don't you know it's bad manners to undress a girl before you've been introduced?'

In the cold light of reason, it was obvious the man loosening the buttons of her high, frilly collar wasn't Sam Whitmore. For one thing, he was ten years younger, his face was more round, and his eyes were dark, where Sam's had been blue. But with his swirling moustache, goatee beard and shoulder-length hair, Buffalo Buck had turned himself into the spitting image of William F. Cody — just as Sam Whitmore had, after travelling the real American West and photographing his hero.

'My mother always said, if you see an opportunity, son, take it.'

'And *my* mother said that when opportunity knocks, pretend to be out.'

With a deep, throaty chuckle, the showman helped her to her feet. 'Feeling better?'

'You mean, reeling better.'

'I assure you, I'm the one who's reeling. From flattery.' He shot her a sideways grin. 'It's not every day that young ladies swoon at my devilishly handsome good looks.'

Julia very much doubted that. She imagined an awful lot of them slept with his billboard under their pillow, and, judging by the crush outside, not all of them terribly young.

'You'll be pleased to know your virtue is safe now. I make it a rule not to undo more than the top four buttons on a first date. Let's step into my office, we'll sit you down and then, if you're up to it, we can do the interview for the paper.'

'This is your office?'

'Don't you like it? I'll have you know, it's the quietest corner of the tent.'

'I assume, since the tent's round, that you're used to cutting corners?'

'Not when it comes to the show, and you can quote me on that in your column. Oh, and you might want to add that it's not so much a gunfight at the OK Corral, more a frosty altercation, in which the outlaws end up with a lot of holes punched in their arguments.'

'Save the quote for later, I'm not from the paper. I'm responding to your request for accommodation.'

'Excellent.' He tipped his hat back. 'The God-fearing citizens of Oakbourne seem stubbornly indisposed to hosting a bunch of desperadoes under their roof, even more so when it comes to the ladies. They have this disquieting assumption that my girls are on the game, and since this is the fourth time I've had to place the advertisement, I am especially grateful to you, Miss —?' He took the proffered visiting card. 'Beg your pardon, *Mrs.* McAllister —'

'Sorry to interrupt, mate.' A delivery driver in corduroy trousers twisted his face. 'You sure this is all the hay you want? Only for a Wild West show, one bundle don't seem very much.'

'My dear sir, that is the exact amount of hay my cowboys need to feed their night mares.'

'Night mares!' The frown turned into a laugh so wide, you could see both of the driver's teeth. 'That's funny. Must tell the Missus, coz she ain't half looking forward to when you open tomorrow.'

'Then here. Two front row seats, on the house.' The showman turned back to Julia. 'Sorry about that.'

'How grateful?'

'Excuse me?'

'You said you were especially grateful for my putting your girls up.'

'Let. Me. Guess.' His dark eyes assessed the clouds of feathers, tulle and fresh flowers perched on top of Julia's head, moved slowly past her pin-striped lavender jacket to the shine on the boots peeping out from her matching box-pleat skirt. 'You wish to double the going rate for board and lodging?'

'No, but in return for having my neighbours think I'm running some kind of bawdy house, I have certain conditions.'

'I trust they're not contagious.'

'Only insofar as you'd have to take the medicine twice a day, Mr —?'

'Buck. Just Buck.'

'Because as long as this tent is in town, I would ask that once a day you drop by my studio and pretend you're my employer with a head cold, and then, between performances, to escort me round Oakbourne and possibly beyond, so that various local shopkeepers see us.'

'Hm.' He twirled his moustache, twizzled his pistols. None of which fooled Julia one little bit. 'Correct me when I go wrong, but your business card reads Whitmore Photographic, yet your name is McAllister, and since you, and you alone, are conducting these negotiations, I assume that you, and you alone, are running the business?'

She held his gaze without blinking.

'Which suggests that your employer is no longer around — I'm guessing died, rather than a moonlight flit, or you wouldn't have a business left to run — and, judging by your reaction to me, he and I share certain physical similarities.'

He turned his eyes on Dodger, whose cheeky-chappie features were now clouded by a scowl, while Avalon studiously packed his fake Chelsea buns into a box.

'Taking silence as affirmative, I'm deducing that you're not the first woman who finds herself swimming against the tide in a man's world, and debts must be mounting. Why else would you offer board and lodgings to a bunch of gypsies, tramps and thieves? Then wait until I've advertised for a fourth time?'

'Which evens the score, Mr. Buck, now that you know I need you as much as you need me.'

'Like I said — just Buck.'

'Very well, Just Buck. Now that we both know where we stand, do we have an agreement? Two female lodgers at the going rate, with you impersonating Sam Whitmore twice a day?'

'Three female lodgers, and I'll be Whitmore once a day.'

'Three, and you live up to your boast of being a twice-a-day man.'

For the first time, the showman's laughter was genuine. 'Deal.' His hand, as they shook, was warm through her glove. 'Now come and meet the girls.'

When Buffalo Bill was invited to perform at the American Exhibition in London, his shows attracted crowds of over thirty thousand, and were so impressive that the Prince of Wales even persuaded his mother to attend. This, remember, was the first time Her Majesty Queen Victoria had attended a public performance since being widowed twenty years before, and was so taken with the experience that she asked Mr. Cody to perform at her Golden Jubilee in front of several other European monarchs.

Following Buck through the labyrinth of bench seating, nine years flew away. Julia and Sam had just settled in Oakbourne, new technology having rendered the need to develop photographic plates within ten minutes redundant. To celebrate the death of their itinerant lifestyle and the birth of a brand new darkroom and studio, they took the train to London, followed the colourful procession to Westminster Abbey, and cheered the Queen as she stood on the balcony of Buckingham Palace. They didn't have a chance to catch Mr. Cody's performance, but Julia very much doubted the Prime Minister would be visiting backstage in Oakbourne. Quite frankly, they'd be lucky to pack three hundred in this pavilion, never mind thirty thousand, and the closest the cast would get to William Gladstone were gladstone bags.

Buffalo Bill would have broken the bank at Monte Carlo. Buffalo Buck would be lucky to break even.

'Annie Oaktree you've already met,' Buck was saying. 'Frizzie Lizzie here is our contortionist. Bending over backwards to help, aren't you, my dear?'

'That's me,' the redhead said. 'Always struggling to make ends meet.'

'I watched you with the three-box trick,' Julia said. 'Your performance was staggering — in every sense.'

'Thank you, and thank you for taking us in,' Lizzie said. 'Frankly, us girls were getting frantic.'

She wasn't the only one. Julia hadn't been entirely truthful when she told Buck she had no intention of doubling the rates. That was the whole point of holding out to the very last moment, hoping and praying no one had answered last night's advertisement. If he posted today, it meant he was desperate! But one look at the showman, and suddenly it was much more than paying off Kuznetsov in instalments. If Buck agreed to her proposal, she, too, could perform magic tricks like the riverboat gambler — starting with pulling the wool over Oakbourne's eyes. With Sam Whitmore once more keeping his appointments, the studio's future should be secure for another three, maybe four years — and Julia could *still* settle up with the Russian, thanks to her boarders.

Sam, it seemed, wasn't the only one who could take the rough with the smooth, roll with the punches, and come up smelling of roses.

'Finally, the third member of the trio. Molly Bannister.'

Molly was pretty much everything the rest of the cast were not. Round as a barrel, plain as a pudding, and only came up to Julia's shoulder. For all that, she had sparkling cobalt eyes and a surprisingly firm handshake.

'Resident comedienne and all-round idiot, me,' Molly said. 'Coz I was going to introduce myself with a boxing joke, only I forgot the punchline.'

'Right then, ladies.' Buck clapped his hands. 'Now that Mrs. McAllister knows what she's letting herself in for, and she has our undivided sympathy, it's back to work, please.'

Julia watched the three women disperse. Lizzie in her tight, white spangled costume that left nothing to the imagination. Annie heading for the Trifle Range, fringed skirt swinging with every sway of her pretty hips. Molly Bannister looking every inch the schoolteacher, as she tried to button a jacket that was five meat pies beyond being fastened.

'You realise what this means, don't you?' Buck said.

'An advance of ten shillings.'

'You drive a hard bargain, Mrs. McAllister.' With a resigned roll of his eyes, he counted the money into her hand. 'What *I* was driving at is that, from now until we strike camp, you are officially one of us. So…' He swept off his Stetson to deliver a theatrical bow that brought his dark hair tumbling round his shoulders. 'Welcome to *Buffalo Buck's Mild West Show*. The only act that brings the hardships of frontier life in Margate to the masses, puts the smiled into west, and where the dead drop twice a day but always get up.'

'My pleasure entirely.' Wasn't that a fact.

'Mind you, for a moment back there, when you talked of conditions —' his dark eyes twinkled — 'I rather hoped you were propositioning me.'

'I do believe you say that to all the women you pick up.'

He was still chuckling when she left the tent, but for a split second, it crossed Julia's mind that he was serious. Which was nonsense. He was an entertainer by profession, and, for his sins, a damn good one. Pushing through a crush of crisp governess starch and matronly hat plumes that had swelled rather than abated, Julia mused how it was every child's dream to run away and join the circus. The excitement! The adventure! The thrills, the spills, the dragons to be slain! The music, the colour, the noise! The trouble was, unless you're born to it, life on the road is rough, tough, and anything but natural, which is why very few stuck with it. Experience proved that those who did stick were invariably running, either to escape atrocity or to escape themselves.

What was the man without a name running from?

He wasn't in this business for the money, that's for sure. After shelling out on wages, board and lodgings, the hiring of labourers and benches, not to mention the cost of running repairs and the hellish amount of dead time travelling between towns, the setting up and pulling down, all in front of intimately small crowds, he'd barely end up with tuppence left over.

On the other hand, as she'd just witnessed with the staggered box trick, things are rarely what they seem.

Julia lifted her head to the leaves unfurling on the oak trees that gave the town its name. To the sun filtering through the clouds and streaming over the red and white striped canvas.

If Buck was running from the law, where better to hide than in plain sight?

CHAPTER 4

After quickly dropping off her newly-acquired ten shillings with her Russian loan shark, Julia raced straight back to her studio, instead of heading to Boot Street police station. While she'd been ready to welcome boarders ever since the first advertisement was published, she'd bargained on two girls, not three.

The decision to prioritise boarders over Mr. Vance's missing son was definitely the right one. No sooner had Julia made up the extra bed than the girls barrelled in, giggling, and out of breath under the weight of their loads.

'Ever so funny, that sign in your window.' Even if Julia hadn't seen the cowboy hat peeping above the mountain of clothing that was bursting out of the crate in her arms, Annie's Welsh lilt was unmistakable.

'And clever.' Equally unmistakable were Lizzie's curly red locks exploding from behind a battered bonnet box. (Just how much luggage did these women have?) '*Shoot the kids, hang the family, frame them all*,' Lizzie quoted. 'Even you're not that funny, Molls.'

'No, but now I've seen it, that gag's mine, all mine. Tell me, Julia. How do you know the toothbrush was invented here in Oakbourne? Coz anywhere else, it would be called a teethbrush.'

Showing them to their quarters, Julia had forgotten how lonely living on her own had become. How the empty rooms had echoed, and how musty they had grown. Still, she'd promised herself to stop taking in waifs and strays — the heartbreak of parting was too bloody painful — and for several months now she'd been true to her word. All the same, polishing the floors and beating the rugs in preparation for guests she'd taken a big gamble on welcoming brought a lightness to her heart. There was pleasure beyond measure in making the bedrooms cosy with aspidistras and fresh flowers, scattering potpourri in the bowls, and stocking the pantry with ham and egg pies, cake and jellied tongue. Now, with the rafters rattling from female chatter, she was (almost) glad her finances had forced her to this, and besides, this was a business transaction, and a short one at that. No time to form attachments. She'd be too busy underpinning the studio's future to become involved in their lives.

And more importantly, there was the little matter of Mr. Vance's missing son! Julia leafed through the *Chronicle*. He was absolutely right. There was nothing in the paper, either, about bodies on the railway, which in itself was odd. The press do love a good —

'Sorry to bother you, but where should I put these?'

'Avalon!' If Annie's skirt was attracting attention, medical help would be needed at the sight of the blonde saloon girl wearing a red silk corset on the outside of her blouse. 'Don't tell me Buck's sneaked you on the lodging list, too?'

'Don't panic,' Avalon laughed, 'these aren't my costumes. Dodge and I will be holed up in Vine Cottage, conveniently next door to the tea rooms, where I hear they serve a scrumptious Welsh rarebit. In the meantime, I thought I'd save the girls a trip, and bring the other things over myself.'

'That's very thoughtful. If you leave them by the counter, I'm sure they can manage to take it the rest of the way themselves.'

'Excellent.' Avalon blew a wayward curl out of her eye. 'What about the rest?'

'Rest...?'

Julia followed the dainty finger pointing at a barrow outside. Which idiot thought splashing Kuznetsov's loan to fill the bedrooms with aspidistras and flowers was a good idea? Together, she and Avalon lugged the remaining boxes indoors, the saloon girl declining the offer of refreshment, tempting as it was, on the grounds that she'd promised to sew the button back on Honky-Tonk Hal's jacket.

'Lizzie offered to do it, but she's all fingers and thumbs when it comes to a needle, and besides, she's got her work cut out here.'

'Hasn't she just.' Spindly as she was, Lizzie had twice the number of boxes as Annie and Molly.

'The residue of two marriages, all that. Heck, it might even be three, and her only twenty-four, as well.' Avalon leaned forward. 'This is just between you and me.'

'My lips are sealed.'

'Then cross your finger none of her husbands finds out that she never filed for divorce,' she whispered. 'Imagine the headlines. *Contortionist can't wriggle out of bigamy!*'

Landing a smacker of a kiss on Julia's cheek, and with a reminder to ask the girls to return the barrow, she was pushed for time, Avalon skipped off, oblivious to the stares that accompanied her progress. Or perhaps simply accustomed. And if Julia thought there was time to lug even one of the boxes upstairs, she was wrong. Hardly had Avalon left than the shop was swamped with the scent of cedarwood as Buck walked in.

'Thought I might scout out the territory.'

'You mean check that you're not paying for your girls to bunk in the coal-cellar on a diet of pigs' trotters and tea?'

'I like pigs' trotters.' Rocking on his heels, Buck studied the photographs on the walls. 'And tea. Which is a hint, by the way.'

'While the kettle's boiling, come with me.'

'My goodness, Mrs. McAllister, if I'd known you were taking me into your bedroom, I'd have worn my best socks.'

'If you're going to be Sam, you'll need to dress like him. Here. Change into these.' She turned in the doorway. 'A word of warning, though. If you tell one living soul about taking your clothes off in my bedroom — and I do mean just one — you and Sam will be sharing more than just shirts.'

'I do hope you're not suggesting the same plot in the cemetery.'

'I'm not suggesting it, Buck. That's a promise.'

She closed the door, deciding he wasn't the sort to keep his socks on, anyway.

Within three minutes of Buck positioning himself in the open doorway, pipe in hand the way Sam had, word got round, and the system was simple. He'd pretend it was too noisy to engage in conversation in the street, so he'd invite the ladies inside, where Julia would hold up a blackboard behind their backs. That way she could scribble down a few salient details, enabling him to address the women by name, and comment on whatever event she had chalked up.

'I am very sorry about your husband, Mrs. White.'

'Congratulations on your new baby boy, Mrs. Dyer. I hope I'll have the pleasure of taking his little portrait soon.'

'Goodness, Miss Webster, I do believe you're looking lovelier than ever. Not long now until the big day — yes, yes, of course. I'd be delighted *to photograph your wedding.'*

His stint might only have lasted an hour, and a short one at that, but it was enough for Julia to abandon any ideas of parading Sam round town. By keeping him in front of the studio, she'd come up with a way for him to actually take portraits. With help from his hapless assistant, of course!

'You were amazing,' she said.

'Why, Mrs. McAllister, if I had a guinea for every woman who told me that when I'm putting on my clothes, I'd be a millionaire.'

'Be careful knotting that tie. You might get choked by your own modesty. And besides, given that you're getting dressed in my bedroom, you should probably call me Julia.'

Actually, no. Next time, he should call her JJ. That was the name Sam gave her, when he found her living rough and needing to change her name, but didn't know what to change it to. JJ was neither a boy's name nor a girl's, he'd said. Rather one that put her on an equal footing, and it wasn't just a new name she was free to choose, either. *Apply your mind, work hard, and the world is yours for the taking.*

She could be anything she wanted to be, he had told her — and that was over the very first meal they'd shared in his horse-drawn darkroom. Julia was fourteen, Sam almost forty, but my, what a team they made!

Once the girls had returned to rehearsals, Julia focussed her attention back on Titus Vance's missing son. A young widower had disappeared off the face of the earth, and while her hope was that he was investing his hard-earned income on showgirls and champagne in the best room the Station Hotel had to offer, she had a bad feeling about this. A very bad feeling, in fact.

After enquiring after Detective Inspector John Collingwood at Boot Street police station Julia was directed to the King's Head just off Cadogan Street. All pipe smoke, mahogany and leather, it could be any public house in London. Behind the bar, shelves running from counter to ceiling were stacked with bottles, their labels facing outwards. The ivory handles of the beer pumps gleamed in the sun. Pewter tankards reflected the bustle in the bar.

Today, the reflections were very different to what normally went on. Usually, you'd expect to see men in top hats leaning one elbow on the bar, knocking back a quart of single stout while perusing the news or filling in the word-squares. Others might be checking the results of the races, debating politics, or relaying their domestic woes to the barmaid. There would almost certainly be tiny fists clutching coins to exchange for porter to take home to their parents, and at least one woman in a ragged bonnet would be drip-feeding her crying baby gin. What you wouldn't expect were uniformed constables wrestling a knife from a blood-soaked drunk, much less a grim-faced detective inspector standing over the body of a woman covered in a bedsheet that was stained an ominous red.

'Julia?' Collingwood turned to look at her.

'I'm so, so sorry, John. When the desk sergeant said I'd find you here, I assumed —'

'I hate these cases.' Collingwood took one look at the ashen-faced customers giving statements to his men, the barmaids sobbing in their aprons, and the landlord who stood open-mouthed, shaking like a leaf, and steered Julia behind the screen that transformed a corner of the pub into the snug. 'Right now,' he said, 'at this precise moment, two of my officers are handing seven children over to the Master of the workhouse.'

Julia's stomach lurched. Most murders were cut and dried, and this was no exception. Armed with a butcher's knife, the thug in handcuffs had followed his wife to the King's Head, fully intending to kill her, and even now was bragging how the bitch deserved it. Without a single thought to how his daughters would be separated from their brothers in the workhouse, and punished if they even tried to talk to each other. Did he even care that seven little orphans (because, yes, oh yes, this man would hang) would be forced to wear the uniform of shame? That they'd be bunked in soulless dormitories until they were old enough to work? And never given the chance to learn to read or write, or indeed have any kind of future?

'Changing the subject,' Collingwood said, 'a little bird tells me that you have a group of travelling artistes boarding above the studio.' The ghost of a smile twitched at his lip. 'What's the collective noun for that? A tightrope of troupers? A shimmy of showgirls?'

'More like a moment of madness.' She puffed out her cheeks. 'If it's not Frizzie Lizzie back-bending on the landing and touching her head with her toes, it's Molly addressing the aspidistra which had to be evicted from the bedroom due to the amount of junk the girls brought with them. *My name, Bannister, derives from the old French word for basket-maker. So you can say I really am a basket case,*' she mimicked. '*Did you hear, the police arrested the World Tongue Twister Champion? Bet he'll get a long sentence.* Honestly, John, I can't decide whether I'm living in an aviary, non-stop chirp, chirp, chirp, or locked in the zoo with performing chimpanzees.'

'In other words, you love it.'

Despite the misery around her, Julia smiled. 'You'll make a good detective one day.'

When Collingwood leaned in, he brought a blast of Hammam Bouquet with him. The distinctive gentleman's cologne inspired by fantasies of sultans cavorting in the steam baths of their harems, and Eastern boudoirs reeking of sex. The same musky blend that used to linger on Julia's sheets long after he had left her bed. 'I've missed you, Julia McAllister.'

Her breath still caught at the memory of his taut, runner's frame under her body, a reaction she could no more control than she could stop her nipples tightening at the thought of his tongue exploring her inside and out. But dammit, that was another promise she'd made to herself, and no matter how desperately she ached for his touch, or how fiercely she hungered for him pulsing inside her, it had had to stop.

'I —' She cleared her throat. 'I realise this isn't a good time to broach the subject, but is it true they found a body on the London line?'

Collingwood's grey eyes narrowed. 'Are you asking me why there's nothing about it in the papers?'

'I am.'

He leaned in closer still, but now his expression was solemn. 'The reason I'm not releasing any details, and you mustn't tell a soul about this, either, is because the poor bugger had chafe marks round his ankles from where he'd been chained up.'

'Dear God! Do you know who he is? Where he came from?'

'Not a clue, but he's well nourished, I can tell you that. And clean, with good teeth. As to whether he jumped from the train, escaped from a canal boat, or was being held nearby, who knows. Did he commit suicide? Did he trip? Did somebody push him? The only thing I know for sure is, if the press get wind of this, it will make news far beyond Oakbourne, and you can trust their lurid reporting instincts to instil fear in the entire British public as long as it sells copies.

They'll have people imagining everything from Frankenstein's monster to Jack the Ripper on the loose. They still haven't caught the bastard, so they'll stir that up again for sure. But you know what terrifies me beyond words? That the publicity will spook whoever was holding him.'

'You mean, the kidnapper will go to ground, and get away with it?'

'I have no idea what the press might trigger, that's the problem. When people are jumpy, especially at night, self-defence results in excessive reaction, and the cemeteries are full enough, thank you. If I can identify the victim, it might lead to why he was imprisoned, maybe even where, but my main fear is that the poor sod wasn't alone. And if that's the case, and this gets out, then there's a chance his captor will kill the others to cover his tracks.' When Collingwood spiked his hands through his hair, Julia noticed a few extra grey strands at his temple. 'My sergeant is putting out feelers with a discretion I thought only royal mistresses possessed, but frankly, it's a needle in a haystack. Why are you so interested?'

'Was this the victim?' As Julia fished out the photograph of Vance's son, a thought flashed through her mind. With the poker-stiff manner of a stock-broker or barrister, Titus Vance was not the type to take liberties with, and there was no trace of family resemblance. Was it really his son who was missing? Or the boy he'd been holding prisoner —?

'No. Our boy was younger, fair-haired, bit on the stocky side, with a mole at the side of his mouth.'

Her sigh of relief could be heard up in Scotland.

'Julia, I'm sorry, but do you mind if we pursue this later?' He nodded towards the bar. 'I need to interview the witnesses, have the body taken to the mortuary, then check up on the children, to make sure it really is their mother, not the result of some rabid hallucinations of an opium-soaked addict who stalked the wrong victim.'

Back on Cadogan Street — where the air should be fresh, but all she could smell was the gagging stench of blood mixed with smoke and stale beer — Julia found it unsettling, to say the least, that a stuffy widower in his early thirties could disappear without a trace. She tucked the picture back inside her reticule, almost wishing it *had* been Vance the Younger whose body was found on the tracks. At least then his father would know what had happened to him.

Instead, the agony was about to be prolonged.

CHAPTER 5

Picking at her lunch, two slices of bread with cold beef and pickles, Julia couldn't put the tableau in the King's Head out of her mind. Walking through the door, she'd been transported back to her childhood in Cornwall. To the tiny cottage they'd called home, until men from the mine turned up, pushing a barrow covered in a similar blood-soaked sheet. Julia had been under the kitchen table, playing with her kitten, wondering why Pa was late home from his shift, and giggling because the miners' black faces were streaked with white — and look! Them boots sticking out from the barrow were exactly like her Pa's!

She couldn't say how much time passed after that before she laughed again, and twenty years on, the pain was every bit as raw. Compounded, today, by the fate of seven orphans.

Julia's mother sacrificed herself on the altar of domestic violence by remarrying to a thug to spare her children from the workhouse, and that guilt weighed on Julia's shoulders every single day, never mind that she was a little girl when her father died. So what if she'd never had schooling? Factory work, the mines, going into service was nothing compared to never hearing her mother's ribs crack, or watching the blood spurt from her brother's nose and mouth, or waiting for the weapon her stepfather kept inside his trousers just for her. Even today, she would take an alternative route to avoid passing the workhouse, and she'd lost count of the times she'd told herself *there but for the Grace of God go I*. Which never had held a ring of truth, not even once. Everything that bastard did was in the name of the Lord.

'Annie!' Forcing a smile, Julia swept the past into a box and slammed the lid. 'Shouldn't you be rehearsing?'

'I 'ad to get away.' The Welsh girl slumped into the opposite chair and buried her head in her hands. 'I can't take much more o' it, I tell you. Worse than performing in a backstreet penny gaff, it is. Same stupid bloody jokes, same stupid bloody tricks, same stupid bloody songs. I'm like a poodle in a three-ring circus, me, an' I'm sick to bloody death of it.'

'Have you told Buck how you feel?'

'Many times, lovey, but you met him, you know what he's like. *Just until the next town*, he says, and because he has a way with him, does Buck, I fall for it every bloody time.'

'Then leave.' Julia poured her a cup of coffee and set another plate. 'Tell him you're off after he packs up in Oakbourne, and make plans now to follow through.'

'Trouble is, I got no money, love, and look at me. Twenty-three's an old maid where I come from in the Valleys, and who'd take on a fairground tramp without a penny to 'er name? No, no, if I'm to start a new life with an 'usband and some nippers, it'll have be somewhere respectable. Suburbs, y'know. Pretend this never 'appened. Which means, see, if I'm to catch myself a solicitor or a bank clerk, I need more money than the rubbish pay this show puts out.'

This time last year, Julia could have offered a solution. American cowgirls, stripping to their boots and doing suggestive things with rifles, would fetch big money in respectable gentleman's clubs. Especially if "Tombstone Tess" posed for a flip book with her lariat. The irony there, of course, being that, this time last year, Julia would have had no need to take in lodgers.

'It's not jus' the money.' Annie sighed. 'There's Avalon, see. She's like a sister to me, that one, and I worry about 'er.'

'She does seem a little absent-minded.'

'Nothing wrong with that girl's brain, pet. It's the oily creep she's married to that bothers me. We all got nicknames. Frizzie Lizzie, pretty obvious that. Honky-Tonk Hal, real name Jeremiah Liddell-Gough from a right posh family, went to Eton, too. Set to be a concert pianist by all accounts, but when you meet him, lovey, you'll see how Roger Wright got his.'

'Dodger?'

'Quick with a grin and ready with a wink, you never met a scrounger like him. Never pays anybody back, and that's a nasty trait, but a piece of advice? Never lend him a single soddin' thing, coz if by some miracle you ever get it back, it won't be in the same condition as you lent it, that's a fact. Aw, she could have done so much better for herself, our Avalon.' She grimaced. 'Still could, for that matter.'

'She seems cheerful enough.'

'An' that's the problem, innit? Can't see the wood for the trees, her. None of 'em can, and that's another reason I need to quit. You wouldn't think of it to look at her, plain as a little pudden, but Molly Bannister's 'ad seven husbands, none of 'em her own, and the consequences haven't always been pretty. Lizzie's got more licences than a string of public houses. Our illusionist's ace at making money vanish, not so hot when it comes to making it reappear — the list goes on and on, but they never bloody learn, and that's the trouble.' Wiping her mouth with the back of her hand, Annie stood up. 'Best get back, before they send a search party. Thanks for lunch, pet. You didn't 'ave to do that.'

'My pleasure.'

Maybe not so much pleasure for the cottage loaf, which was down to its last crust and a couple of crumbs.

'Thanks for the gossip, too. Real nice treat, havin' a bit of girly talk without any of the bickerin'. For a small troupe, it can get pretty bloody brutal, no wonder girls don't stay with us long.'

When the shop door closed behind her, it was like a gale force wind dropping suddenly and the lights going out at the same time. Julia should have known the peace was too good to last.

'I know what I forgot to tell Mr. Whitmore this morning —'

'You just missed him, Mrs. Winters. Can I take a message?'

'A little bird tells me that Mr. Whitmore is back —'

'He was never away, Mrs. Spence.'

'I'd like to book an appointment for a family portrait —'

'Of course Mrs. (Henderson / Cartwright / Robbins / Cooke), let's see, now. When would suit you best?'

So much for a quiet lunch! Reaching for a fresh box of visiting cards under the counter, Julia was surprised to see a pair of shining brogues below a knife-edge pleat.

'Mr. Vance. I didn't expect to see you quite so soon.'

'You said you were headed straight to the police station. I wondered if you had any news?'

Poor sod. Ramrod straight. Immaculate clothes. Talk about stiff upper lip. But Julia had seen the same thing many times, when she'd been photographing loved ones in their coffins. Widows, widowers, children, lovers — you'd expect the bereaved to be a mess, uncaring about their appearance, yet so many turned up as neat as a new pin. Was it a means to distract themselves from grief? Channelling their pain into something constructive? Or was it a mark of respect for the deceased? Proof of how much they still loved them? Julia imagined that, for Titus Vance, carrying on as normal was as much for his own sake as his son's. If routine was their bedrock, constancy would be paramount, and let's be honest, what better way to stabilise emotions after trauma?

'Miss O'Leary! I'll be with you in a second.' With Oakbourne's top busybody hovering one yard away, this wasn't the time to throw Mr. Vance's life into even deeper turmoil. Julia leaned across the counter to whisper. 'Detective Inspector Collingwood was out at a crime scene.' For once, it wasn't a lie, but to tell him the body on the railway wasn't his son's would surely do more harm than good. 'The instant I have news, I will telephone —'

'Pah! I don't subscribe to any of that modern fandangery, but it is a great comfort to me, knowing the time and effort you are investing in this, Mrs. McAllister, I really do appreciate your support.' He bowed. 'Thank you.'

She wondered how much of a comfort it would be, knowing there were far more important calls on police time than a thirty-three-year-old male going absent without leave. But as she wrapped a Yorkshire terrier for Miss O'Leary's nephew — 'He would so love a real, live doggie, but the hairs, oh my! His mother finds the mere idea of them sticking to the furniture utterly distressing' — Julia reflected that, when you boil it down, it's not a question of whether bad things happen to good people. It's how good people deal with bad things that's important.

Please God, she'd done the right thing by not telling him.

Early the following morning, hunched over, Julia mused that most women would be content weighing out flour with butter and sugar, adding beaten eggs, currants and nuts. Instead, here she was, measuring out three and a half ounces of sulphite of soda to mix with metol salt, hydroquinone and water, then combining the solution with equal parts of potassium carbonate, more water and bromide.

She laid the plate in the developing bath and agitated gently. After a few minutes, an image began to form on the glass of a little boy in a rented suit, eyes wide, staring at the camera. In the crook of his arm was a wooden toy soldier.

'Julia?'

The knock made her jump, she was miles away. As luck would have it, she'd already fixed the negative in the developing fluid, but when she opened the door, the stench of acid was instantly trumped by cedar. 'Quick.' She pulled Buck inside, to avoid compromising the darkroom.

'My goodness, Mrs. McAllister, if I'd known you were going to drag me into a cupboard, I'd have washed behind my ears — holy mackerel, what's that stink?'

'My perfume.' She washed the plate, dried it with a chamois leather and drew back the curtain to let in some light. 'Now then, since it's the crack of dawn and you don't have a key, would you mind telling me why you broke into my house?'

'I had no choice.' Buck shrugged. 'The door was locked. Nice looking boy, by the way. Birthday portrait?'

'Not exactly. He's dead, and this is the only picture his parents will ever have of him.'

'Are you pulling my leg?' Long, frontiersman locks fell forward as he took a close look. 'This kid looks very much alive to me.'

'Trust me, I will not be touching any part of your anatomy, but that's the point. I rented him a suit, borrowed a wooden Grenadier from the toy shop on the corner, then spent half the night painting his closed eyelids to make it seem like they're open, and colouring his little cheeks and lips.'

'Surely he has his own toys?'

'If only. Both his parents were injured in last year's explosion at the mill, and since neither has been able to work since, destitute doesn't begin to describe their situation.'

'Yet they splash out on a portrait?'

'Actually, they don't. When I found out Georgie had died, I told them *momento mori* were gifts from the church in circumstances like this — and crossed my fingers that they wouldn't ask which church.'

For the same reason, she'd rented the suit from her own funds, but that was what photography was about. Not pandering to rich businessmen, wanting puffed-up pictures of themselves to display on their mantelpieces, or retired officers who couldn't let go of the Army. Photography was about capturing emotions and feelings. 'What are you doing here, Buck?'

'I've lost my Annie Oaktree.'

'That's very careless of you.'

'We always run through a full dress rehearsal on the day we open, starting early to be on top form for the paying public, and it's not like her to turn up late. You haven't seen her, have you?'

'Not since yesterday evening.'

'Lizzie and Molls haven't spoken to her since last night, which isn't unusual. Molly's — let's just say an acquired taste, and Frizzie Lizzie's working on another husband.'

'Your riverboat gambler?'

'One thing about Lizzie, she never mixes business with pleasure. But since no one can shed light on my missing sharpshooter, I was wondering if you know what time she left this morning?'

'I didn't hear her come or go, but then I was in the studio all night, with little Georgie.'

'You don't mean he's still…?'

'Where else could I make him up and stage the photos? Which reminds me. I had a hell of a job, wrestling him into that suit.' Dead weights are next to impossible to manoeuvre, even little children. 'You couldn't give me a hand changing him back into his own clothes, could you?'

'I've done some rum things in my time, but undressing a corpse is a new experience.'

'And here's me, thinking you'd lived life to the full.'

Georgie's parents wouldn't be round to collect their son for a while. Ample time to check Annie's room, in case she'd slept in.

'The bed is still as I made it yesterday,' Julia said after leading Buck to the room. 'Is that unusual?' Showgirls and morals were rarely compatible.

'Honestly? I have no idea what she does in her own time.'

'But you know she wants to quit the circus life?'

'She has mooted the possibility,' Buck said, sifting through the pile of costumes at the foot of the bed. Pioneer bonnets. The infamous fringed skirt that set off her hips. 'More than once, as I recall.' He picked up what looked, to Julia, like a genuine Cherokee headdress and frowned. 'This shouldn't be here.' He didn't put it back, instead ran his fingertips across the intricate beaded browband. 'Did you know that war bonnets are made from tail feathers pulled from young eagles still in the nest?'

'I did not.'

'They can be plucked three times, before the feathers cease to grow back.' He stroked the rabbit-fur drops that hung down the sides of the bonnet. 'The resilience of nature, human and otherwise, is truly amazing, wouldn't you say?'

'Are we discussing eagles, or Annie's opposition to being talked out of leaving?'

'Maybe both, but right now, although I may not show it, I am, to quote every inhabitant of New York and Boston, kickass furious that she's let the production down. Sulking is not an admirable quality.'

'Perhaps she's hoping you'll fire her?'

Annie hadn't packed up and left, that much was certain. Her hairbrush, comb and mirror were neatly laid out on the dressing table, ditto a crisp, white five-pound note issued by the Oakbourne & Southolt Banking Company and anchored by a pink ceramic clock.

'That's not how I operate, Julia.' He laid the headdress on the bed. 'I do confess, though, I am disappointed in her. I truly believed she was better than that.'

A scene flittered through Julia's mind. Vance's son cavorting with a cowgirl on a bed of rose petals, whooping it up with whisky and wine.

'I shouldn't worry, Buck.' You don't live life on the road without becoming shrewd and resourceful, and she should know. 'Annie will turn up.'

Odd how two people had gone missing in a matter of days, though.

CHAPTER 6

No parent should have to carry their dead child home in a handcart.

Life had improved dramatically for the middle- and upper-classes, thanks to the rapid industrial expansion and the export of British goods. Child mortality was seen as a tragedy, rather than the norm now. Not so the poor.

Especially a mother so horribly disfigured that she'd lost nearly all the use of her arms, and a father blind in one eye and missing a foot.

Julia's fingernails bit into her palm as she watched them drag the barrow up the street. The Poor Law wouldn't cover Georgie's funeral. A family needed to be in the workhouse to qualify, while the Workers Compensation Act was in its second — correction, third year of trying to be passed. Little Georgie's coffin would be tossed in a pit thirty, forty feet deep, without ceremony or service, with others below and above him until it was full. Headstones were out of the question. The poor don't merit a marker, or even a spadeful of earth between coffins, so any visits to his grave, at least until it was sealed, would be marred by the stench of the noxious effluvia seeping from those who shared the pit with him.

What his parents *would* have, though, was a photograph to remember him by, and while it was tempting to slot his picture in a silver frame, Julia resisted the urge. This pair were so poor, they'd have no choice other than to sell it, then hate themselves for betraying their child. Whereas a thin, wooden frame with no monetary value would give them comfort for the rest of their lives.

Talking of cadavers, a familiar face had appeared at her doorstep. 'Sergeant Kincaid, what a pleasant surprise.'

'Last time we met,' said a voice roughened by equal measures of tobacco, porter and war, with a face to match, 'you coshed me over the head and trussed me like a chicken. I think that's earned you the right to call me Charlie.'

'Why don't you join me in a cup of coffee and a nice thick slice of Battenburg, and tell me what brings you to my doorstep this bright and sunny morning?'

As it happened, two slices fell victim to Kincaid's voracious appetite before he felt inclined to talk shop, meanwhile taking his definition of the word thick to a whole new dimension. Where he put the cake was a mystery. Tall and gaunt, his legs were thinner than the average house spider's.

'Is this about the body on the railway line yesterday?'

'Partly.' He cut a third slice for good measure. 'If you could drop by the hospital mortuary and take his photograph, I'd be grateful. With luck, someone might recognise the victim, though I should warn you, mind, the 6.48 train wasn't kind to the boy.' Dawn was just breaking, he explained, and in the half-light, the driver didn't see anything on the tracks until he was almost upon him. 'He braked, but those locomotives take half a mile to stop.'

Ice rippled down Julia's spine. That poor driver, knowing what was about to happen and powerless to stop it. She shivered. How many months before he'd stop going to sleep wishing *if I hadn't been so keen to run a punctual service ...* even though it wasn't his fault.

'What —' she cleared her throat — 'was the other element of "partly"?'

'Ah, well. Yesterday's dawn didn't have a monopoly on sad stories. When the sun came up today, it revealed a woman's body hanging from the bridge over the canal.' Suicide, self-murder, self-suspension, call it what you like, death didn't come quickly. It took five minutes, if you were lucky, closer to ten, choking on a line… 'Nothing to say who the poor cow was, which is the other reason I'm here.' His face twisted. 'The only thing in her pocket was your business card.'

'Why do so many people choose to end their lives in public, Charlie? There's no dignity in hanging like a pheasant, being gawped at by the public, while children throw stones and laugh.' Was it a shout to the world, *look at me*, because nobody ever had, until then? Was it to punish their families, their lovers, their husbands, their wives? There! I told you I'd do it. Or was it because these poor souls had reached the end of their endurance, and simply didn't care anymore?

'If I knew the answer to that, Miss, I'd be a priest or a poet.'

'Come, come. I'm sure being coshed on the head and trussed like a chicken has earned *you* the right to call me Julia.'

'Believe me, I called you a lot of names at the time.' His chuckle was like gravel washing over cobbles. 'Anyway, if you wouldn't mind taking our suicide's picture while you're at it, I'll have the boys pass that round, too. See if we can't put a name to the face.'

Better that way, Julia decided. If the police could identify the victim, it was easier on her loved ones to hear the news in the comfort of their own home.

'Of course,' he said, 'she might be a customer of yours, in which case we'll be doing the tax payer a favour, by saving the cost of your fee.' He grinned. 'No taking her picture, mind, then suddenly remembering that she's been a regular for five and a half years.'

'Spoilsport.'

He put his cup down, and the smile dropped from his face. 'Do you know what breaks my heart into tiny little pieces about these suicides?'

'How young they usually are?'

'Only the young can turn the all-consuming intensity of love into an all-consuming bleakness when it's gone.'

'Impulsiveness is youth's blessing and its curse, Charlie.'

'Romeo and Juliet. I know. It's why young men rush to war, I've done it meself.' He stood up and reached for his bowler hat. 'Mind you, I'd still have ten fingers and both ears, had I known the Sudan was full of foul-smelling, ill-tempered buggers that keep spitting at you.'

'Ah. Camels.'

'I was thinking more of the men in my squad, but yes, camels, too.'

Sergeant Kincaid was just the ticket when it came to lifting spirits. He'd seen things — probably done things — in the Royal Horse Guards that no human being should have to confront. Yet, like a fishing boat in a storm, he bobbed on the sea of life, and his resolve never wavered.

And since time was of the essence when it came to identifying victims, Julia tucked her tripod under her arm, picked up her mahogany camera, and heaved the bag of photographic plates and equipment over her shoulder.

Inside the infirmary, orderlies scrubbed floors, carted soiled sheets to the laundry, and helped the injured balance with crutches. As her footsteps echoed down the long hospital corridor, Julia's stomach churned, and not from the stink of carbolic. Like Charlie Kincaid, she had kept the tone light, and, just like Charlie, it was an act. Coffee and cake was the buffer between coping with sudden death and the possibility that she might — *please God, no* — be somehow responsible for a young woman taking her own life.

Who on earth would have just her business card, nothing else, when she tied a noose round her neck and then jumped? Julia could hardly be the next-of-kin contact. She had no family, at least no one who knew where (or who) she was. And if you don't make friends or let people close, then you can't be hurt when you, or they, leave.

Wild theories flew as she dodged the starched headdresses of the nursing sisters, and tried to close her ears to the moans and groans from the wards, the chinking of metal instruments against dishes, the creaking of trolleys and whispered exchanges between hospital staff.

Suppose it was Miss Webster, lying in the mortuary? Only yesterday, she was radiant and blushing with excitement at the prospect of hiring a wedding photographer. Had she rushed home, told her parents what she'd done, only for her mother to be furious that her daughter had sabotaged her own plans for the wedding? Were words said that were so hurtful, they would never be forgotten or forgiven? Surely all the more reason to start a new life with her husband! The fiancé, then. Had she discovered something terrible about him? Bad enough that she couldn't live with the knowledge? Had he died, making her own life not worth living? Had he broken off the engagement and, rather than sue for breach of promise, she'd avoided humiliation by killing herself —?

Julia passed a waiting room crammed with old men bent double in pain, women clutching babies with faces that were either too red or too pale, and children bundled inside bloodstained rags. In one of the side rooms, four impossibly young doctors were holding down a male patient, whose boots thrashed in violent protest. The hems on the nurses' uniforms were crusted with blood, and a young girl in a wheelchair was weeping into her hands.

Death Houses, her mother used to call them. Kill more than they cure, she insisted. Less havens of healing, more gateways to the grave. Indeed, no matter how hard Julia's stepfather beat her, she refused to set foot inside a hospital until the time, when Julia was nine, she'd had no choice but to spend three days in a hideously overcrowded ward, her agony on display like some gruesome freak show, all the time insisting she'd fallen on the rocks — while her bastard husband brought flowers he'd picked with the same hands that put her there in the first place.

The memory was so raw that the pain of it threatened to engulf Julia all over again, and that was the bugger. The crushing sense of helplessness at being forced to cower in the corridor like some voyeuristic ghoul, because children weren't allowed to visit the sick, had never gone away. Even today, just like when she was little, nursing sisters still crunched along corridors painted the most depressing green, oblivious — all right, let's be charitable and say impervious — to the distress around them. It was almost a relief to reach the oppressive, airless room, where, God willing, it *wouldn't* be Miss Webster laid out across the wooden bars, waiting for a different kind of photograph to be taken, and the unfortunate boy on the railway line *wasn't* too horribly disfigured.

Forcing a smile, Julia introduced herself to the mortuary attendant. She didn't have a specially designed tripod like the Parisian police, since the chief superintendent argued that crime scene photography inclined more towards indulgence than necessity. Detective Inspector Collingwood, on the other hand, had no time for cases that didn't end with guilty verdicts. Young and ambitious, he took the view that the more evidence that was gathered, the more airtight the case, and when it came to promotion, science was indispensable.

'The best way to record a scene is if the camera is pointing downwards, rather than straight ahead,' Julia advised.

Consequently, he had commissioned, out of his own pocket, a standard tripod to be adapted so that it could be positioned directly above whatever evidence needed to be recorded. And left it to Julia to contort her body in ways that Frizzie Lizzie would be proud of, in order to take the bloody photo.

Taking a deep breath, then instantly regretting it — the chemicals in her darkroom had nothing on mortuary brews — Julia clenched her teeth as the attendant drew back the sheet.

'I can see why you don't want to snap him propped up,' the attendant was saying. 'Not much to prop.'

Charlie Kincaid wasn't kidding when he said the 6.48 had done the victim no favours, because a locomotive hurtling down at fifty miles an hour is going to do a lot more than break bones. It's going to rip skin and muscle from their anchors, turn soft organs into juice, and the wheels had severed both his left arm and his leg.

'The examining surgeon concluded that the poor bugger was alive when the train hit,' the attendant added, confirming Collingwood's hypothesis that it was impossible to tell if he jumped, fell, or was pushed. 'The doc reckons he was half-on, half-off the track, which explains the mess on the left side.'

Julia had visions of him frantically trying to haul himself out of the way as the train thundered down, unable to break free because maybe his hand or his foot was caught under the rail, or because his limbs had been weakened by being held captive too long. 'Death is rarely quick, it's rarely easy, and I know this was incredibly painful,' she whispered to the boy. 'I hope, for your sake, the agony was purely one brief, split second.' The alternative was too horrendous to contemplate.

Julia turned to the sheet on the other slab, and the woman whose head lay supported on its unforgiving wooden pillow. She hadn't photographed a victim of hanging before, but was well aware that the aftermath wouldn't look as though the deceased was sleeping and that a death grimace was the very best she could hope for.

'Ready,' she told the attendant.

Don't let it be Miss Webster. Julia had watched her blossom from a gawky, giggly schoolgirl into a charming young woman, and was genuinely overjoyed at the prospect of photographing her wedding.

It should have come as a relief.

The body wasn't Miss Webster.

All the same, it hurt far more than it should have done, to see Annie Oaktree lying there.

CHAPTER 7

'My God! My God, that's terrible!'

Julia had taken Buck aside from rehearsals to break the news, leaving Lizzie handcuffed inside a sack tied with a rope, then stuffed inside a trunk.

'Why didn't I see this coming?' He pulled off his Stetson and wiped his forehead with the back of his hand. 'You're sure it's her?'

Her. That was what brought a lump to Julia's throat in the infirmary, and kept it there right the way home. After all that had happened, she didn't even know "Annie's" real name. 'Positive.'

'This is dreadful. I should have —' His jaw was slack, his skin waxy as he stared at his boots. 'Definitely her?'

'Feel free to make the identification yourself, but yes. I'm so sorry Buck —'

'I don't know what I'm going to do without her.'

What do you say to a man who has lost everything? Nothing about him hinted at the depth of his feelings but if they had been in love it explained why he kept talking her into staying with the circus. 'If there's any way I can help, any way at all —'

'Yes! Yes, of course, why didn't I think of it?' He grabbed both of Julia's arms, and now the light was back in his eyes. 'You're the same height and shape. You're perfect to stand in —'

'What? No! For God's sake, aren't you even a *tiny* bit sorry she's dead?'

'Emotion won't pay the backstage labourers' bills, regret won't put food in the mouths of my troupe, and letting down four hundred eager punters certainly won't bring her back.'

'Tell me you're not planning to go ahead with the show. Not when the blood in her veins is still warm.'

'You think I'm heartless?'

'Was that a question?'

'Then let me ask you one, assuming you can hear me on that high horse of yours. Are you prepared to disrespect her memory, throw the whole show into chaos, and disappoint a ton of kids on account of something you can't change? I thought not, so run home, change into Annie Oaktree, then report back for rehearsals. You have —' he glanced at the illusionist, standing with his booted feet apart on top of the trunk — 'precisely ten minutes.'

'To hell with that! For one thing, I have a photograph to develop, and for another I wouldn't know where to start.'

'We'll guide you. Every step of the way, I give you my word.' His voice softened. 'Please, Julia, I am begging you. Hundreds of people are depending on this.'

She couldn't see any holes in the trunk, but if there was even the slightest chance of Lizzie suffocating, presumably the riverboat gambler wouldn't be swinging his watch chain with such nonchalance.

'Very well.' She dragged her eyes away from the magician, and suddenly the smell of cedar was no longer appealing. 'But just for today.'

'Thank you. I appreciate it.' He tipped his white Stetson. 'Nine minutes.'

Out of breath from racing home, Julia scrambled into the fringed cowgirl skirt, half-expecting orderlies from the asylum to come barging through the door. Here she was, rummaging through a dead girl's belongings, still in shock from her visit to the mortuary, sickened that despair had bottled up until it exploded at the end of a noose, saddened by the loss of a vibrant young life, repulsed by the insensitivity that the show must go on — but most of all, ashamed that she was complicit in it.

You met him, you know what he's like. Annie's Welsh lilt echoed in her memory. *He has a way with him, does Buck.*

Annie admitted that she fell for it *every bloody time*; well, she wasn't the only one. What about the other poor sod in the morgue, whose photograph needed to be developed? Surely his death took priority? Yet with a recklessness she couldn't explain, Julia had agreed to stand in at rehearsals, despite the fact that everything she knew about showbusiness could be written on the wing of a fly. When it came to musical comedy she knew even less, and too often her singing had been compared to a walrus with piles.

She pulled on the cowboy boots, which were surprisingly soft and annoyingly comfortable. Maybe if she and Sam had seen the genuine Wild West show, she might have something resembling a clue. Instead, the closest they got was the corner where it played in Earls Court, scoffing Gunpowder Pies, so-named for the vast amount of pepper to disguise the contents.

Grabbing the Cherokee headdress that Buck, as an afterthought, had asked her to bring, Julia was tempted to book herself into the asylum and save the orderlies a trip.

'Nonsense, you'll be great.' Back at the circus, Avalon's confident smile almost reassured her. 'Between us, we'll deliver all of your lines for you. You only need to watch for your cue, then follow a few simple instructions. I can write them down, if you like?'

'Pinning prompts to the sleeve of my forearm isn't what I'd call a life-saver, but when you're drowning, even the smallest log is worth clinging to. Thank you.'

'Not at all, I —' Avalon was cut off by the Prince of Wales lookalike, who'd been holding up the Grand Canyon yesterday.

'Aha, the war bonnet!' It must be difficult to whoop with a cut-glass accent, but somehow the Eton boy managed. 'Small wonder we were unable to find it.'

'That's coz Annie asked Avalon to take it over, didn't she, darlin'?' Dodger shot a smile at his wife as he tied on his giant holsters.

'Did she?'

'You said she asked you to put it in the box with her things. We both thought it odd, if you recall.'

'Tch!' Avalon's lovely eyes rolled. 'My memory's like a sieve these days.'

'Well, whatever Annie wanted it for, it's back, innit.' Dodger turned to Julia. 'Roger Wright, aka Roger the Dodger, the Hot Cross Kid, Wild Bill Hiccup and the blind Indian seer, coz although his wife's pretty, he's blind and can't see 'er. Welcome aboard, love!'

Blue eyes, dimpled cheeks and an easy manner made him an attractive proposition, whatever he was called — and Julia imagined a lot of ladies would be tempted to call him quite often. Lucky Avalon! 'Thanks, but it's only for —'

'On account of the beast I spend more time tuning than playing, they call me Honky-Tonk Hal.' And to think the Prince of Wales could have been a concert pianist! 'Delighted at the prospect of developing our act, m'dear.'

'It's only for —'

'Lizzie and Molls you already know,' Dodger said, 'while this handsome cove is —'

'The Great Mississippi Moonlight Magician at your service, *madame*.' The riverboat gambler, in gold jacquard waistcoat and a black coat that fell halfway to his knees, scooped up her hand and kissed it. 'What happened to the old Annie?' he asked Dodger.

'Took ill, apparently. Buck didn't say what — but here, you must've seen her, Snaps. How's she doing?'

Buck hadn't told them? 'I think I heard someone say that she'd been taken to the hospital.'

Was he worried her death would put the cast off their game? Did he fear a drop in attendance? And honestly, was Snaps the best that Dodge could come up with?

'So what do I call you?' she asked the illusionist. Close up, he was even more attractive, with his glossy dark locks and deep penetrating stare. 'The Great MMM?'

'Diamond Jim, when I'm flipping decks behind my card-sharp moustache, and Texas Jack, when I'm walking on water.'

'And exactly which part of Texas would Jack be from?'

'Wolverhampton.' He winked. 'My best illusion yet, pretending that I've ditched the accent. Like Hal, I very much look forward to working with our new Annie Oaktree.'

'It's only for —'

'I believe this is yours, though.' He dangled the little watch that was pinned to Julia's jacket when she called to break the news earlier to Buck.

'How did you do that?' She hadn't even been close to him.

'That, my dear Snaps, is what puts the Great in the MMM.'

'Come on, back to work!' Buck's showman's voice must have carried to central London, if not Canterbury, Oxford and Hove. 'Places, please.'

Rehearsals resumed at exactly the point where they'd left off. With Lizzie once again handcuffed and stuffed inside a sack, which was then tied and sealed in the trunk. Fascinated, Julia watched as the magician stood on the box and unravelled a shimmering gold sheet, matching his waistcoat, that hid the box as well as his body. Hal tinkled out a few bars of *Oh, Susannah, don't you cry for me* — but only a few — while the sheet shivered and shook in the magician's hands, before it slowly lowered to reveal Lizzie on the trunk, and the illusionist nowhere to be seen. Julia gasped, as the audience no doubt would, when Lizzie opened the lid to reveal the riverboat gambler, trussed inside the sack, exactly as his assistant had been.

And as Hal went to Alabama with a banjo on his knee, all the niggles that had been grating at the back of Julia's mind suddenly clicked into place.

Annie Oaktree didn't kill herself.

She was murdered.

CHAPTER 8

'I know you won't believe me, John, you'll think me certifiable —'

'Julia —'

'— and I realise you have dozens of cases to investigate, on top of the railway victim and the woman in the pub —'

'Julia, slow down.'

'— and I know I don't have a single shred of evidence, but there were so many things about her suicide that didn't make sense, the way she talked about her life, the plans she had, the five-pound note on her dresser, but it wasn't until I saw the illusionist in action —'

'Stop.'

'Please, John, at least hear me out.'

'Why am I here?'

'What? Because I sent a messenger, asking to meet, and said it was urgent.'

'I run a city police station with a fleet of overworked officers, who are habitually bludgeoned, spat at, punched, kicked and spewed on. Everything's urgent,' Collingwood said. 'So instead of following up on robberies, rapes, pickpockets and assaults, why am I standing in the wings of a circus tent, while my scene-of-crime photographer cavorts in a skirt that passes for a pelmet — and, just out of curiosity, why is she holding a sketchbook?'

'Annie Oaktree draws really fast.'

'I should have known better than to ask.'

Had the audience been able to see behind the screen, they wouldn't have thought it odd that a showgirl was engaged in conversation with a gentleman in a grey worsted suit that matched the colour of his eyes to the nuance. With most policemen hailing from working-class families and lacking a decent education, the audience would blithely assume he was just another stage door johnny. But that was the genius of the show. Even if Julia and Collingwood were in full view of the crowd, every eye would be on the performance.

'Take a close look at the stage, John.'

The assistant-in-the-sack wasn't purely a question of the quickness of the hand deceiving the eye. It was the speed with which Lizzie and the magician executed the illusion.

'Can you imagine the forethought and planning that goes into that trick? The rehearsing, the precision, the timing?'

The professionalism with which they pulled it off was eye-watering. Right down to the gold sheet rumpled apparently artlessly on the floor, but was in fact hiding the drop-down panel through which Lizzie rolled out and the magician rolled in. And while the audience gasped and clapped as his assistant twirled on the lid of the trunk, spangles glinting in the light of two dozen naphtha flares, the Great MMM was busy closing the flap, wriggling into the sack, tying it from a hidden cord inside, and clipping on the cuffs, all at lightning speed.

'Should I add to the excitement, by arresting your riverboat gambler while he's still handcuffed, or wait until he's taking his bow?'

'I'm not suggesting Texas Jack killed her. It was seeing how the trick was pulled off that made me realise that Annie didn't kill herself. She was lively, excited, looking forward to planning a future away from what she felt was a demeaning freak show, but most importantly, there was the matter of the —'

'Five-pound note.'

'You're Buck's mind reader now?'

'As a policeman, I'm trained to have an especially good memory. All it takes is for you to tell me something three hundred times and hey presto, it sinks in.' He inclined his head towards the stage. 'Isn't that your cue?'

Dammit. Now he'd head back to Boot Street, and any leads would be stone cold by the time he picked them up. *If* he bloody well picked them up. 'It was murder, John. You have to believe me.'

With the honky-tonk tinkling and the crowd roaring, Julia bounded into the spotlight, but the only sound she could hear was Collingwood's reply.

'If you'd let me get a word in, you'd have known that's why I'm here.'

Did it feel strange, horsing around in a dead woman's costume? The very sort of clothes that the smutty picture brigade would pay good money to see being peeled off?

Did it worry her, that half of Oakbourne was packed into this grandstand, and that most of them knew her by name, if not sight?

Did she feel stupid, clopping in on a hobby horse?

Hell no. This was exhilarating with a capital E, and if Julia was nervous — make that terrified — about performing in public, that changed the second she ran onto the stage. Hiding behind a disguise helped. In fact, she barely recognised herself under the soft, cowgirl hat, with her hair bouncing round her shoulders like the real Annie Oakley, and cheeks reddened with rouge like a clown. But to see how the show lifted the spirits of everyone from stokers to solicitors, machinists to moguls, small boys to old men, eclipsed every trace of anxiety.

'According to the *Denver Times* —' Buck was in his element, holding up the newspaper — 'Annie can shoot the tip off a cheroot while it's between a man's lips, hit the thin edge of a playing card from thirty paces, and let's see, what else does it say? Ah, yes. Hit a bullseye from looking in a mirror.'

You could almost hear the audience slide to the edge of their seats.

'What do you say, ladies and gentlemen? Shall we ask Little Sure Shot to give us a demonstration?'

Cheers almost lifted the roof, but Buck wasn't done yet. 'Did you know, Annie shot a cigarette clear out of Kaiser Wilhelm's mouth? And hits flying targets from a galloping horse? So come on, Annie. Show us what you've got!'

Bawdy chuckles echoed round the tent, as Buck fanned out a deck of cards and Julia positioned herself sideways, one hand on her hip, the other pointing a gun directly at Buck.

'Stop!' Up ran Dodger, dressed as the Kid. 'You've hired the wrong Annie.' The paper he was waving was blank, but no one could see. 'It says OAKTREE on the contract. Little Miss POOR Shot.'

Pantomime time: *'Oh, no, she isn't...' 'Oh, yes, she is...'*

'If that woman threw herself on the floor, she would miss — look, I'll prove it.' He flung open his jacket, to reveal a target pinned on his chest.

That was the cue for Julia to pull the trigger and a flag reading *Bang!* to drop down.

Dodger let out a theatrical gasp, clutched his chest, and "fell dead".

Buck displayed a mass of holes in the playing cards.

Julia wondered if she hadn't found a new vocation.

Julia's euphoria was short-lived. Once the clapping had died down and the crowd had dispersed, nothing had actually changed. A young woman had been murdered, and her death staged to look like suicide, which meant a killer was still on the loose. More than likely someone she knew.

'I'll collect her personal possessions later,' Buck had whispered. 'After dark, so as not to arouse suspicion.'

'Why haven't you told them?' Julia had hissed back, but he was already striding away, not a care in the world, to congratulate Molly on initiating a new act with a gunswinger holding a big sack marked "pepper", and warning everyone to be careful *that man's packing heat.*

Was this simply another case of how good people react to bad things?

Or was there a more sinister reason for covering it up?

If so (and what else explained his haste to collect the dead woman's belongings?), Buck had picked the wrong landlady. Julia had no intention of allowing evidence to be taken away or destroyed, and since Collingwood hadn't hung around for the show and the light was already fading from the sky, there was no time to waste.

...if I'm to catch myself a solicitor or a bank clerk, I need more money than the rubbish pay this show puts out... Annie's words floated back as Julia drew the curtains out of respect for the dead, *...who'd take on a fairground tramp without a penny to 'er name...*

So where did that crisp five-pound note come from? Tempting as it was to suggest Annie had resorted to the age-old fall-back to raise the necessary funds, who stumps up the equivalent of a copy clerk's monthly wages, however good the services rendered? And considering it was so precious, why simply anchor it under the clock? Unless Annie was in such a hurry, that she came home, changed out of her costume, then, without even time to squirrel it away, dashed straight off again.

Distasteful or not, Julia sifted through Annie's clothes, and, halfway down the trunk, found a thick envelope wrapped in a shawl.

...trouble is, I got no money, love...

And yet she had. A lot of money, actually. There was something else tucked inside the shawl, as well. A copy of a birth certificate for one June Margaret Sullivan, registered in Dublin. Julia leaned back on her heels.

...twenty-three's an old maid where I come from in the Valleys...

The dates tallied up, but was she really such a good actress that she could keep up a Welsh accent without letting it slip? And since she worked for "rubbish pay", why bother?

'Julia?' Footsteps clunked up the stairs, giving her just enough time to stuff the envelope in the waistband of her skirt before they reached the landing. 'If you persist in breaking into my home,' she trilled, pretending to pack hosiery, chemises and bloomers in the trunk, 'I will have to call the police.'

'Let me save you the trouble,' a familiar voice drawled. 'Not that an open door is considered to be breaking and entering, although I have to say, Mrs. McAllister —' Collingwood stepped forward, bringing the scent of Hammam Bouquet with him — 'I'd be more than willing to take down your particulars.'

'My particulars are staying right where they are, Inspector.'

In the darkened room, urges swirled. She wanted him to pull her into his arms, press his lips to hers, throw her on the bed. 'How,' she croaked instead, 'did you know it was murder?'

For a moment, he stood motionless. Would he lean in? Coil his little finger round a strand of her hair? Draw her to him? Julia swore she could hear dust motes hit the floor.

'*Livor mortis.*'

'I noticed it at the mortuary. I assumed rigor mortis merely established that she'd been dead for several hours, rather than an indication of foul play.' Working at crime scenes, she was getting used to how the body starts to stiffen a couple of hours after death, commencing with the muscles in the face, neck and shoulders.

'Livor, not rigor,' he corrected. 'When the heart stops beating, the blood stops pumping and gravity takes over. With a hanging, I would expect to see discolouration on the lower extremities, but Annie Oaktree's back was purple.'

'You told me once that lividity changes if the body is moved up to eight hours after death.'

'Six hours, but yes. Theoretically, she could have died anywhere except under that bridge, and for that reason I alerted the coroner, and what do you know? The doctor found fingerprint bruises on her neck.' He paced the room that still held the spirit of a vivacious brown-eyed showgirl. 'Annie Oaktree was strangled, and her murder staged to look like suicide.'

'Then why aren't you investigating?' Who wouldn't be tetchy when the man who'd shared your bed, your breath, your secrets, your soul, was colder than the other side of the pillow. 'Any other murder, and you'd be stamping all over the suspects, lifting stones, rattling cages, checking alibis —'

'Or.' There was unaccustomed steel in his voice. 'I'd take a more subtle approach, so as not to spook the killer.'

Ah. Like the victim on the London line, the police weren't making this public, either.

'Right now,' he was saying, 'you're the only civilian who knows this was anything other than the tragedy it seemed.'

Maybe it wasn't Collingwood. Maybe it was the death of a young woman with everything to live for that rattled Julia's composure. The fear, the frustration, the wickedness, the waste, that left her stomach tighter than a sailor's knot. 'Her name was June Sullivan. She told me that she was brought up in the Valleys, and her accent was certainly strong, but look at this.' She held out the birth certificate. 'Why pretend?'

'Who said she was pretending?' He squinted at the paper in the semi-dark. 'The Irish flooded into Wales by their thousands to escape the potato famine, most of them ending up in Cardiff, Swansea and Merthyr Tydfil. Very much the Valleys.'

'That was fifty years ago. She was only twenty-three.'

'Put it into context, though. Even if they'd been spread across several cities, not just a handful, thirty thousand immigrants is a large number to absorb. Especially when the majority were unskilled, illiterate, and that poor, they were known to sleep fifty to a room on occasion.' Collingwood blew out his cheeks. 'Rumours were put about that they were child-killers and sucked the blood out of sheep, in a bid to drive them away, and even now, in some parts, the Irish are still hated, despised and distrusted.'

'That only explains why she hid her background.'

'Yes, but trust, or lack of it, cuts both ways. I can think of a number of reasons why Annie's — sorry, *June's* — mother gave birth in Ireland.'

'She went home, because it was safer?'

'A distinct possibility, as is the Sullivans being neither first generation nor refugees, but caught in a situation where the father follows the work, the wife's too heavily pregnant to travel, but joins him after the birth. Far more likely, although I'm no expert on Irish paper, that certificate is forged. Which would make sense if the child was born out of wedlock.'

It was, after all, rare for someone to go to the trouble, not to mention outlay, of obtaining a copy of their own birth certificate.

'The chances are we'll never know,' he continued, 'though I'm hoping for better odds when it comes to catching her killer, which is why I'm here. This is a dangerous situation, and you need to take care. It's probably someone she knew —'

'I'm well aware of that, and as much as I appreciate your concern, I can look after myself.'

'And the best way to do that is to cut your ties with the show, which includes throwing out your lodgers.'

'No.'

'With immediate effect.'

'It doesn't matter how many times you don't listen to me, John, the answer's still no.'

'Being strong-willed is an admirable trait.' He flung open the curtains, and began riffing through the dead girl's possessions. 'Stubbornness is not.'

'I prefer to think of it more as perseverance.' Take away the costume changes, there was very little by way of personal items here, and those clothes Annie had owned were worn thin, and had been mended over and over. 'Especially,' Julia added, 'when there's no one better placed to bring this monster to justice. Besides.' She watched professional fingers probe the pockets, shake the folds, tap the trunk for hidden compartments. The same fingers that used to snake down her spine. Ripple over her skin. Explore every inch of her body, inside and out. 'You've drummed it into me enough times that the Three Musketeers of detection are motive, means and opportunity. Since everyone in the cast had numbers two and three to spare, we need to focus on motive.'

'For Christ's sake, Julia, are you related to mules? For the last time, there is no "we" about this.'

'So you don't want my thoughts about how a girl with threadbare underclothes might get hold of this kind of money?' Julia tossed him the envelope.

'How she got it isn't the point,' he said, counting the contents. 'Robbery clearly wasn't the motive, since the six hours her body was left on its back gave the killer ample opportunity to relieve her of her savings, and the five-pound note would also be gone.'

'Not necessarily,' Julia said slowly.

Why else would you offer board and lodgings to a bunch of gypsies, tramps and thieves, Buck had asked. At the time, she'd dismissed it as part of his patter, but suppose there was more to it? Watching the speed with which he switched the deck of cards for the holed ones in the act, the riverboat gambler didn't have a monopoly on light fingers…

'Suppose Buck and June were running a scam? He steals the items, she fences them?' It explained why he was so keen for June to stay. Why he genuinely didn't know what he'd do without her — and suddenly, his distress had sod all to do with suddenly having a gap in the cast. By holding back from telling the others, he'd bought himself time, and collecting her belongings under cover of darkness allowed him to pocket the cash without attracting attention. 'If Buck discovered she'd been short-changing him, I'd say betrayal is as good a motive for murder as any. Wouldn't you, Inspector?'

CHAPTER 9

The change between the afternoon audience and the evening crowd was extraordinary. Vendors lined the path of the Common, tempting the punters with jellied eels, hot potatoes, and bowls of pea soup. There was sherbet for the ladies, beer for the men, and the queue for admission coiled right round the tent. If any of the spectators mourned the absence of freak shows and peep shows, they were masking it well, and the drop in temperature after sunset merely heightened the excitement, as the swelling crowd snuggled together to keep warm.

Inside, Hal pounded the honky-tonk to build anticipation even higher. On the stage, the Great MMM tapped out timing with Lizzie, crucial when it came to swirling the cloak that she would wear to the guillotine. Molly was checking the inside of her fingertips, where she'd inked the order of the jokes she intended to deliver, while Avalon had transformed from saloon girl into Cherokee squaw, and was trying to balance Dodger's war bonnet, which had a tendency to tilt to the left. Julia could have told her she was wasting her time. In that short, tight, buckskin tunic, not a single member of the audience would notice if the eagle feather headdress took flight and flapped right out of the tent.

'Are you comfortable?' Buck tested the rail that would keep the crowd from his exhibit. 'Still time to swap with Avalon, should you wish.'

Lying flat out on a tiny tin tray, with a rod sticking down her left arm and along each of her outstretched legs, the word comfortable didn't immediately spring to Julia's mind. Especially when she was dizzy with concentration, trying to keep her balance. Then again, if it was a toss-up between being the floating angel or having to engage in theatrical dialogue, no contest. 'Comfy as a kitten,' she trilled.

'Good. Because it's time to open up.'

Watching the showman stride towards the entrance, whistling as though he hadn't a care in the world, it was easy to picture him leaning forward to kiss a lady's hand, and, hidden by his curtain of hair, sliding her ring into his mouth. Turning a manly handshake into an exchange of homes for a ticket-holder's bulging wallet. Loosening a gold half-hunter from its watch chain…

'Ladies and gentlemen, children and vampires, welcome, please, to the greatest show in Oakbourne.'

With a swish, he pulled aside the flap, making sure that the illusion was the first thing they saw as they surged to take their seats. And it was masterful. No one could see the contraption that held Julia rigid inside her tight, white, feathered costume. Only the angel that hovered in mid-air, where the only part of her that touched the ground was her shining silver wand, complete with shining golden star where it met the earth.

'Is she real?'

'She is, son,' Buck assured the goggling child. 'Straight from heaven, aren't you, Gabrielle?'

'Devon, Buck,' Julia tutted. 'How many times do I have to tell you? Straight from DEVON.'

Again, there was no question of being recognised. Julia's face had been plastered white, as had any part of her skin that was on show, while the white wig and halo masked much of her face. That wasn't for Julia's benefit. Like all small circuses and shows, the cast was kept to a minimum, with each performer playing several parts. The trick was to make the troupe look bigger than it was.

'The gallows will testify that there's no honour among thieves,' Collingwood had warned before she set off for the show. 'But the scaffold trembles under the weight of killers who will go to any lengths to cover their tracks.' He would not, he insisted, stand by and let her throw herself to the wolves.

'Have faith, Inspector,' she'd said, pinching his cheek. 'Who knows? I might just come home leading the pack.'

If the whole point of the Mild West Show was to fool the audience, then the last thing they'd expect was to be taken in themselves. As far as Buck, indeed all of them, were concerned, here was a woman struggling to keep her head above water in the shark-infested seas of business, happy to help out when one of her lodgers was indisposed.

Although the concept of *you scratch my back, I'll scratch yours* held a certain irony for floating angels. The Spanish Inquisition's iron maiden had nothing on this.

'You did really well,' Avalon said, once the audience was seated and the curtain screening the illusion had fallen. 'It's quite a challenge, balancing in thin air.'

'I have lost all feeling in my hands and feet, and I'm pretty sure half my ribs are broken.'

Out on the stage, Molly was setting the mood. 'I'm so unlucky when it comes to love,' she was saying. 'My first husband died from eating a batch of poisonous mushrooms, and the second died from a fractured skull.' She paused. 'Stupid sod wouldn't eat the mushrooms.'

The laughter nearly took the roof off.

'I felt the same way, the first time they laid *me* flat out in mid-air,' Avalon said, easing the device to vertical from horizontal, before releasing the buckles holding the angel in place, then unfastening the costume that hid the metal rods. 'But it's a clever contraption, and very, very safe. You'll soon get used to it.'

Safe? Julia had never felt so vulnerable in her life. Poles strapped to her outstretched arms? One leg up, one leg down? The only thing she had control over was her face and voice, but that's the thing about illusionists. You have to trust them.

And there, as William Shakespeare said, did lie the rub.

Molly had finished her warm-up routine — *show me a piano dropped down a mineshaft and I'll show you A-flat minor* — and now, lit like Paris by a score of naphtha flares, the Great MMM was demonstrating to his open-mouthed audience that this was a genuine, working, and indeed perilously sharp guillotine. So much so, that Julia suspected many of them would never eat their greens again, hearing the head of cabbage thudding onto the boards.

'Ready?' Avalon whispered.

Julia nodded. Barely had she scraped off the thick, white paste than she was scrambling into a pioneer woman's frock, pulling the ugly bonnet down low to obscure her face. Avalon was wearing a similar dress, not an easy feat on top of her squaw costume, but quick change was paramount in this show. At Hal's musical cue, they grabbed Lizzie, also in frontier attire but with the addition of a billowing cloak, threw a sack over her frizz of red hair, and dragged the prisoner, struggling and screaming, towards the platform.

At which point, timing was everything.

Halfway up the steps, the condemned woman tries to make a break. Her two wardens thwart the escape, grab her firmly by the shoulders to stop her struggling, then lay her on the guillotine. In silence, the executioner mounts the platform. Without a word, he releases the rope. The blade whizzes down.

The head falls in the sack. Stepping forward, he pulls off his mask — except, wait! It's the red-headed prisoner!

'Well done,' Buck said, as the curtain floated down. 'Your performance was impeccable.'

'All I had to do was hold her,' Julia pointed out.

'Right angle, right timing, right amount of dramatics. No mean feat for a first-timer.'

What could she say? That there was no time to think about whether she was doing it right or doing it wrong? Underneath the billowing cloak, and disguised by the frontierswoman frock, was a massive cushion designed to resemble a body. When they'd reached the halfway point on the steps, Julia and Avalon weren't grabbing an escaping prisoner's shoulders. They were shaking the cloak, so Lizzie could slip her head out of the sack, wriggle free of her costume, and drop into the gap opened by the trapdoor in the stairs. With all eyes on the drama, no one noticed the executioner merge into the blackness, and while the cushion was being laid on the guillotine, the riverboat gambler was helping Lizzie into an outfit identical to his own.

Or should Julia come right out and say it? Annie Oaktree was murdered, please swear he had nothing to do with it, or, if he did, it was an accident, he panicked, then tried to cover it up.

She couldn't, of course. Partly because you can't strangle someone "by accident". Yes, you might lunge for their neck. Yes, you might squeeze. But it takes several minutes — and extreme effort — before the last breath leaves their body. If the killer had lashed out, causing Annie to fall and hit her head, that might be different. Then again, only might…

Also, John Collingwood hadn't reached the rank of detective inspector at such a young age for nothing. Building cast-iron cases was his stock-in-trade, and if he was keeping this murder quiet, like the body on the railway, he had good reason.

'Well, you know what they say at the guillotine, Buck. Can't let your heart rule your head.'

And she mustn't. As the showman strode off to introduce the next act, Julia couldn't afford to let her guard down by assuming he'd killed Annie. Molly was short, Lizzie was skinny, Avalon was wholesome personified, but to work in this troupe, strength came with the territory. It was the same with the men. The Great Mississippi Moonlight Magician was an intentionally comical tongue-twister, and, like Dodger and Hal, the man from the Midlands was lithe, lean, funny and fast, but more than anything, he was adaptable.

Right now, he was in the spotlight, head to foot in black, playing the Gumswinger — *do you want peppermint or spearmint?* — and facing down Dodger, a.k.a. Willy the Kid.

'You're kidding!'

'No, just Kid. My parents couldn't afford the other four letters for the birth certificate.'

'Isn't that for telegrams?'

'I was a quick delivery.'

The crowd was in stitches, and as Julia ran on stage for the musical finale, *I wish I was in Brixton, hurrah, hurrah*, she couldn't help but wonder how someone in this group could invest so much of themselves into making people happy, and at the same time be a cold-hearted killer.

CHAPTER 10

In his office on Boot Street, Detective Inspector Collingwood stroked his cheek where Julia had given it an affectionate pinch.

'Have faith,' she'd said. 'I can look after myself.'

Could she? He capped his fountain pen, pushed his reports to one side, and leaned back in his chair. She'd sailed close to the wind when she was being framed for murder, and photographing victims at a crime scene had only fired her sense of injustice. Nothing wrong with crusades. He rubbed the bridge of his nose. Providing they posed no risk.

The smell of hot mutton pies floated up from the street. Where better to stand with a tray of steaming pastries than outside a busy police station after last orders?

The trouble was, this case presented threats at every turn. At its heart was a killer who was cunning, bold, organised, clever, and, most importantly, very much on their guard. If she hoped to outwit her adversary, that confidence was very much misplaced — but since when did Julia McAllister listen to reason? And there was more at stake than physical danger. Did she have any idea what would happen if someone found out that she was effectively a police spy? As things stood, the public mistrusted plain clothes officers as a matter of principle. In the communal mind, their sole role was to watch, search, scrutinise and report back on personal individuals, rather than examine and detect crime. Should word get out that she was working covertly for the police, Julia would have bricks thrown through her window, paint, eggs and filth thrown at her in the street, her business was effectively ruined.

Claiming to understand the risks was reckless in itself. Ignoring them was simply pig-headed.

On the floor below, the cells were fast filling up with drunks, thieves, street-walkers and vandals, every last one of them loud, aggressive and angry. The desk sergeant would be battling false names and addresses, while one constable patched wounds and another swabbed floors awash with urine, blood and puke. Which was the conundrum. One detective inspector in charge of two sergeants, sixteen constables and a jurisdiction in uproar had no leeway to offer protection to a girl in the firing line.

'Crikey,' rumbled a gravelly voice. 'If you was any deeper in thought, sir, you'd be in Australia. Something wrong?'

'No. Not really.'

Charlie Kincaid closed the door behind him. It barely dulled the din. 'You having second thoughts about the girl under the bridge?'

'When travelling shows roll into town, Charlie, you and I both know they bring trouble with a capital T. The Mild West is no different, which is why we're still working at — good grief, eleven twenty-five.' No wonder his stomach was rumbling.

'Buffalo Bill Cody brought a hundred Indians across the Atlantic, Gawd knows how many Gauchos, Arabs, Mongols and Turks, whole herds of horses, and let's not forget the buffalo and them elk. All that passed peaceful enough.'

'Only because the men responsible for all that stunt riding, calf-roping and lasso work doubled as the show's private security, and were not the type to be tangled with.'

'That, and the threat of being scalped,' Kincaid acknowledged with a chuckle. 'The worst Buck can throw at the punters is a pie from Custard's Last Stand.'

Collingwood wished he hadn't mentioned pies. 'That's the thing, though, isn't it? The big shows, like Lord George Sanger's, travel with trainloads of equipment and a squad of labourers. This lot fits in a steamer trunk by comparison.'

'They're not touring Europe.'

'They're not coining it in, either.'

One heavy shower plus one small hole in the canvas, or one tent pole that had been shoddily fixed, was all it took to turn grass into mud, seats into paddling pools and bring a soggy pavilion down on their heads. The fact of life was, most showmen died penniless — and they were the lucky ones. Naphtha flares lit the stage beautifully, but they were unstable and dangerous, and canvas is anything but fireproof. This was why Collingwood had insisted on the municipal fire brigade being stationed outside, on standby. More than one impresario had gone down with his ship, trying to salvage the props. 'Have you met him? Buck?'

'Not yet, though the missus is hell-bent on dragging me along for tomorrow night's performance. Want me to introduce myself?'

'No, no, you and Clara deserve a night without work intruding.'

'Then let's hope and pray we don't find another poor soul hanging from the bridges.' Kincaid packed his pipe with tobacco and lit it. 'I have a theory about your Annie Oaktree,' he said slowly. 'Are we sure it was murder?'

'Two words. Livor and mortis.'

'I know, but bear with me, sir. What if it started out as a lover's tiff? She might have been getting clingy. Maybe she tried to blackmail him? Perhaps he told her it was over, he'd found someone else?'

'Or the other way around.'

'Nope, and that's what I'm coming to. Whichever way it went, they argue, he clamps his hand round her neck to — I don't know, make a point, show her who's boss, or what he's capable of? Anyway, for whatever reason, he's not a killer. He doesn't follow through.' Kincaid puffed on his pipe. 'Say he then throws her down like rubbish. At that point, Annie realises it's over, and hangs herself in desperation?'

'You wouldn't be after my job, would you, Sergeant?'

'As it happens, I've tested the chair, it's certainly comfy enough, but I'm not sure I'd fancy Her Madge looking over my shoulder night and day.' Kincaid pointed his pipe at Queen Victoria's portrait on the wall behind Collingwood. 'I've seen warmer expressions on an attacking Doberman.'

'Well, I'm glad my livelihood's not under threat, because, as theories go, yours is very colourful, but doesn't explain away the lividity on her back.'

'Does, if he came back to apologise and found her swinging from the rafters, tent pole, wherever this happened, although I'm guessing the pavilion, on account of the rope she used to tie the knot.'

Collingwood hated to admit it, but that scenario was sound. Love might have died, but affection did not. Her lover wouldn't want her seen like that, not by her closest friends, and spends the next few agonising hours wondering what to do, now that he's cut her down. Finally, he decides his only option is to pretend she took her own life someplace else.

'Any of the others could have done it. Hell's bells, it could even have been two different people, and not necessarily a man. All sorts of shenanigans go on with them travelling shows, remember that circus four years back? Jeezus, I'm broad-minded, but that clown and the —'

'Stop!' Collingwood held up a hand. 'I haven't had my dinner yet, and you've just ruined my appetite.'

'Good.' His sergeant's laugh could pass for the creak of a gallows chain. 'Consider it payback for making me miss a glass of porter and a cuddle with the missus, on account of working the railway victim case. Which, by the way, is why I popped my ugly head round your door in the first place. To give you an update on what I've found.'

Collingwood jolted upright in his chair. 'And?'

'Nothing.' Kincaid grimaced. 'Absolute bloody nothing.'

CHAPTER 11

The bell of St. Oswald's chimed four. It was the in-between time. That deep, dark, tranquil period which exists only once the last, defiant spurt of adrenalin has popped, and before the first, faint spike of recuperating energy has stirred. The limbo hour, when yesterday seems a million miles behind, and tomorrow feels like it will never come. The loneliest, most desolate of times.

In her studio, Julia pegged the photographs of the railway victim up to dry. 'You didn't deserve this,' she whispered to the boy. 'But we'll find what you were escaping from, I promise.'

A tall order? Perhaps. Without hope, though, there's no purpose, and while she'd produced a decent enough portrait for Sergeant Kincaid to pass round on the off-chance that someone might recognise him, she'd also taken photographic records that testified to the poor boy's captivity.

None of it made sense.

Young — she doubted he'd even reached his majority — he wasn't what you'd call handsome, but he was well-nourished, and his clothes, while not Savile Row, fitted well and were clean. Telling herself in the mortuary that, attached or not, a limb was a limb, just take a deep breath and do your job, she'd made photographic records of both ankles. Examining them now, she remembered how his muscles showed he was strong, yet his hands were soft. If he'd been put to work, it was not manual labour. Holding the pictures to the light, she peered at the chafe marks on his ankles, which were numerous, layered, and faded. Being chained was a protracted occurrence, then?

Also, the grazing on one ankle was fainter than the other, proof that the poor lad had been restrained one leg at a time.

'At least death came quickly for you.'

It may not have been instantaneous, but when the locomotive struck, it would have either rendered him unconscious, or disorientated him from shock.

Unlike June Margaret Sullivan.

Julia swiped the hair out of her eyes with the back of her hand. She wished, now, that she'd taken photographs of June's corpse. At the time, of course, it wasn't a crime scene. Kincaid had merely wanted the suicide identified. She had duly obliged. All the same, Julia couldn't put the girl's suffering out of her mind. The frantic struggles. The pain. The fear. The terror. The fevered belief that she would, dammit, fight off her attacker. The torture of realising she could not...

In a way, Julia wished June *had* taken her own life. The troupe was so close-knit that they were effectively her family, and the idea that one of them could crush the life out of her was horrific.

I'm like a poodle in a three-ring circus, me, an' I'm sick to bloody death of it.

Not enough to hang herself from a bridge, though. Despite what someone went to great lengths to make people believe.

Worse than performing in a backstreet penny gaff, it is. June's words floated in the stillness. *Same stupid bloody jokes, same stupid bloody tricks, same stupid bloody songs.*

Except the Mild West wasn't like the penny gaffs. Not remotely. Those were cheap, cramped, one-room affairs, churning out lurid occult melodramas and outrageous theatrics. Yes, they had gags, and yes, they had tricks, but there was little repetition. The whole purpose of the penny gaff was to entertain folk who couldn't afford other kinds of entertainment — or at least, who thought they couldn't. In reality, they were money-spinners *par excellence*. A con of the very sharpest order. By hooking the audience with cheap admission and fresh material, the crowds parted with more money by attending several times than they'd have spent on taking in a dozen professional shows.

The real difference with the penny gaffs, though, had nothing to do with bad acting, lack of space and second-rate beer. It was the audience, where rough would be putting it kindly. If the jokes weren't vulgar, performers were booed off the stage. The stench of tightly packed unwashed bodies was gagging. Pickpockets and groping was rife.

Which begged the question: what prompted a respectable girl from the Valleys to make such a wild comparison?

The cry of the muffin man, the clop of hooves, and the tinkle of bicycle bells in the street was the equivalent of Oakbourne's dawn chorus. Setting out the china plates for breakfast, Julia detected the splutter of a passing motor car, a far more common sound than this time last year, yet a sight that still drew a decent crowd.

'Top o' the mornin', me darlin'!' Molly barrelled in through the shop, cobalt eyes twinkling as she laid a hot loaf on the table. 'The baker's boy sends his regards.'

'Molly! You didn't —!'

'Him? Lord, no, the kid's only thirteen. I've been to the doctor's on account of me fever, swollen glands, cough, and shortness of breath. Must admit, I was scared, but the doc told me not to worry, it's just a case of Paracoccidioidomycosis. Well, I said, that's easy for you to say...'

Julia laughed. You couldn't help it with Molly. Even so — 'Tell me you didn't spend the night with the baker?'

'Someone had to make sure his dough would rise.' Molly chuckled as she unbuckled her shoes. 'Civic duty, I'd say.'

Seven husbands, none of 'em her own — Annie's words came flooding back. Especially when the baker's wife was away, visiting her ailing sister in Sussex.

'Lizzbells up yet?'

'I haven't heard her,' Julia admitted, and what do you know? There was a good reason for that, as well. Grinning and dishevelled, it seemed Lizzie had also taken it into her head to spend a night on the tiles.

'Here.' Lizzie tossed a rolled-up newspaper for Julia to catch. 'I picked up the early edition on the way home.'

This wasn't fair. The *Chronicle*'s presses, two showgirls and a crime scene photographer had all been hard at it through the night, yet only two of them enjoyed it. Julia felt a twinge of jealousy at the girls' freedom and high spirits. Would there *ever* come a time when women would be as equal here as they were in the Wyoming Territory? She filled a giant pot with coffee. Twenty-five years had passed since women were given the vote out there — a quarter of a bloody century! — yet in Britain, nothing changed. In fact, one of the reasons Sam had modelled himself on Buffalo Bill was Mr. Cody's approach to female emancipation, and Julia could recite by heart the newspaper clipping she had saved.

These fellows who prate about women taking their places make me laugh, Buffalo Bill told the reporter. *If a woman can do the same work that a man can do, and do it just as well, she should have the same pay.*

In reply to the question as to whether women should enjoy the same liberties and privileges as men, he was equally unequivocal.

Most assuredly. If they want to meet and discuss financial questions, politics, or any other subjects, let 'em do it, and don't laugh at 'em for doing it. They discuss things just as sensibly as the men do, I'm sure, and I reckon know just as much about the topics of the day.

That's why Sam felt his studio was in safe hands when he bequeathed it to Julia, and in theory, he was right. As a widow, she was perfectly entitled to own property and sign contracts — which was fine, had she been able to verify her status. Considering Julia had never married, and it wasn't her real name, anyway, proving the death of a fictitious husband without a birth certificate, marriage certificate, or death certificate was two doors down from impossible. Worse, as she very soon discovered, forgeries don't come cheap, which is what set her on the road to taking smutty photos in the first place. Also, Wyoming is a long, long way from Oakbourne, where no self-respecting head of the household would dream of entrusting a mere woman to take the family portrait.

Sam hadn't taken any of this into account, for the simple reason that he'd never been at the blunt end of the contempt and suspicion that single, independent women were viewed with. Every day since he'd died had been a battle for survival. Not all of it financial.

'Right then.' Julia unrolled the newspaper as two ravenous vultures pushed aside the kippers to heap their plates with kidneys, scrambled eggs, bacon and devilled chicken. 'Let's see whether our great nation has won any more medals in Athens.'

The inaugural Games of the I Olympiad (to give them their proper title) were proving such a success, that the follow-up in Paris in four years' time would —

'Oh, dear God!'

One look at Julia's expression and Molly was snatching the paper from her hands. Her face turned white, and Lizzie gasped as they read the headlines: *SHOWGIRL MURDERED! Made To Look Like Suicide.*

'*SHOWGIRL MURDERED! Made To Look Like Suicide*,' Sergeant Kincaid's eyes stood out on stalks as he read the paper Collingwood had passed him. 'Sir, you're telling me the Boss himself tipped that to the press?'

'The chief superintendent believes this is exactly what people should expect, when the circus comes to town.'

'You told him your reasons for wanting to shush it up?'

'In person and in writing, but that's the benefit of being top dog, Charlie. The authority to ride roughshod over anyone, providing you can claim it's in the public interest.'

Whether Miss Oaktree was a woman of loose moral fibre or not, Chief Superintendent Blaine had argued that people would believe it to be the case, and while he acknowledged that the consequences were tragic, he also felt that they were pretty much inevitable.

'That's only his puffed-up, out-of-date, out-of-touch opinion,' Kincaid growled. 'There's no evidence to back any of it up.'

'The cells are overflowing,' Collingwood pointed out.

'With misdemeanours, not violent crimes.'

'The perfect distraction, according to the Super, to get away with murder.'

'He doesn't think that headline might escalate any tensions that travelling fairs always bring?'

Collingwood scrubbed his fingers through his hair. He felt a hundred and two years old. 'The top brass are of the opinion that, if we rattle the Mild West's cages hard enough and loudly enough, they'll pack up early and take their riff-raff act to someone else's jurisdiction.'

'With headlines like that following 'em, the show won't last long, wherever they wash up.'

'That, Charlie, is the whole idea.'

Music halls were multiplying faster than mice force-fed with aphrodisiacs and, through a variety of by-laws, building regulations and planning committees, fell under the control of both central and local government. Travelling shows, on the other hand, were a force unto themselves, attracting undesirable criminal elements, rarely declaring accurate takings and, more often than not, posing serious fire hazards, thanks to naphtha flares, candle chandeliers and dodgy oil lamps. Collingwood wasn't without sympathy, but to promote a girl's murder for political gain was inexcusable.

To the point, in fact, where he'd slammed his fist down so hard on his boss's desk, that ink spurted out of the inkwell and two pencils fell on the floor. 'This is as unnecessary as it's alarmist.'

The fat man hadn't so much as blinked. Merely rolled his cigar round in his mouth, before reminding his inspector that, after an entire day of getting nowhere fast, Collingwood was more in the bloody dark than the damned victim in the morgue, so if putting law-abiding people on their guard was sensationalism, better that, than a string of bloody corpses.

Somewhere in that tirade, Collingwood remembered, the chief superintendent brought out a police whistle from his desk drawer, laid it on his blotter, and thrown in the suggestion that, if Collingwood didn't like it, he'd be more than happy to make arrangements for him to return to patrolling the streets at the regulation two miles per hour. It would certainly be faster than his current progress.

'Our superior officers like to think they're making Oakbourne safer, by moving this rabble on,' Collingwood told Kincaid, 'and in some respects, they're right.'

There were, however, two points that Detective Inspector soon-to-be Constable Collingwood took issue with.

Firstly, people loved the thrill of travelling shows. Admittedly, it led to increased volatility, but danger was part of the attraction. From stockbrokers to stokers, barmaids to bankers, nine to ninety-year-olds, every single person who rolled up to these extravaganzas felt they were stepping into a world where anything might happen, and two thousand of Buffalo Bill's wild mustangs wouldn't keep them away. Nor, in Collingwood's opinion, should they.

Primarily, though — 'To muscle the troupe out of Boot Street's jurisdiction means moving the killer on, as well.'

He was damned if he'd stand aside while a murderer walked free.

CHAPTER 12

Clearing away the abandoned breakfast, Julia thought it was easy to dismiss Molly's and Lizzie's reactions as a combination of shock, bewilderment and grief.

'Seems only ten minutes ago she was borrowing my soap.'

'Wish I hadn't teased her so hard about her nose.'

'Remember that night in Canterbury, when her skirt caught on a nail on the hobby horse?'

'The look on that vicar's face in Oxford, when she asked him if he had an alter ego?'

All the same, watching the girls race back to the pavilion, Julia couldn't shake the feeling that guilt would have a similar effect. If *you* were convinced you'd got away with it, wouldn't *you* gasp, or feel the blood drain from your face, when you saw the murder splashed across the papers?

How the press got wind of it, Julia had no idea, but now it left Collingwood no choice other than to investigate. Still, from first-hand experience, when she was his prime (indeed only) suspect when her models were being picked off one by one, Julia knew Collingwood was too smart to show his hand. More likely, he'd capitalise on the sensationalism, and pass the murder off as random. Then, on the basis that such killers are rarely caught and these were simply witness statements that he was collecting, he'd hope that whoever was responsible grew complacent enough to let their guard down. That's when mistakes were made. That's when he'd swoop.

That's when the gammon joint in Julia's larder would sprout wings and fly.

'My deepest apologies, if you felt I was abusing your good nature, Mrs. McAllister.'

'I thought no such thing, Mr. Vance.'

'You really are very kind, it's just that — oh my goodness, I see you have an admirer.'

Where else was Julia supposed to put the flowers that had been evicted from the bedrooms due to lack of space?

'Widows do tend to receive a certain degree of attention.' She was damned if she was going to admit that she'd bought them herself. 'How's the search coming along? Any news?'

Stupid question. His mouth was tighter than a warship's hull, his eyes were dead, and who could blame him? The death of a child was torment enough, but to have his boy vanish, with so much heartache already behind them, and the police indifferent since he was an adult, and a wealthy one at that...

'Regrettably, none, and that's the reason I failed to call yesterday.' He smoothed the silk of his lapels, tinkered with the kerchief in his breast pocket, shot his cuffs. 'It would have been remiss of me, as a father and a human being, not to check the hospitals and, dare I say it, mortuaries further afield.' Clasping his hands behind his back, he turned to the photographs on the walls. Was he looking past the calm agricultural scenes and tranquil lakeside shots to happier times? Or hoping to absorb some of their serenity?

'I'm very sorry, Mr. Vance.' What do you say to a man whose hours hang heavier than lead? Who trails round hospitals, for God's sake, in a bid to feel useful, when in fact he's completely powerless? 'I can't promise Lady Luck will lay her hand on your shoulder and tell you everything will be fine, but I can promise that a raised hare pie and a chunk of Wensleydale will take the edge off.' When was the last time he ate? Julia bet the skeleton displayed in the pharmacy's window had more meat on its bones.

'No, no, I couldn't possibly impose —'

'Through there.'

If he wondered why she was directing him to the kitchen, rather than the dining room, he was too polite to say. Which was just as well, considering that, along with the drawing room, the morning room, indeed every other square inch downstairs, had been taken over by darkrooms, studios, equipment and store rooms.

'You have an impressive collection of china dogs in your window, Mrs. McAllister.'

'Ah, well.' She laid out the spread and indicated for him to help himself. 'A dog's bones may Rottweiler spirit lives on.'

Corny as the joke was, it was sufficient to soften the rigidity of his gaze. 'I am something of a collector myself.'

'Fine art?'

'Is there any other kind?'

Feeling comfortable enough to open up about himself was an encouraging sign, but — sod's law — before she could exploit the breach and let him talk out the anguish, the shop bell tinkled.

'Mr. Whitmore's not here right now, Mrs. Levinson. He's delivering a portrait, but he should be back in, ooh, twenty minutes. Maybe half an hour? Excellent. See you shortly, I'll tell him you called.' She returned to the kitchen. 'Sorry about that.'

Vance was on his feet, though, the napkin neatly folded on the table, reminding Julia of that time a fishing boat was lost in a storm off the Cornish coast. She was twelve, maybe thirteen, but it was seared in her memory, the scrubbing, the cleaning, the laundering, the polishing of the woman whose husband

and three sons were missing. As she recalled, it was less than a day before they found bits of wreckage floating on a now spitefully calm sea, but that woman's compulsion to keep moving stuck with her.

'I see you are something of a perfectionist.' He indicated the neatly stacked box files, prints and catalogued plates in the adjoining room. 'An admirable quality, Mrs. McAllister, if I may be so bold. On top of that, you are generous, kind, witty … perhaps when my son returns I might have the honour of introducing you to him?'

'I —' You can hardly say not bloody likely to a man who's had his heart and soul ripped out — 'very much look forward to that, Mr. Vance.'

If he'd nibbled a mouthful, she'd be surprised, and she felt a pang of guilt at the relief that swept over her once he was gone. Only a real bitch would judge a man whose life was torn to shreds and scattered to the winds, and who knows? Titus Vance might not always have been so stiff and starchy. Tragedy plays havoc with emotions, and not everybody copes well with the aftermath. On the other hand — and whoops, an even bigger pang — she couldn't help wondering if the son hadn't reached breaking point under the suffocating atmosphere.

Julia also wondered how keen Vance would be on welcoming a daughter-in-law with a talent for snooping.

Was it disloyal, trawling through Lizzie's spangled costumes? Was rifling through Molly's underclothes deceitful?

Julia couldn't say these girls were friends, but then again, she couldn't argue that they weren't. The crucial factor though, and the one that swung the balance, was that Annie Oaktree had been sharing Julia's roof, and if that didn't make it her responsibility, what did? Collingwood would be pulling out every stop to find her killer, but Julia was in a unique position to help with the investigation, and in a way that the police were unable.

There wasn't time to lose! She knew Buck well enough now to know he'd be along any minute to fulfil his obligations to pose as Sam. Last night, exactly as he said he would, he'd collected Annie's possessions under cover of darkness, including the money and the birth certificate that Collingwood had meticulously replaced. Whether Buck was a killer, a thief, or neither, unless he had a black rock in place of a heart, the cash would at least secure the girl a proper burial — unlike little Georgie. Goose pimples rippled Julia's arms at his parents stumbling up the street, pushing their dead son's body in the barrow, knowing that the next stop was to watch him being tossed in an open pit, with the best thing they could hope for was that the pile was nearly full, so earth might finally be laid on top of him.

In brutal irony, the Salvation Army chose that moment to march down the street, singing *All Things Bright and Beautiful* to a loud orchestral accompaniment on tubas, drums and trumpets. It was the very kick Julia needed to stop wallowing, and, starting with Lizzie, dived into the mountain of lace and silks, wondering how on earth any girl could accumulate so many petticoats. Or would want to. All with a waistband the size of the average handspan!

'I'm so flexible, I strain myself getting into a colander,' Lizzie would quip.

Except this wallet containing three marriage certificates for one Elizabeth Pitt, without any record of divorce, was no joke.

Did that make the redhead a hopeless romantic? There was no shortage of jewellery and trinkets from (presumably) her admirers, and enough books, mainly poetry, to put the Library of Alexandria to shame, most inscribed with fond wishes from a variety of men, none of whose names cropped up on the certificates. Or was there a more sinister motive? The classic black widow, who kills her husbands to claim the insurance money? Lizzie clearly had a taste for the fine things in life. Silk petticoats don't come cheap, nor do fine kidskin gloves — and oh my God, was that wrap Russian sable? The most expensive and sought-after of furs, its silver strands glinting like sun through a stained-glass window among a whole box of chinchillas and mink? Did Annie find out? Was that why Lizzie needed to silence her?

Oh, for goodness sake! Julia pushed the skin-tight costumes back in their trunk, and secured the lids on the hat boxes and furs. The Brothers Grimm penned less lurid tales.

Turning to Molly's boxes, where the waistbands here were stressed to breaking point and buttons had been moved more than once, Julia was surprised that rooting through other people's belongings wasn't half as distasteful as it should be. Then again, why should it? A woman had been murdered, and maybe her killing was planned, maybe it wasn't. Either way, there was no getting round the hideous manner of her death, or the callous nature of the cover-up, and if sifting through her friends' personal effects proved that one of them was her killer, then justice had been done.

Of course, if it helped to rule them out, so much the better.

Sensibly, in Julia's opinion, Molly was neither a lover of fine pieces or a hoarder.

Seven husbands, none of 'em her own.

Make that eight with the baker, but Julia didn't believe it was because none of Molly's lovers had ever given her gifts. She might be plain, she might be dowdy, and Julia suspected that everywhere Molly went, women would look her up and down, and think poor cow, who'd marry her? Women, that is, who would call themselves respectable, and feel themselves superior, when in reality their lives were dull, their outlook narrow, and their personalities more shallow than their shadows.

Molly laughed her lovers into bed and left warm memories behind, which is the big attraction with married men. She could love 'em and leave 'em, no strings attached, and that included tangible reminders. Life on the road, as Julia knew from travelling with Sam, needed to be simple. The worst accusation you could throw was hypochondria — all those nasal sprays for the relief of seasickness, hay fever and congestion brought on by colds and flu — which meant Molly's possessions, by and large, were both predictable and boring.

At least right up to the clipping from the *Manchester Times* that dated back twelve years recording how one Molly Bannister, aged ten, died when she lost her footing in a quarry.

With rehearsals in full swing under the red and white canvas, only a mind reader of the highest order could divine that there had been a death in the family, never mind a violent one.

'I'm taking this jar of vinegar straight back to the shop,' Hal was saying.

'Why's that, Honky-Tonk?' Molly continued.

'Look at it, old girl. It has lumps in it.'

'Those are pickled onions.'

'Stop right there.' Buck held up his hand. 'Your timing's excellent, Hal, but you need to project your voice more. They won't hear you at the back.'

'Those should be Annie Oaktree's lines,' Avalon whispered to Julia. 'Instead, poor old Hal's been roped in, and ducks have never taken worse to water.'

'Keep going,' Buck was saying. 'Just remember to project from the diaphragm.'

Hal nodded. Molly took up from where they'd left off. 'Be careful when you talk to Wild Bill Hiccup over there.' She pointed an exaggerated finger at Dodger, twirling his pistols with a maniacal grin.

'Why? Is he dangerous?'

'Dangerous? That man's so wild, he'll plug your novel.'

'Nope.' Buck stepped forward. 'Look, I know you're accustomed to exercising your fingers, rather than your vocal cords, but the joke's lost if no one can hear you, Hal.'

'I'll do it,' Avalon piped up. 'If you swap the next two acts around, I can play Molly's stooge in the pioneer frock I wear for the guillotine, and still have loads of time to revert back to a Cherokee squaw for our next skit.'

Buck turned to Dodger. 'Your wife's a genius, did you know that?'

Dimples popped in Dodge's cheeks. 'So she keeps telling me.'

Within what seemed like half a second, Hal was back at the ivories, Avalon was on stage, and Molly was saying, 'Did you know the Mild West Show used to have a human cannon ball?'

'What happened?' Avalon asked.

'Buck fired him.'

'Excellent!' Buck held up a triumphant thumb. 'Not so loud that freeloaders outside the tent can hear, but perfect for all those squashed in at the back. Good work, Avalon. Well done.'

Watching their professionalism coping under the strain, admiring the easy way the troupe had adapted to change —

including murder — Julia found it hard to believe that someone here could be a cold-blooded killer. While the girls were going through their new routine, the Great MMM was passing a hoop across his levitating assistant to prove there were no wires or rods holding her up. Once again, how he pulled that off, Julia had no idea, but did his hand shake? Did it hell. The coordination was as perfect as his handsome features. On the board, Lizzie lay as stiff as the hypnotised creature she was playing. Not a tremor. Even her hair had been tamed under a blonde wig, and as for Buffalo Buck, if a reporter came in now, they'd think the worst problem the showman had to deal with was making sure the tear-drop pinch in his Stetson was symmetrical, and that the diamantes studding its leather band caught the light.

Could it be that they simply didn't care? *Girls don't stay with us long*, Annie had confided over lunch, so perhaps, like Julia, the cast also avoided making friends, since loss was hard to come to terms with? Some of them might feel that way, just as others might brush off murder as terrible-but-these-things-happen, while some might even agree with the chief superintendent, dismissing it a risk that goes with the job.

Or was pretence so entrenched in their collective psyche that armour plating came as standard?

That was something else Julia understood. She'd worn hers for nearly thirteen years, and dear God, was that suit heavy! Surely, though, none of them would have to carry the deep, dark, terrible secret that she'd had to live with. Watching the riverboat gambler pass the hoop back and forth over his floating assistant, a chill filled the pavilion. Did Julia regret killing her stepfather? Not once. It was his life or theirs, and even taking family out of the equation, simple mathematics said saving two lives at the expense of one was justified. The regret came from letting the bastard get away with it so long, and not saving her mother and her brother earlier, and never mind that she was only fourteen.

Julia turned her attention back to the comic routine. According to the *Manchester Times*, ten-year-old Molly Bannister had been playing in the quarry with her three brothers and their friends when she fell. So who was Molly Bannister? And why was she so important that "this" Molly stole her name?

Julia thought back to when the girls barrelled into her shop (was it really only two days ago?). *Ever so funny, that sign in your window*, Annie Oaktree said, pointing to "Shoot the kids, hang the family, frame them all." To which Lizzie had quipped, *even you're not that funny, Molls.* As Julia recalled, the comedienne's reply was something along the lines of *no, but now I've seen it, that gag's mine.* Quite right. Inspiration was the lifeblood of creativity, and as names went, Molly Bannister was both catchy and unusual. Who wouldn't be tempted to use it as a stage name, having read it in the paper? Which didn't explain why she kept the clipping…

'Did you know that Buffalo Bill named his Springfield rifle *Lucretia Borgia*, after the famous Italian poisoner?' Molly was saying.

'Why did he do that?' Avalon asked.

'Because, just like his rifle, Lucretia Borgia was beautiful but deadly.'

'Then why does Buffalo Buck call his rifle *Fart*?'

'Buck's is silent but deadly.'

Extra rehearsals weren't a ploy to take people's mind off the shocking news. Now the cast was one member short, they were a necessity, since there was no room for improvisation where acts were tightly choreographed and the players dependent on one other for timing and support. All for one, and one for all. Just like the three musketeers for solving murder. Motive, means and opportunity...

'The Boss'll never say, Snaps —' Dodger quietly sidled up to Julia so as not to interrupt the flow on stage — 'but he's dead grateful that you agreed to stand in again today.'

'What happened was horrible. I'm happy I am able to help.' Help hang the snake who'd throttled the life out of a defenceless young woman, then tried to pass it off as *her* choice.

'We've had to drop some of the acts,' Dodger said, 'change Annie's role into non-speaking parts, and add a couple of extra illusions.'

'Like the hoop trick?'

'Like the hoop trick. But if one more person says the show must go on, that's what Junie would want, I say bugger that, pardon my Français. Junie would want to still bloody be here! Oops, 'scuse me. Avalon's going off set, to change costumes, that's my cue.' He bounded on stage, leaving Julia unsure which surprised her most. The bitterness in his voice as he talked of Junie. Or the carefree expression that masked it, when he addressed his would-be audience: 'When I asked my brother what he'd like for his birthday, he said I'd like a bookmark. It broke my heart when I heard that.'

'Why's that, love?' Molly asked.

'Because he's twelve years old, and he still can't remember my name is Sylvester.'

Suppose it was a case of mistaken identity?

Molly Bannister's 'ad seven husbands, none of 'em her own, Annie had said, suggesting she'd ruined more marriages than Monday night football practice. This wouldn't be the first time that an angry, hurt and disconsolate wife would want to kill the bitch who'd stolen the love of her life. Unaware that Molly was the love-'em-and-leave-'em type, it was easy to picture the aggrieved wife following her man across the Common. Watching him sneak inside the tent. Hearing giggles. Whispers. Sounds that were no longer heard in her own bedroom. What if he emerged — smiling, laughing, smug, who knows? — and the next person to come out was Annie Oaktree? No one wants to think their husband has deceived them with a short, fat frump. Before you know it, two and two have added up to five, and the wrong woman is dead.

Then again. *Lizzie's got more licences than a string of public houses.* Three hardly constituted a string, but it was definitely a pattern, suggesting more a string of broken hearts. Suppose one of them felt betrayed by her shallow idea of love? Or couldn't cope with the fact that he'd been duped? Was it such a leap to then imagine he'd baulked at doing the ugly deed himself, but paid a third party to kill the woman who'd shamed him? Who tragically gets the names muddled up? Or the humiliated lover fails to mention the colour of her hair…?

These were possibilities to consider, and that was just the start, but for now it was Julia's turn under the spotlight. Nervous to the point of shaking in case she fluffed it, Annie Oaktree barely noticed the backdrop had turned the stage into a saloon, while Buffalo Buck's banter was nothing but babble.

'The trick is to show teeth,' Avalon whispered. 'Lots and lots of teeth.'

'My top lip's already stuck to my gums,' Julia lisped back.

'Perfect!' Avalon giggled. 'That way, the audience won't see the screwed up concentration in your eyes. They won't see your stage fright. All they'll see is your dazzling smile, where smile equals confidence, confidence means they're getting a good show, good show equals value for money, which equals more bums on seats for us tomorrow.'

Julia understood why Buck felt the Mild West would falter without her. She watched the impresario, twirling his pistols to the delight of the imaginary crowd. From the wings, she could see that the polished walnut grips were intricately carved, but not whether they were inset with ivory or mother-of-pearl. They were fine pieces, though, that much was sure.

Dressed top to toe in black, and wearing a false moustache, the magician strode on stage, flipping the deck, fanning it, shuffling the cards so fast, that the pack blurred one into the other.

'That's an impressive display, Diamond Jim,' Buck said. 'But what's that up your sleeve?'

The gambler seemed shaken. 'Are you calling me a cheat?'

'Let's see, shall we?' He grabbed Diamond Jim's coat, where two cards fluttered on to the floor. 'Queen of Spades,' he said, showing them round, 'and the Ace of Hearts. How do you explain that?'

'It's a mistake,' the gambler insisted.

'A mistake? You, sir, have been cheating poker tables all the way from Firewood to Stodge City! What we need, folks, is a heroine.' Avalon nudged Julia forward. 'Annie Oaktree will run this villain out of town, won't you, Annie?'

While Julia wondered if she'd ever be able to straighten her face again, Buck was addressing the invisible audience behind his hand.

'She used to partner with her husband, y'know, until he suggested she fired straight at him and he'd catch the bullet between his teeth. I tell you, ladies and gentlemen, that was the last time he'd shoot his mouth off.'

'How dare you accuse me of being a card sharp!' The gambler snatched both cards out of Buffalo Buck's hand, but not before Julia had pulled her gun and fired. Down fell the flag that read *Bang!* She fired again, and a second flag fell down that read *Bang! Bang!* Diamond Jim pressed his hand to his heart and staggered, but it wasn't the gambler who had been shot. In his fist, the Queen of Spades and the Ace of Hearts were peppered with holes.

'And on that subject, my friends, tomorrow I'll tell you about our lovely Indian princess, Poker Hottest, and how she got her name playing five-card stud in the saloons of Clacton, Scarborough and Poole. But for tonight — that's all, folks. Thank you all for coming, and please don't forget to tell everyone how you had a wonderful evening. But this wasn't it.'

As Buck closed the show with a sweep of his Stetson and Hal played out the imaginary audience with a foot-stomping *Polly Wolly Doodle all the day*, Julia decided that the idea of a stranger committing murder was a million times better than the prospect of one of the cast calmly plotting some kind of tragic accident, should they get wind that she was closing in on them.

Unfortunately, as attractive as the idea sounded, Julia also knew that, from now until the show moved on, she'd be locking her bedroom door at night, and checking for string across the top of the stairs.

CHAPTER 13

Steadying her tripod, Julia slotted the glass plate inside the camera. Usually, when the shutter opened, it captured a unique moment in a person's life, one that could never be recreated or repeated, and froze it in perpetuity. This, however, wasn't a family portrait or a wedding, where the emphasis was on individuality beneath the formality. This was pure pleasure.

Around her, groundsmen mowed the grass, pulled up weeds, and rolled the gravel walkways. Birds sang with the exuberance that only spring could produce. Blossoms unfurled on the trees. Before disappearing under the heavy cloth, Julia took a long look around. With its mature trees, rare plantings, broad stone steps and reflective ponds, a stranger would be forgiven for thinking this was Oakbourne's botanical gardens, rather than the land of its dead. Proof that not everything from the Industrial Revolution was overshadowed by poverty, misery and the threat of eternal damnation if you weren't buried close to a church.

She lined up a shot of a cocker spaniel lapping at the edge of the pond and, like the residents of this place, absorbed the peace and tranquillity of her surroundings. Just as photography requires patience, and the perfect shot is made from many, so concentration empties the mind. Injustice cannot thrive while you're bringing a marble lion into focus. Disquiet withers when a thrush perches on a headstone with a beak full of wriggling worms.

'You should have said you'd be working,' a gravelly voice rumbled. 'I'd have helped carry your equipment. That stuff's heavy.'

'Tell me something I don't know, Charlie.' Julia wriggled out from under the cloth. 'By the time it's my turn to lie under this grass, I'll have arms like a circus strongman.'

'As long as it's just your arms.' Kincaid's cadaverous features twisted. It was only once you got to know him, that you recognised the changes as a grin. 'Coz the only strongmen I've seen were as bald as coots.'

'Why do you think I wear a hat?'

'And there's me thinking it was to keep your brains in. Ah, thanks.' He took the photograph of the railway victim. 'Hopefully someone, somewhere will be able to put a name to the face, and if they don't...? At least it rules out a local.'

That was another thing Julia liked about Charlie Kincaid. No matter how dire the prospects, he always found a bright side, and as much as her mind could have emptied equally well, sharing coffee and buns in her studio, the last thing she wanted was to be seen dealing with the police as anything other than a witness. So far, none of the cast knew about her crime scene connections, including Buck, and she'd very much like to keep it that way.

Though wasn't it odd that the showman didn't question why she was at the morgue in the first place, to identify Annie Oakley's remains —?

'Nice camera, by the way.'

'The best, Charlie.' She rubbed her hand over the carefully crafted dovetail joints and the fine grain of the Spanish mahogany casing. 'Pure precision.'

'More than that. I'd say, it's a work of love.'

'I wish I could share your enthusiasm when I'm polishing the damn thing. That's almost as hard work as musical comedy.'

'Not funny, then?'

'Not remotely.'

'The jokes are.'

'The skits are.'

'The illusions are mesmerising,' he said. 'But —?'

Counting out the timing? Listening for cues from the music? Taking cues from the cast? Having to stand in a specific spot, at a specific moment, holding yourself at a specific angle? 'The level of concentration beggars belief, and there's no room for error, Charlie. One mistake, and the whole act goes down like a house of marked cards.'

'Ah, well. Takes practice to make things look easy, least that's what my mum reckoned, God rest her soul.' He pointed past an explosion of bright yellow forsythia. 'Buried right there, as it 'appens. Probably watching us now.'

'Then let's make her day.' Julia picked up her camera, indicating for Charlie Kincaid to collect the rest of the paraphernalia. 'Whereabouts exactly?'

'You're not going to —?'

'Photograph her grave, so you'll have a permanent memento? Of course I am, and no charge, before you start opening your wallet and letting the moths out.' She set down the tripod and curtsied. 'Pleased to meet you, Mrs. Kincaid. Now then. How about a nice wide smile for your son?'

It was odd. Surrounded by death, yet everything about this place was uplifting. Thanks to first the cholera epidemic, then the high mortality rates from heavy manufacturing, traditional churchyards filled to saturation point, forcing the creation of new burial grounds with a whole new fresh approach. Reminiscent of country estates (except with a chapel, as opposed to a mansion), the idea was to stop people associating cemeteries with decay and departure, rife with body-snatching, gambling and prostitution at night. Instead, they were treated to exquisite settings, where their loved ones could truly rest in peace, where they could talk to the deceased, tend their graves, and re-live happy times. On Sundays, families congregated with picnics, lovers strolled the gravel paths, and factory workers found respite from the non-stop pounding of steam hammers and the incessant clank of machinery. Some visitors were even known to bring blankets, and spend the night.

'Any luck with the search for Mr. Vance's missing boy?' Julia asked, sliding the plate cover from its holder.

'Name don't ring a bell.' Kincaid brushed fallen blossoms from around the headstone. 'How old's the kid?'

'Thirty-three.'

His laugh was like gravel swishing around in a tin. 'I'll follow that up straight away,' he said, with a mock salute. 'Once I've found the bastard who chained up this poor sod. Chased up a string of robberies. Find the pig who assaulted an old woman in her bed. Nailed a couple of fraudsters. Put paid to that spate of burglaries by the viaduct. Found a missing librarian. Arrested the scum who's stealing from the homeless while they sleep. Cracked down on the pilfering from the bargees — it's fast reaching vigilante point, that. Oh yes, and proved, God knows how, that Mrs. X (can't tell you more) is actively poisoning her old man. I could rattle off a dozen more, but I think you get the drift.'

'You forgot that little matter of Annie Oaktree's murder.'

'Rattling that particular cage is the inspector's job, and he's very welcome to it, and here, while we're on the subject, you want to be careful, Julia. I know you say there's no one better placed to find out what's going on inside that tent —'

'There isn't.'

'Maybe not, but the closer the access the closer the danger.' He jabbed his pipe in warning. 'We're not talking about someone who lashed out in anger. This was very, very carefully thought out.'

'I can look after myself, Charlie.'

'Pound to a penny the dead girl used them very same words.'

'I appreciate your concern,' she said, giving his shoulder an affectionate shake. 'But haven't you got arsonists or a counterfeit gang or something to run to ground?'

'Listen, love, if you think them crimes I mentioned is going to stop me and the boss from worrying, you're wrong.'

'I may have my faults, Charlie, but being wrong isn't one of them. Now kindly leave me and your mum to finish our chat, this is girl talk, and you're interrupting.'

With his laugh echoing down the tree-lined path, Julia turned back to her camera. She understood why the police would put a missing adult at the bottom of their list, but if Titus Vance found out that they weren't even *looking* for his son, it would be a knife to the chest. She took a long, hard look around. There was nothing dismal or foreboding about the marble lilies and stone angels, or the smiling cherubs, curled-up lambs, and open books. Quite the opposite. There were far worse places for a man to lay his son to rest — but at least he'd have a grave to weep over. Right now, he was tortured by uncertainty, with every scenario more terrifying than the last, and, since a father's only job was to protect his children, he'd be wracked with guilt and shame.

Julia uncovered her lens, then quickly covered it again. The plates were highly sensitive. A fraction of a second was enough to capture Mrs. Kincaid's headstone, and what a beautiful monument it was. God willing, Titus Vance wouldn't be ordering a similar marker any time soon, but the more days that passed, the harder it would be to find answers. If he had any chance of finding peace, he'd need help.

Satisfied with her shot, Julia gathered her equipment, and tucked her tripod under her arm. No more waifs and strays, she had promised herself. No more involvement in other people's problems. Fine in theory — but she couldn't just stand by. Like it or not, she'd just have to pitch into the mystery of his disappearance herself.

Exactly *how* Julia was going to fit this in might be the biggest mystery yet, because if it wasn't one problem, it was another. Judging by the comments and sneers she overheard on her way home, the girls' dawn return hadn't passed unnoticed. The coalman told his wife, who told the haberdasher, who told the milliner, who told the greengrocer, who told the pharmacist...

'Is there ANYONE in Oakbourne who doesn't think Whitmore Photographic has become some kind of bawdy house?' she asked Buck, rolling her eyes.

'Oh ye of little faith,' he laughed. 'While you were out, snapping whatever it is you people snap, your Sam was smoothing out their worries, ironing out their fears, and neutralising every single snip of vicious gossip.'

'In short, you disappointed three hundred upstanding matrons of our illustrious community.'

'I'll have you know, Buffalo Buck *never* disappoints a lady, ma'am. Sam merely explained how his boarders offered to run errands in return for a portrait, and crossed his fingers that no one thought to question why the ladies ventured outdoors at that time of the morning in their finery.'

'They're showgirls, Buck. Respectable society wouldn't expect anything less.'

It all boiled down to the same old issue, though. The whole business could have been avoided, if this wretched building had a back entrance. Unfortunately, since Julia had never had two farthings to rub together, she couldn't afford the piece of land behind the studio that would give her access to the street beyond, much less pay to have holes knocked in a thick stone wall and have a door put in. Such a shame! After all, what was the point in building up new contacts for selling saucy pictures, if she had no way of taking the bloody things? Previously, she'd operated from a secret studio across town, something she couldn't set up again, even if she had the money, since it required a man to sign the lease. With a back route in and out, she wouldn't need to wait for England to catch up with Wyoming on the matter of equality. Her models could come and go any time they pleased without arousing suspicion — and everybody's reputation would be safe.

'By the way,' Buck was saying, changing out of Sam's clothes into his own. 'That detective inspector, who interviewed the rest of us earlier, called while you were out. Said he'll come back later to take your statement.' His brow furrowed. 'Felt sure I'd seen him before.'

Julia hoped that chatting to Collingwood in the wings yesterday wouldn't just pass the audience by — every eye on the illusionist, and all that. She'd also assumed Buck would write him off as another stage door johnny. *Damn.* 'Did he say if he was any closer to finding June's killer?' she asked quickly.

'He's working on the theory that she was most likely chosen at random, in which case, such crimes are virtually impossible to solve.'

'The idea of someone getting away with murder is awful.'

'I imagine a lot of people get away with it.' Buck leaned forward, dark eyes boring into hers. 'It just takes planning,' he whispered.

The breath caught in Julia's throat. She saw her stepfather. A wife-beater. A bully. A rapist. She heard quotes from the Bible.

The sun shall be turned into darkness and the moon into blood — She heard bones crack. More quotes. Old Testament. New Testament. His fists didn't care. *They that wait upon the Lord shall renew their strength* — His boots certainly renewed their strength as they slammed into her brother, and suddenly, she was lifting a gun from its hiding place. Digging a grave. Making an assignation that implied the two of them were running away…

'Sorry, Buck, must dash. Need to develop these as a matter of urgency.'

Running to her studio, she slammed the door, and slowly slid down the wall. *The sun shall be turned into darkness* — Was that why her darkroom had become her sanctuary? So the moon wouldn't be turned into blood? After a few minutes, maybe five, she stopped shaking.

After another few, maybe ten, she wiped her eyes, blew her nose and stood up. Demons can't live in these sorts of conditions. They need fear to thrive. They need chaos and turmoil and guilt, and there was none of that here, inside Julia's darkroom.

Only the certainty that, if you kill a man in cold blood, you hang.

For that to happen, though, someone has to find out.

CHAPTER 14

Twelve fifteen. Julia made a quick calculation, and decided that, if she played it right, she could avoid Detective Inspector Collingwood, pick Avalon's brains, and treat herself to a lunch that didn't involve preparation, cooking, then washing the dishes, before following up on a theory she had about Vance the Younger, fitting the whole lot in before the afternoon matinée started.

Plans, however, have a way of tempting fate. Admittedly, catching Avalon at the boarding house was a long shot. Knowing her, she'd be sitting cross-legged under red and white canvas, gluing wayward feathers to the warbonnet, spot-cleaning the costumes, or polishing the spurs. *I honestly couldn't imagine this show without her*, Buck had said right at the start, and Julia believed it. From mixing pots of greasepaint, straightening costumes, sewing on buttons, running to the shops if Hal ran out of tobacco, or if she just felt a bag of custard creams would go down well between the dummy runs, Avalon was the grease that kept the Mild West running smoothly. What Julia *hadn't* bargained for was the landlady's frown, which had nothing to do with a young woman in a midnight blue bloomer suit standing on her doorstep beside a bicycle.

'Who?'

'Mrs. Wright.'

'Not this boarding house, lovey.'

'Mr. Roger Wright and his wife, Avalon…?'

'So she found her Mr. Right, did she? Bully for her,' the landlady said. 'Still no one here by that name.'

'This *is* Vine Cottage?'

Conveniently next door to the tea rooms, Avalon had said, *where I hear they serve a scrumptious Welsh rarebit.* The very treat Julia had promised herself for lunch!

'Says so on the plaque, don't it?'

The landlady's patience was growing thin, but everyone on the road keeps secrets. Suppose these lovebirds were only pretending to be married? Suppose Dodger used a stage name because his real name was Whiffing, Leech or Crapper?

'Young couple, very handsome. She's blonde and slender, he has dimples in his cheeks —'

'Save your breath. There's no couples here, full stop.'

Before Julia could thank her anyway, the door had shut in her face, and damn. There wasn't time to circle back to the pavilion, as well as follow up on Vance's son. How important was it to pump Avalon about Lizzie? She stared at the shiny, bright brass knocker, still rattling against its plate. Was she reading too much into Lizzie, asking if she could have the vacant room on the grounds that it had a better view for one thing, and when she lost the toss over who would be sharing, she had no idea that Molly snored? No one kills just so they can have a room to themselves, for what, a couple of days, a week, at the most! She'd spent the night out, anyway, or was that the point? With Husband Number Lost-Count currently being lined up, what girl wouldn't want as much privacy as she could get, given that hotel rooms weren't an option on her wages?

Even so... Sharp little rats' teeth gnawed at the back of Julia's mind.

Suppose Lizzie *had* killed her colleague? The motive could still have been to silence her, but if she suspected Annie had hidden something — something that incriminated her, that she hadn't been able to find in earlier searches — switching rooms made sense. Especially if she was despatching the men for money, in which case no divorce papers were *ever* going to be found.

Avalon? Vance's son? Lunch? Still undecided, Julia was so busy turning her bicycle away from the boarding house, that she failed to notice a boy with patched trousers and felt cap until he cannoned into her. In one grubby fist was the string of a top, which he'd been whipping down the street at full pelt. In the other, the iced bun he was munching at the same time. Disengaging herself from rope, crumbs and the sort of gleeful chuckles that could only come from a child bunking off school, she was suddenly struck by the spectre of another young boy.

Her brother, Cador. He has been just eight years old when their father's crushed and bloodied body was wheeled home from the mine. Julia was only six, but even as kids, they were conditioned to accidents. Ropes broke. Rocks fell. Blasting through granite with gunpowder increased efficiency (what used to take a group of miners six days with a pickaxe now effectively took minutes), but every year, men died in these explosions. It was just that, until then, accidents had happened to other people.

Some mines had lifts, but many, like the one her father worked, relied on ladders where, after a ten-and-a-half-hour shift in dust poisonous with arsenic, the miners then had to haul themselves up to the surface. Was he exceptionally exhausted that day? Did someone shout, tell a joke, call his name, that made him lose concentration? After rain, the tunnels ran wet. Was the ladder slippery from the boots of the men up ahead? Julia would never know. Only that, as he reached the top, Pa lost his grip, and fell three hundred feet straight down the shaft.

Suddenly, Julia knew exactly which direction she'd be taking. Wondering why he slipped, running through his last thoughts and dying moments, haunted her still, and that same lack of resolution would be torture for the parents, maybe a wife, brothers and sisters, who were missing a young man with fair hair and a mole at the side of his mouth — and was eating Titus Vance alive, too. Uncertainty trumped any niggles she harboured over Lizzie's request for a room to herself, even the death of the girl whose bed she'd taken over. Harsh as it sounded, solving murder was the job of the police, and not only was Collingwood a bloody good officer, he had the entire Boot Street police force at his disposal. Whereas a missing adult, with no seemingly suspicious circumstances surrounding his disappearance, had no one in his corner, except his father.

Cycling along the towpath, Julia was amazed that her bloomer suit, ending as it did just past the knees, didn't attract the same outrage from the bargees as it did on the road. If anything, she'd expected women in huge, heavy bonnets and frumpy frocks to sneer at best, spit at worst, but prejudice is an ugly trait, and shame flared her cheeks. The bonnets they wore kept off the sun, the frocks were made for hard work, not fashion. Besides, their dress code, like the painted roses and castles that coloured the boats, gave them a unique identity and bestowed individuality. Just a shame that the women on barges heading west were scooping buckets of the same water to wash their clothes that women from barges heading east had emptied their chamber pots in. No wonder cholera was still rife on the narrowboats.

'Nice legs,' one of the stokers shouted across, wolf-whistling her shapely stockinged calves.

'They run in the family,' she yelled back.

'Ha, ha, you should be in that Mild West Show!'

Putting smiles on faces meant Julia's time on earth wasn't wasted, but dear God, wouldn't it be wonderful to do it without having a bag packed, ready to run at a moment's notice, or not be constantly looking over her shoulder? She'd cut a deal with Collingwood. In exchange for certain favours during the last murder case she'd assisted with, he'd agreed to stop looking into her past, and she trusted him. He'd given his word, and his word was his bond — but he wasn't the only policeman on the force. Charlie Kincaid was affable and kind, but he was sharper than lime, and more ambitious than he made out. Also, if Collingwood got wind that premeditated murder was involved, he'd put justice above a promise any day.

And then there was the moneylender. The big Russian from the Ukraine, whose interest rates were spiralling out of control, and whose thugs took a great deal of pleasure in their work...

She waggled her fingers at a baby harnessed to one of the decks, and watched it kick its feet and chuckle. Anyone who imagined these ribbons of water were silent carriageways was in for a shock. Sixteen unbroken hours spent loading and unloading from the factories and mills, redistributing the weight, maintaining the engines, or seeing to the horses for those that hadn't switched to steam meant sixteen unbroken hours spent barking orders or snapping out complaints, and that's without the clang of winches, the pounding of pistons or the creak of chains and pulleys.

Amid such a turbulent lifestyle, there were very few people whose occupations were both static and yet in a position to monitor and observe everything that happened on the canal. One such job belonged to the lock-keeper, another to the canal inspector, though two more different roles could not be imagined — or viewed in diametrically opposite camps. Julia glanced at the lock-keeper, chatting to the boat people, laughing and joking, making small talk and banter as he opened the sluice gates. Once clear of urbanisation, mile upon mile of this watery network passed without a single manned lock, making men like him a mainstay for itinerant bargees. Their north star, if you like. The lock-keeper would certainly give Julia the information that she wanted. What he wouldn't be able to give her was much of his time.

'Mr. Nicholls?'

As luck would have it, the inspector was just heading back to his canal-side cottage, swinging his bowler hat in his hand.

'I was, when I woke up this morning, although maybe I'm still dreaming. No one ever approaches me. In fact, they usually run, hide or throw things. How can I help?'

Julia passed him her card. The one that listed her services as a crime scene photographer.

'My, my.' He rubbed a hand over his little bald head. 'Doesn't this lift the tedium! Mind, there's precious few crimes round here, dear. Leastways, not of the nature I imagine you'd be recording.'

For a man who was universally hated and despised for prying into peoples' private lives, she hadn't expected the inspector to boast such a jolly smile, or imagined there'd be a spring in his step. In fact, water off a duck's back was the phrase that sprang to mind.

'It's more a crime that I'm unable to record,' Julia said. 'A man has gone missing, there's no logical reason for his disappearance, yet at the same time, there are no suspicious circumstances, either.'

'I'm not sure where I fit into that — oh, excuse me a sec. That's another of the little sods off.' He cupped his hands round his mouth and shouted. 'Don't think I didn't see that!' His voice carried further than a foghorn and came over twice as loud, which she supposed it would have to, to override the shouts and shunts of canal life.

'Sorry, am I keeping you from your work?'

'Not remotely, dear.' Green eyes twinkled behind his spectacles. 'The boaties see me coming —' he tapped his tell-tale clipboard — 'and think they can outsmart me by making the kids jump ship before they tie up, but the law's the law. You can't fight it or outrun it for ever.'

Ouch. 'In what way, Mr. Nicholls?'

'If it's not me who's checking that the number of people on board complies with regulations, the next inspector down the line will, and they can't keep pretending those aren't all their kids, or that their eighteen-year-old daughter's well-formed for her age, and honest, guv, she's still under twelve.' Nicholls shook his head. 'Buggers think it's perfectly decent to have a full-grown woman sharing a cabin twelve foot long that doubles as kitchen, living room and bedroom with her parents, but it isn't.' He laughed. 'I know, I know. You think these peoples' lives are short and careworn enough as it is, without some government official prying, and spying, and writing it down.'

'Funnily enough, I don't think that at all.' Travelling the country with badly overcrowded cabins was one thing, and why the law made a fuss of who slept where and at what age was a mystery. But the inspector's primary role was making sure the kids had access to schooling, and, more importantly, that they weren't being put to work. 'Child labour sailed with the ark, Mr. Nicholls.'

'Actually, it sails on half the bloody barges that pass through. Leastways, it would, if it wasn't for the likes of me.' He tapped his little round nose. 'They don't outfox Nicholls. Every boat stores drinking water, and with the crew busy loading and discharging, it's the nippers' job to fetch it. I simply wait by the water pump.' Busy folk have blissfully short memories, he chuckled. Once they moor, nosey inspectors are instantly forgotten. All he had to do was follow the little ones back along the towpath, after which there was no escaping officialdom. 'So while we wait for this next lot to pull their dodges, tell me about your missing gentleman.'

There wasn't much to tell, Julia admitted. That was the trouble. 'But if someone fell in accidentally, say lost his footing in the dark, couldn't swim, and drowned —'

'The water's shallow, dearie. Someone would have seen the body, they're a sharp-eyed lot, these boaties. That's how so much stuff gets nicked. Believe me, light-fingered doesn't begin to describe 'em, and that's why no one likes 'em.'

'These warehouses are tall, they cast permanent deep shade, and the water's far from clear. If he also happened to be wearing dark clothes…'

'You fall in, you drown, three days later, there or thereabouts, your body fills with gas and up you come.' The inspector twirled his bowler hat in his hands. 'Seen more than my fair share of that in my time.'

'Your there or thereabouts changes with heart disease, though. Should the heart suddenly compress, the corpse will still sink, only it takes longer to come back up to the surface.'

'Still don't see how your gentleman could fall in and part of him not catch on a hull, a rope or a pole.' He swept his arm around. 'Look at the amount of traffic, dear. Next to impossible, I'd say.'

'Next to is good enough for me.'

'In that case, you might try under one of the bridges. Some of 'em are pretty wide, and when they're wide they're dark, and when they're dark, the boaties hug the side so's not to bang into one another. Oops. Excuse me.' He donned his little bowler hat and tapped his clipboard. 'Water pump time. But if I was you, I'd say my best bet was the middle of one of them dark bridges. Good day to you, Mrs. McAllister!'

Julia watched him saunter off, whistling (*Abdul Abulbul Amir*, unless she missed her guess), and thought, that was fine. Finally, she had somewhere to look.

Only how was she supposed to go poking around under dark bridges at night, without a boat, or the ability to walk on water?

CHAPTER 15

'This wasn't part of the original schedule,' Avalon confided to Julia. 'It was just that, suddenly, we couldn't sell enough tickets to accommodate everyone, so Buck had a brainwave.'

A brainwave, Julia wondered, as she squeezed through the palisade. Or part of the plan? Ghouls descend on murder scenes like wasps to ripe fruit — but would the showman really kill one of his own cast to double the takings? *Girls don't stay with us long*, Annie had said. Maybe Collingwood should look into that.

'He had a word with the City Council yesterday, and they agreed we could fence off the pond on the Common, with admission for paying customers only,' Avalon said. 'Eddie, Buck and Hal spent half the night setting this up.'

'Impressive,' Julia said. 'Who's Eddie?'

Avalon pointed with the pasty she was munching.

Surely not! 'The Great MMM is called Eddie?'

'Eddie Cox to be precise.'

Gone was the shimmering gold jacquard waistcoat. This afternoon he was top to tailcoat in black, wearing a black mask over his nose and mouth. No one would even think to link him with the riverboat gambler, making the mid-section of his assistant disappear, or cutting her head off at Madame Guillotine, just as they wouldn't see him as card sharp, Diamond Jim. Surrounded by half of Oakbourne squashed inside the fence, Julia wasn't worried about being recognised, either. True, her soft brim was pulled low over her face as a precaution, but with her long hair loose, a lasso in one hand, a pistol in the other, and her fringed cowgirl skirt swinging each time she moved, even her own mother wouldn't make the connection between Annie Oaktree and the photographer's lowly assistant.

'I called at Vine Cottage earlier. I thought we might take lunch in the tea rooms next door, my treat, only the landlady hadn't heard of you.'

'She wouldn't.' Avalon giggled. 'I got the whole thing completely muddled up. Again! Vine Cottage is where Eddie and Hal are staying. Dodge and me are at the White Lion Inn, and honestly, my memory's such a joke these days, Molly's even worked a gag in. *How long have you suffered from memory loss?* she asks, to which I have to say *as long as I can remember.* Ooh, I've just thought of a way to make this skit even funnier.'

She scampered off, saloon girl feathers waving in the breeze. On the makeshift stage by the duck house, Molly was warming up the crowd. 'What's your favourite childhood memory?' she asked the audience. 'Skipping? Football? Tying ribbons on puppy dogs' tails? Mine was building sandcastles with my grandmother. Leastways, until Dad took the urn away.'

'Hey,' Buck shouted, as Dodger swaggered forward. 'Aren't you Marshal Kwyatt Burp?'

In reply, Dodger let out a theatrical belch.

'Ah. Not so *quiet*, then,' Buck said, pulling a face. The crowd lapped it up. 'What brings you to this part of Stodge City?'

'I'm bringing in Texas Jack. He's wanted everywhere from Land's End to John O'Groats.'

'How many people has he killed?' asked an astonished Buffalo Buck.

'None,' the marshal said. 'It's the ladies who want him.' He waited for the laughter to die down. 'Say, you haven't seen him, have you?'

Suddenly, a mass of red feathers popped up from the bushes. With a comical gesture, the saloon girl indicated that the coast was clear. The masked outlaw then stood up to join her, where they pretended to brush greenery off each other and straighten their hair and their clothes.

'Stop!' Dodge yelled. 'In the name of the lawn, I order you not to move!'

Avalon clapped her hands to her face in mock horror. 'Run, Texas Jack, run!'

'You'll never catch me, Kwyatt Burp!' With Dodge in hot pursuit, he raced towards the pond, pulling up with a comic teeter at the edge.

'Trapped at last.' The marshal twirled his fake moustache. 'Unlike my wind, but there's no escape now.'

'To arrest me, don't you have to lay your hand on my shoulder?'

'Correct,' said Dodger. 'Which is why you, sir, are under arrest.'

He stretched out his arm, but to the gasp of the crowd, Texas Jack started to walk on the water. 'Come on, Marshal,' he taunted, 'what are you waiting for?'

As he inched towards the middle of the pond, Dodger started to follow — only to sink deeper and deeper into the water. Even the ducks seemed to be laughing. Reaching the other side, Texas Jack bowed, waved his Stetson, then legged it out of the palisade, while a girl with red flounces and her corset on the outside cheered him on and the marshal waded slowly back to shore.

The crowd got their money's worth with this one.

Once word got round that Texas Jack could walk on water, that was it. Jellied eels and beer stands popped up faster than you could blink, children scaled the trees for a free view of the spectacle, and any disappointment about the lack of fortune-telling ponies, scalped frontiersmen, or Cherokee squaws who caught cannonballs in their hands was forgiven, now that bowls of whelks and cockles were in the equation.

By the time the evening show came round, Buck didn't need a speaking trumpet to pull the crowds. The Common had become the scene of a stampede, where feathered hats knocked against straw boaters and cloth caps, the wheels of bicycles and perambulators spun so fast the spokes blurred, and it didn't matter whether little legs were encased in delicate white stockings or itchy woollen socks. Class was unimportant when it came to buying tickets. What mattered here was elbows.

Buffalo Bill's extravaganza included rope tricks, sharp-shooting, and re-enactments of real events, such as the battle at Little Big Horn that was Custer's last stand. He recreated the hardship that frontiersmen and women had to suffer, he simulated buffalo hunts, and even staged a train robbery. Julia looked around the inside of the palisade, to the pond lit by flickering naphtha flares. There were no bronco riders here. No arrows hissing through the air. No stagecoaches to be saved from bandits. Just the smell of fish and chips, tobacco and cheap scent mixed with carbolic drifting on the air, and the satisfaction that all the elk, moose and buffalo in the actual West couldn't compete with a damned good belly laugh.

'Put me out of my misery,' Julia begged Dodger, about to reprise his role as Kwyatt Burp. 'How does Texas Jack walk across that pond?'

'Buck'll skin me like a rabbit if he finds out I'm talking to the enemy —'

'Hold on! I clomp around on a hobby horse, shoot holes in playing cards with a flag that reads *Bang!* and dangle on a pole dressed as an angel, and Buck calls me the enemy?'

The dimples in his cheeks pitted as he grinned. 'Theoretically, anyone who hasn't signed to secrecy is the enemy, but if you'd been rehearsing alongside, you'd have seen how it's done anyway. See that red post?' He pointed across the water, shimmering in the torchlight. 'That marks the far end of the wire stretched just below the surface.'

'Crikey. He has to run on wire that he can't even see?'

'The whole show runs on trust, Snaps. We have each other's backs every single second of the day, which is why we drill more than the bleedin' army do, and why it's so successful.'

'Takes a lot of practice to make it look easy?'

'Bloody right, and that's why we cordon off the area with a high fence, not a rail. No one can see us attach the wires. And you clomp very nicely, by the way.' The smile dropped from his face. 'Y'know, seeing you dressed up in costume, and what with that copper asking questions earlier, really got me thinking. It sounds a rotten thing to say, but...'

'But?'

'Well ... in an odd way, I'm glad Junie didn't top herself. Don't get me wrong,' he added hastily, 'I'm not glad she's dead, I miss that girl like crazy — no offence, of course. You're doing' a grand job! It's just that —'

'I'm not Junie.'

'Exactly. She was something special, her. A real live wire, no pun intended, and it would've been unfair, if the only way she'd have been remembered was the stigma of self-murder.' His nose wrinkled. 'I know they don't confiscate their worldly goods no more, or drive stakes through their hearts, or bury 'em at crossroads. Bloody barbaric, that. But even so —' He swallowed. 'Junie deserves a decent, Christian burial and a decent, Christian burial is what she'll get. Here, you couldn't lend me sixpence, could you, Snaps? Forgot to eat between performances, then forgot to slip a coin in me pocket as I was dressing up.' There they were again, those little dimples. 'Getting as forgetful as the missus, me!'

Watching Kwyatt Burp swagger into his scene, Julia remembered her mother, not a religious woman by any stretch of the imagination, crossing herself every time the subject of her aunt came up. The aunt, it seemed, suffered from morbid melancholia, and hanged herself at the top of the stairs, aged sixteen. Julia's mother, at the time, was only four, which put the whole ugly pageant of suicide burial within living memory. The grave (if you could call it that) deliberately dug too short, so the corpse would be as uncomfortable as possible in the afterlife. Shallow, too, with just a covering of lime. The objective was humiliation, pure and simple. Thank God attitudes had changed, but Dodger was right. Self-murder, as many liked to call it, was still widely deemed immoral and unnatural and, like Dodger, Julia felt that June Margaret Sullivan had suffered enough humiliation, thank you very much.

'Mind if I join you?' she asked Hal. His tinkling couldn't carry to the duck pond, so, like Annie Oaktree, he was sitting out the walk-on-water act in the tent.

'Be my guest, old thing.'

'Thanks. Don't stop playing on my account, though. What is that tune?'

'A little piece I wrote m'self.' Kind eyes smiled at a point over Julia's shoulder. '*Cardiff Lullaby* I call it. One might think it odd, composing a commemorative number on a piano that one is obliged to keep slightly off-key. For me, it remains a fitting tribute, one that is both unique and personal, for the wake.'

'You were fond of June.'

'Why would I not be?'

He rippled a few more bars on the upright that Julia discovered was kept deliberately untuned, to give it that distinctive Western saloon sound.

'As a matter of fact,' he said, 'after the show, it is my intention to take a bouquet of lilies to the bridge where she was found.'

'Do you know where it was?'

'Oh, dear. What a ninny you must think me. Now you mention it, old girl, I have absolutely no idea which direction to take.'

'Would you like me to show you?'

'I say, that is most gracious of you. I would, indeed, very much appreciate the help. Thank you.'

Did those long, thin fingers wrap round June's neck, and squeeze until the last breath left her body? Lilies smacked of remorse, but what motive did he have? A delicate Eton boy, who could have gone on to become a concert pianist, his public life was an open book. What might he be harbouring that he felt he had no other option than to silence her?

Those eyes. The tender way he touched the keys. The sense of belonging when he played, man and piano moulding into just a single instrument. None of those attributes hinted at a viciousness lurking in the shadows of his mind, but the same applied to all the cast. Especially to Buck.

Julia found it difficult to reconcile him killing Annie for nothing more than cold hard cash, or because she was holding out on him. On the surface, he was flippant and funny, but underneath he took his show, and his responsibility for the crew, very, very seriously. He was a hard businessman, a perfectionist, and if anyone could stage a suicide, it was him. All the same, she was convinced that, had there been any thieving going on, the proceeds would have been directed straight back into the Mild West.

She thought of Dodger's dimples, Avalon's wide smile, Molly's chuckle, Lizzie's openness. Not forgetting the Great MMM's undoubted charm, of course.

None of them came over as a cold-blooded killer, and yet one of them, she was sure, was harbouring a secret. One so terrible, that it was worth killing for.

Why couldn't it have been some bloody random act?

CHAPTER 16

'Half the population,' Hal said, swinging his cane with jaunty precision, '*view* chimneys belching out the Devil's smoke as symbols of oppression, consigning their harried workforce to an early grave after a wretched and meaningless life.' The narrowboats were already moored up on the opposite bank to where he and Julia were walking, ready for a quick start through the lock gates in the morning. Those that were still drawn by big, black Shire horses had tied up close to the stables, though Julia and Hal still had to guard against piles of manure. 'The other half count their blessings that their lives are enriched by steam.'

Steam was the future. No doubt about that, Julia thought. It powered everything from railways to ships to yes, these ugly factories towering above them, opening up not only Britain, but the world, ushering in an exciting age of science and exploration, and — rather pertinently at the moment — entertainment.

'Don't know about you, old thing, but I am definitely in Camp Two.' Hal adjusted the tie that matched the red striped ribbon round his boater. 'Thanks to Old Man Steam and the knock-on prosperity, there are over three hundred music halls in London alone, cutting through class and the division of the sexes in a way nothing else has even the faintest hope of achieving.'

It was true. They didn't just entertain people through magic, acrobatics, male and female impersonators, and ooh-er-innuendo, they kept the audience informed of current events through clever, catchy songs, and, as the Mild West proved, no one went home miserable after a night of musical comedy.

'You support equality, then,' Julia said.

'Like the good William Cody, I also fail to see why one should be judged on one's race, religion, gender or status.'

'Then you are wasted in musical comedy. I suggest you run for Parliament, instead. I'd vote for Jeremiah Liddell-Gough. Had I the right, anyway.' Cradling his bunch of lilies in the crook of her arm, she expected him to smile, return the banter, even admit that it crossed his mind more than once.

'Who gave you my name?'

Listen hard, and Julia could almost hear the nerve that she'd touched.

'Don't bother answering! I know it was your predecessor. Who else gossiped like an incontinent fishwife?'

Quick! Change the subject! If she persisted — asked, say, questions about Eton, or why he chose this life over that of a concert pianist, he might clam up altogether. Or worse. Be leaving lilies at the place where her body was found. 'Look,' she said, pointing to lights twinkling through the fug. 'That's the new variety theatre. I haven't been inside yet, but I'm told it boasts gilded ceilings and pillars, too many chandeliers to count, and a carpet that cost one thousand guineas.'

Hal's mood switched in the click of a finger. 'A thousand guineas. Imagine.' He tossed his cane in the air with his right hand, catching it in his left. 'When fewer than half of the performers will earn a guinea a week.'

'I hear they get free drink, mind.'

Hal's laugh echoed in the darkness. 'Lord save us, that surely is a gift to be grateful for, Snaps, but ask Buck. Who takes to variety for the financial reward?'

'Or the drink?'

'Not so fast, old thing. Why do you think they style themselves Champagne Charlies? Come!' He linked her arm with his, little realising that tunnel ahead was where Annie Oaktree was found. 'What say you and I join this prestigious club, right here, right now? Sing with me, Snaps. *Two lovely black eyes* — You're not singing.'

'Be grateful. Unless you want to know what a frog stuck in a trumpet sounds like.'

'Nonsense! The boat people are fast asleep, and their shutters are closed tight. No one can hear the trapped frog, except me. I promise you, you and I shall create entertainment at its sublimest (dearie me, is there such a word? does it matter?) *Oh! What a surprise!*'

Should she warn him about the tunnel? He was in such a happy mood, why spoil it? And for goodness sake, it was only two hundred yards. '*Only for telling a man he was wrong,*' she joined in, and he couldn't say he hadn't been warned. '*Two lovely black eyes!*'

The chorus was echoing gloriously as they entered the tunnel when Julia heard a dull thud. Hal dropped his cane and put his hand to his face.

'Blasted loose brick,' he said, rubbing the side of his head. 'One would expect the authorities to undertake better maintenance of these archways. That could have been a child, and would you look at that. Blood over my finest tweed suit. Damn you to hell, Oakbourne Council!'

'Did 'e just swear?' a disembodied voice asked reasonably.

'Now you mention it, Joe, reckon he might've.'

'Drunks,' Julia whispered. 'Ignore them.' Not that Jeremiah Liddell-Gough struck her as the sort to go around picking fights in the dark.

'Swearing's a terrible thing, especially in public. Fucking terrible, wouldn't yer say?'

'I would, Joe. Right fucking bad manners. 'Specially in front of a lady.'

'Of course, if he apologised to 'er, that'd square it.'

'Very well,' Hal said, ignoring the warning jab from Julia's elbow. 'I apologise for swearing in public, and in front of a lady to boot. Now kindly step aside, sir, we have business to attend do.'

'Oh. So she ain't no lady, after all? Well, well, well. Don't that put a different slant on things.'

'You take that back, sir!' Hal put up his fists. 'You take that back right now.'

'Ooh-hoo. The toff wants to box.'

'Well, Joe, he did say he wanted two lovely black eyes.'

'Boxing?' Hal snapped. 'What would you louts know about the Queensberry rules? Some old queen's rules, more like.'

The mood shifted. Julia felt the hairs rise on the back of her neck. 'Hal,' she hissed. 'Let's go.'

Was he deaf, or just stupid?

'What's the matter, "Joey"? Cat got your tongue?'

She tugged at his sleeve. This wasn't some Eton rugby scrum, or a post-performance tussle. These men were dockers, or packers, maybe railway workers, who thought it would be funny to goad a swell and his lady, and they didn't really take Julia for a prostitute. They simply saw them as symbols of the oppression Hal had talked about earlier, and, in their drunken haze, decided throwing insults and stones would level the score. That the "toff" took the bait was a bonus.

'Or is it that you can't take being on the receiving end, sir? Because that's what this is about, is it not? You chaps hanging around bridges at night — receiving end being the right phrase, I imagine?'

The punch to Hal's kidney came out of nowhere. With an agonised yelp, he fell to his knees. A boot smashed into his ribs.

'You wash yer dirty mouth out.'

'What say we wash it for him, Joe?'

'That's enough,' Julia said. Could they hear her heart thumping? 'We're leaving, so let's just call it quits.'

Hardly a case of quitting while they were ahead, but calling for help wasn't an option. The barges were moored well out of earshot, and in any case, like Hal said, shuttered tight.

'You leave when we tell yer to leave,' a voice snarled, tossing her off Hal as though she was a blanket, and heaving him to the edge of the canal. 'As for you, mate, I reckon you must've had yer 'ead pushed down a toilet twenty times a week at that fancy school your Daddy sent yer to. So let's see how long you can hold yer breath, eh?'

'Cowards,' Hal spat. 'What are there? Three of you? Four? Not one of you with the balls to fight like a man.'

For God's sake, Hal, are you mad? Then Julia remembered what she'd heard about boarding schools. The jeering, the sneering, being beaten up in the dormitory. Was Hal trying to apply the principles of Eton bullying to rough, tough men having their manhood questioned not once, but twice? Bullies bore easily. Julia knew that from experience. If you don't fight back, they'll find someone who does. Hal had blown his chances with this bunch.

'When I said that's enough, I meant —' Julia dipped into her reticule and produced her British Bulldog — 'that's enough.'

'Ooh-hoo. The strumpet's got a *toy*.' A hand skimmed Hal's boater into the canal. 'Well, shoot this, luv.'

Fair enough. Julia shot it straight through the hat band.

Which was worse, Julia asked herself later? The ear-splitting crash when the weapon discharged? The endless echo? Or the silence that followed?

Was it staggering home with a man who'd come down from the dizzy heights of Adrenaline City, only to discover that lobbed missiles, kicked ribs and a punch in the kidneys suddenly hurt worse than hellfire?

Or that, when they turned off Cadogan Street, it was to see flames leaping high on the Common and fire crews pumping like crazy, the smoke too thick to tell if the tent had gone up, or something else was the cause?

Funnily enough, it was none of those things. It was finding herself naked in bed with a man with a lean, runner's frame and piercing grey eyes, who left the scent of Hammam Bouquet over every inch of the bedsheets.

'Tell me again —' Collingwood took a handful of her hair and buried his nose in it, not caring that it reeked of smoke — 'how you carried a grown man half a mile after he'd passed out from head wounds.'

'He was fully conscious the entire way, and it was a bump.'

'Don't forget the six broken ribs.'

'Bruised.'

'Excellent! The training has paid off! My favourite crime scene photographer has finally become Boot Street's expert on cracked ribs.'

She was an expert long before that, isn't that so, Mama? 'I'm your *only* crime scene photographer.'

'I suppose it's too much to ask what happened to the lilies.'

'This isn't funny.'

'I'm drunk. Everything's funny.'

As moonlight flooded the bed, Julia felt stone cold sober, but clearly she wasn't, or he wouldn't be here — and since when did "never again" mean "just this once"? The trouble was, seeing him pumping alongside the fire crews, his grey worsted jacket as black as his face, she could hardly let him walk off without scrubbing up first, though, with hindsight, she should have wheeled out the Courvoisier in the kitchen. It was just that the girls had left the place in such a mess, dirty dishes stacked every which way, remnants of food on the table, paper bags and rubbish strewn on the floor, not to mention a load of frizzy red hairs, that common sense dictated taking the bottle upstairs. And indeed, everything was going fine until his mouth went tight, his jaw tighter, and he admitted that the only reason he was out at two in the morning, and thus able to pitch into fighting the fire, was because this was his deceased daughter's birthday, and no twelve-year-old should have to spend it alone and cold in her grave.

'It's called poor decision making,' Julia murmured, straddling Collingwood for the second time and placing his hands on her nipples.

He'd needed release, she'd needed release, and when it came to sex appeal, God had given generously to Inspector John Collingwood. Not that Julia was short of admirers herself. Buck, for one, made his feelings clear every time they met, his twinkling eyes raking her from top to toe and back again, and at a speed that made snails look like cheetahs. God had contributed liberally to him, too, but kissing the showman would be like kissing Sam, which in turn would be like kissing her father. Maybe if Buck cut his hair? Shaved off the goatee? If Sam hadn't been her confidant, mentor and friend —?

'Are you deliberately trying to shorten my life?' Collingwood said, as they lay sated and panting. 'Christ, Julia, what were you thinking, showing Hal the place where the body was found at two o'clock in the bloody morning?'

'Cabaret keeps strange hours, and I wanted to see how far, and how easily, it would be to transport a body from the tent to the bridge.'

'With a gun?'

'Yes, with a gun! You know damn well I carried that revolver when I was being framed for those girls' murders. I had no intention of heading down a dark towpath, in the early hours, with a man who might be a killer, without some means of protection.'

The scariest part was once the echo died down. In the silence, her mind raced, trying to decide if they'd rush her, who to shoot first, and where. Mob violence is terrifying, but she could have saved herself the tight chest and pounding heart. The yobs hared off like greyhounds round the track.

'I'll have a constable patrol the tunnel,' Collingwood said, stroking her thigh. 'But I doubt they'll come back.'

'Much as it pains me, for once I agree with you.' She reached for the biscuit tin she kept under the bed. Custard creams weren't the stock accompaniment to fine cognac, but whether it was the danger, the fear or the sex, she was ravenous. 'That fire…' She couldn't get over the moment her stomach flipped when she and Hal turned the corner. 'Was it arson?'

'Too soon to tell,' he said, licking the crumbs off her breast. 'Flares don't have wicks, which means liquid fuel runs down to the burner, rather than up, and gravity is fine as long as the flare is secure … there's no wind … the taps are properly controlled … and someone doesn't knock it over, accidentally or otherwise.'

'You *do* think it's arson.'

He poured a dribble of cognac into the dip of her collarbone and licked. 'What I think is that we have one violent crime involving the show, followed by a fire two days later. Is it coincidence? Well, madam, that's what Her Majesty's police force is here to find out.'

'You won't find the answer in the dip of my collarbone, any more than you'll find it at the neck of a bottle.'

He recoiled at her tone, and she instantly regretted it. 'I'm sorry. I didn't meant to bark, I'm simply worried that you'll do what you did last time, to numb your grief.'

His drinking had become so bad that he'd come close to losing his career — and a whole lot more besides.

'You know, Mrs. McAllister, I've half a mind to arrest you on suspicion of double standards.' The words were starting to slur. 'You can worry about me, but I am not allowed to worry about you?'

'Come, come, John. There's no point in having double standards, if you don't live up to both.'

His only reply was a snore.

CHAPTER 17

Lining up the backdrop of a balustraded terrace on a country estate, positioning her sitters, and photographing Captain Wills with his wife and seven, no, eight children, should have absorbed every ounce of Julia's concentration. Small boys are notorious when it comes to standing still for longer than fifteen seconds, babies have a tendency to yell, and toddlers? Well, guess why they're called that. Three times she'd had to reclaim little Mabel from the properties stored behind the backdrop, which reminded her, she really must dust the props more often. Cobwebs and ringlets don't make for a good combination.

If Julia wasn't so distracted, maybe Mabel wouldn't be chasing dust bunnies, small boys might actually stand still, and eight-year-old girls would know better than to moon at strangers. Unfortunately, as long as the grass still smouldered inside the palisade, Julia could not focus on anything else.

Collingwood might be keeping an open mind on arson, but Buffalo Buck was a perfectionist. Forget all that police nonsense about fuel evaporating in preheated burners, until the temperature reached between 80 and 100 degrees Celsius, at which point the naphtha gives off a flame, and turns into a fire hazard of Biblical proportions, should the flame go out and puddles of fuel then form on the ground.

'If you want to be scientific,' she had told Collingwood as he had climbed into his clothes that morning, 'the vast majority of circuses and fairs use them, and Buck is conscientious to the nth degree.'

The reason that form of lighting was so popular was because the flickering added to the magic and mystique. The pong was irrelevant, and generally overridden by stale fish and chips in any case. What mattered was the pulsing contrast between light and dark, playing with the senses to create almost dreamlike illusions that disassociated people from reality. In short, they were hooked before they even saw the show.

'If there is a point to that comment,' Collingwood said, 'could you make it a little quieter, please? The Hammer Concerto is playing inside my skull, and the percussion section appears to be exceptionally enthusiastic.'

'What I'm saying, John, is that you might lose your eyebrows trying to light these bloody flares, but Buck doesn't leave the opening and closing of taps to chance. We all have to check on them, there's a set rota, to ensure accidents do not happen.'

It was arson — but why? Was it to distract the police from the murder? Surely that would have the opposite effect, especially now the word was getting round that Annie was a random target.

One thing was certain. The arsonist wasn't Hal, and it wasn't the impresario, either. Buck was livid when he saw the devastation — or, more accurately, the fact that the firemen might have cottoned on to how Texas Jack could walk on water. According to Collingwood, the relief on his face was something to behold when the hoses were unravelled. He could, of course, be putting on an act — God knows showmen are experts in the field — but he couldn't be certain that the fire crew would swoop so quickly. Not so long ago, insurance companies employed their own brigades to extinguish fires on properties covered by the firm. In those days, the chances of two fires raging at the same time for the same company were small to non-existent, and the response time was predictable.

Now that municipal fire brigades took the brunt, Buck couldn't possibly estimate how many other calls there might be on their resources. Admittedly, there wouldn't be many cats stuck up trees that time of night, but this was early spring, the nights were chilly, chimney fires broke out all the time — and for pity's sake, what reason would he have to sabotage his own show, anyway? Unless...

Julia emerged from under the heavy sheet and removed the glass plate from the holder.

Unless the motive wasn't sabotage, but investment. The higher the drama, the more the crowds flocked. Funny how it always came down to money, when Buck was in the equation...

'That's perfect, Captain. Thank you, Mrs. Wills. Children. We'll have the portrait developed and framed for you by tomorrow.'

'Admirable of Mr. Whitmore to show you how to take the photo, what.' A blue serge arm grabbed little Mabel before she could find another cobweb. 'Of course, and I beg you not to take this the wrong way, m'dear, but if ... how can I put this, if...?'

'You're not satisfied?' Julia smiled. 'Then you and the family come back, Captain, Mr. Whitmore will personally take the portrait, and you won't even have to pay for the frame.'

She was laying herself wide open here. Of course, it was vital to exude confidence — but giving Captain Wills an opportunity to have the portrait done for free? Was she mad? Never mind that, if he took her up on it, the man he thought was Mr. Whitmore couldn't take a hike, much less a photo.

'The portrait will be fine, dear,' Mrs. Wills whispered, as she brushed past.

Later, strolling across the Common disguised as Annie Oaktree, Julia couldn't decide whether she'd imagined that conspiratorial wink from Mrs. Wills, or whether it was a trick of the light, but one thing was certain, she knew a fellow suffragist when she saw one. For God's sake, how long before the Great British Empire caught up with Wyoming!

Approaching the tent, she heard the unmistakeable sound of sobbing. Following the sound, she found Avalon hunkered in a ball behind the pavilion, writhing in pain. 'What's wrong?'

'It was my fault, my fault, all my fault, that fire. I'm so stupid. I got mixed up again, I — I — thought Dodger was checking the flares, and — and — instead —' she howled into her hankie — 'look what I've done!'

'Avalon —'

'I could have killed someone, Julia! The whole tent could have gone up! I'm so sorry, I am, I truly am, I didn't mean for this to happen, and I wish I could make it right, but that's the thing, I can't!'

Julia's reply was cut short by Dodger running up, scooping his wife into his arms and rocking her tight to his body. 'Shh. Darlin', shh, shh, shh, this *isn't* your fault.'

'I got muddled up —'

'I know, I know, but we all make mistakes, love. Accidents happen, the fire engines were here in no time, and there's no damage to speak of, just a patch of burned grass.' He kissed the top of her head. 'If the papers were full of that walkin' on water lark before, they're doubly keen on covering it now. In fact, Buck reckons the takings will double, thanks to this.'

'So I did him a favour, nearly burning the town down?'

The sobbing turned into a fully-fledged wail. Dodger held tight and Julia stroked her hair, until the outburst ran its course.

'Come on, sweetheart, big blow in Dodge's hankie, atta girl. Now, let's get you scrubbed up and looking pretty, eh? Show starts in an hour.'

And hey presto, it was magic! Seeing Molly standing in front of the Grand Canyon, which had been hurriedly nailed to a makeshift frame to draw the eye from where the grass had caught, no one in the crowd could guess how wretched Avalon was feeling when Molly called Lakota Sioux and her husband, Broken Nose, forward.

'But I haven't got a broken nose,' the warrior protested.

'Give me two minutes,' Avalon trilled, hefting a stick. 'And by the way, my name isn't Sue. It's Three Ponies.'

'That's an unusual name,' Molly said.

'Not when you get to know her,' Dodger replied. 'Nag, nag, nag...'

This time, it was Lizzie's turn to play the saloon girl in the bushes with Texas Jack, and the Grand Canyon turned out to be a blessing in disguise. The screen was the reason they could fit the extra skit in, allowing Dodger to pull off his costume to reveal his gunslinger outfit underneath, swap the war bonnet for a Stetson, and swagger into the arena as Kwyatt Burp.

Were the roars and whistles louder, because of this extra sketch? Or was Dodger right about the crowd doubling in numbers? Floating in the air, the angel that was Julia couldn't help noticing the unedifying clamour for admission to the tent, the second Texas Jack had made his getaway. Feather hats were knocked squiffy. Small toes were trodden on. Leg o'mutton sleeves became chops. This was every Prince of Wales checks for itself.

'Before I forget anything else,' Avalon said, easing the angel out of the contraption and rubbing the feeling back in her ankles, 'here's the sixpence Dodger borrowed.'

'Thanks.' Julia slipped the coin in Annie Oaktree's pocket. 'There's something I wanted to ask you about —'

'Oh, no! What a time for Molls to have one of her wheezing fits.' Red in the face, the comedienne was hacking into her handkerchief. 'Hang on, I'll fetch her throat spray, works a treat. Back in a jiffy, Snaps.'

Julia should have known better. Thanks to Molly's voice reduced to a croak, the cast were forced to adopt Plan B. Or possibly J, P or T, there were that many mix-and-match combinations. Instead of Molly quipping jokes and making asides, the Great MMM swung into action, alongside the very girl Julia had been wanting to talk to Avalon about. And part of the show or not, she was starstruck. She watched wide-eyed while two boxes were wheeled out on the stage, then, to a tinkle of Hal's ivories, Lizzie danced in, wearing silver spangles and very little else, waving a shimmering fringed turquoise shawl.

'Ladies and gentlemen,' the riverboat gambler announced, 'what you are about to witness is the vanishing lady.' The idea, he said, was that his lovely assistant would stand on this box — he pointed to the one on the right — he would wave his magic cape, *voila!*, and she would re-appear in this box. He pointed to the left. 'No trapdoors.' He'd demonstrated that right at the outset. 'Simply the powers of yours truly, the Great — no, let's be honest, the *Greatest* Mississippi Moonlight Magician.'

The audience cheered him on. Lizzie stepped on the box. Capes were waved. Notes were played. Then came the usual abracadabra and, with a flourish, he opened the lid of the box on the left. *Empty!* As one, the crowd craned their necks forward.

'Oh dear, oh dear,' he muttered. He flung his arms wide in puzzlement. 'Where is she?' He lifted the lid of the box on which Lizzie had been standing. Also empty! 'It seems I have a problem. Every time I say abracadabra, my assistant really does disappear!'

'No, I haven't.' Lizzie stood up from the middle of the audience. 'I'm right here!'

As the crowd clapped and cheered — remember, this had all taken place in a matter of seconds — no one noticed that the assistant was a different woman. All they saw were spangles covering very little of her modesty, and a turquoise shawl that clashed with wild red curls, that, if you looked closely, was a wig. They certainly didn't notice that it took two men to carry the box on the right off the stage, instead of the one man who'd carried it on.

Unfurling herself from the hidden compartment, Lizzie puffed out her cheeks. 'Talk about an open and shut case,' she giggled. 'I could hardly breathe in there. How did Avalon get on?'

'Exceptionally well,' the riverboat gambler assured her. He turned to Julia. 'Even the folk in the rows right behind didn't spot her throwing off what, to all intents and purposes, looked like a dull paisley frock, but was in reality a wrap-around shawl.'

'Let me guess. The inside lining was turquoise?'

Julia had to hand it to the cast. When it came to professionalism, they scored ten out of ten.

Out on the stage, Buffalo Buck had the audience eating out of his hand. 'My father was a magician, you know. He was constantly boasting that he could slow his heart until it stopped, but for all his bragging, what do you know? He only did it the once.'

Solidarity, fellowship, trust and support. The foundation for any good team.

But the quickness of the hand deceives the eye.

What, oh what, had she missed?

Julia wasn't sure which surprised her the most when she got back to the studio. The smell of coffee, wafting through from the kitchen. The steak and ale pie on the table. Or Detective Inspector Collingwood scribbling notes in a little book balanced on the arm of her favourite velvet sofa.

'John? How did you get in?'

It was enough that Buck had picked the lock. Weren't the police supposed to be above that kind of thing?

His grey eyes danced in the flickering light. 'You gave me this, remember?'

Julia snatched the key out of his hand. 'And now I'm ungiving it.'

'Someone's in a good mood.' The eyes still danced. 'What happened? Did the greasepaint melt?'

'It's not lard, suet and lanolin any more,' she snapped. 'That's wig paste. These days, it's a base of minerals, which lasts longer, doesn't go rancid, and best of all, doesn't stink.'

'Unlike your mood.' Still with that annoying half-smile plastered on his face, he folded his papers. 'I take it the matinée did not go well.'

'The matinée went very well, that's the problem.' Irritation usually subsided as quickly as it flared. Today, a team of oxen couldn't drag the damn thing away. 'Molly had some kind of coughy-wheezy fit, apparently it happens a lot, just not on stage, and what do they do? Carry on as if nothing had happened, with Buck delivering the lines instead of Molls, the Hot Cross Bun Kid trying to sell Texas Jack a half-price saddle,

146

because that's all it is, a saddle cut in half, and Avalon cartwheeling in to steal the scene with a knife-throwing trick that might or might not be dangerous, I couldn't bloody tell.'

'Is that it?'

'No. Buck wrapped up the show by promising the audience that tomorrow he'd tell them how Sitting Pretty courted his lovely wife, Running Bare, and three encores later, with the sound of feet stomping and voices lifting the roof with *Oh, Susannah, don't you cry for me*, and *then* that was it.'

Collingwood stood up and wrapped his arms around her. 'So that's what's under your skin. You're seeing another Annie Oaktree situation — one man down, yet nothing changes — and you're angry.'

'I am not angry.' Julia shook off the comfort. She did not — NOT — want a relationship with this man. How many times must she tell herself that? 'All right, yes, I *am* angry. I'm angry, because of the way they slot everything in so seamlessly. It's as though they don't care, but that's the trouble. They *do* care. They care very much, and that's what makes me mad. They're much more than a team, John, they're a family —'

'And families don't kill each other?'

For a second there, she saw the gun. Felt blood spurting hot on her skin. Heard the gargle in her stepfather's throat, as he lay dying — 'In passion, yes. Papa comes home, catches Mama *in flagrante*, kills the lover.' Never the wife, you understand. Only the innocent party. 'Or Papa finds out his brother's been molesting his son, beats the brother to a pulp. But these acts are heat of the moment. Families don't plan murder to look like suicide.' She ran her hands through her hair. 'There's something I've missed, John, and the problem is, I don't know where to start looking. But watching how the show rolled smoothly without Molly, it worries me that history might repeat itself and —'

'What are you doing?'

'Telling you what bothers me, what does it sound like?'

'Not that. The frantic grubbing around in cupboards, like a bull in a china shop.'

'If you must know, I'm looking for my little willow pattern gravy boat.' More drawers were turned out. 'Blue, bone china —'

'I know what willow pattern looks like, Julia, and it won't be in the cutlery drawer. Just calm down a minute. Take a breath —'

'I don't need to take a breath, I need to find this wretched pot and put the key in it for safekeeping.'

'Safekeeping? Really?' He stopped himself from laughing just in time. 'You see the irony, I assume?'

'What I see is you in my way, and I don't know whether the girls have been stealing things —'

'Gravy boats are highly prized by fences.'

'You mock, but all manner of things have gone missing recently. Now maybe they've moved them, they're not the tidiest of girls, but my blue fountain pen's gone, a hand mirror from my dressing table, and now this.'

'Are you sure a sprinkle of Avalon hasn't rubbed off on you?'

'Bad memories are hardly contagious.' Julia thumped the table so hard, the pie dish jumped. '*Nothing wrong with that girl's brain*,' she mimicked in a Welsh accent. 'Annie Oaktree told me that, sitting right here at this kitchen table, but oh, there is, John. There's something very, very wrong with that girl's brain.'

Being forgetful is one thing. Not paying attention, in one ear out the other, well, you can get away with that, too. But

Avalon? Julia was reminded of the book-binder's grandmother. Lovely old lady — never remembered your name, though, or how you'd spoken with her only five minutes earlier, or that she'd left a pan of cabbage on the cooker, and it had boiled dry.

'Suppose Avalon's been doing things, horrible things, that she can't remember,' she said. 'And because she has such an open, helpful nature, it wouldn't cross her mind that another part of her might be capable of such acts?'

'As wild theories go, that one should be released on the Serengeti without delay.'

'One individual with two simultaneous streams of thought is not unheard of, though, where actions occur outside the knowledge of that person.'

'Hardly my field of expertise, but isn't that sleepwalking?'

Hardly Julia's field, either. In fact, her only experience was Dr. Jekyll and Mr. Hyde, but this didn't seem quite the right time to quote R.L. Stevenson's novel. 'Suppose, John, she enters a state where one personality takes over, but the other has no recollection of what has taken place, and vice versa. Believe me, she was distraught when she found she'd nearly set Oakbourne on fire.'

'I have no intention of frogmarching Mrs. Wright to the asylum and asking a psychiatrist to put her into a mesmeric state, simply because she absent-mindedly singed a duck's tail feathers.'

'And I wouldn't dream of suggesting it, but that's my point. Avalon's mental state is one among numerous leads I should have been pursuing, except I got distracted, went off course, and completely lost sight of the priorities here.' She slumped into the chair. 'I just felt so sorry for him.'

'Who?'

'Titus Vance.' She told Collingwood what she'd told Charlie, and how the more time goes on, the more the widower was distraught. 'He's been calling at Boot Street twice a day, as well as following up among friends and acquaintances, enquiring at the railway station, the *Chronicle*, the bus stops, and his son's place of work, but no one's seen anything. His son has vanished into thin air, and as Charlie made clear, a grown man going off falls very low on the list of priorities.'

'So you thought you'd become Mrs. Sherlock Holmes?'

Working with the police gave her a different perspective on crime, she said, unaware that she'd scoffed a quarter of the steak and ale pie until she reached for another slice. 'I've been giving Mr. Vance the proverbial tea and sympathy, but under the circumstances, and him holding his emotions so tight, it felt terribly inadequate. Then it occurred to me: suppose his son suffered a sudden compression of the heart while taking a stroll, and stumbled into the canal. Now suppose this happened to take place, say, under a bridge after dark? The body wouldn't be noticed by the bargees until it surfaced.'

'From now on, you may call me Doctor Watson.' Collingwood gave a mock salute. 'What leads?'

Julia shook the coffee pot. How on earth did that become empty? 'Huh?'

'You said Avalon's mental state was one among numerous leads.'

'Ah, well!' She reached for the Victoria sponge cake. 'I'm wondering if there wasn't something going on between Dodger and Annie Oaktree.'

The familiar way he said her name — Junie. If that wasn't intimate, what was? Then there was the bitterness he expressed at her death. *If one more person says the show must go on, that's what*

Junie would want, I say bugger that, pardon my Français. Junie would want to still bloody be here!

Without doubt, Dodger was devoted to Avalon ... which isn't to say her state of mind made her easy to live with! He could still love his wife, but at the same time seek refuge in the arms of a Welsh girl. The opposite side of that same coin could well see Annie disguising her feelings for Dodger by pretending to dislike him. Telling Julia that he was a scrounger and a layabout to deflect attention, just as the guilt of sneaking around behind Avalon's back explained an overstated desire to protect her.

The lady doth protest too much, methinks. The quote was from Hamlet. From a play within a play. Was any line more pertinent here?

'Hmm.'

'Hmm, what?'

'I'm just thinking about how you always make my work interesting,' Collingwood mused, scribbling notes. 'In this case, for instance, while taking statements about a random act of murder, I somehow need to work into the conversation with a married member of the company as to whether he was engaging in adulterous activities with the victim.'

'Diplomacy is your middle name, my dear Watson.'

The coffee wasn't the only thing that had gone. As Julia brewed another pot, she realised that her bad mood had evaporated along the way, too.

'Here. I have a present for you.' Collingwood tossed it across.

'A whistle?'

'A police whistle, to be pedantic.' His grey eyes hardened. 'You can't swan around town with a revolver, simply because it suits your purposes, Julia. I know you carry the damn thing for protection, but I'm sorry. You can't just go around shooting things.'

'It would have been bloody hard to whistle a hole in Hal's boater. Or did you expect me to spit the pea at it?'

'I'm serious. It's against the law to carry a gun. This is the last time I'm turning a blind eye. If you're in trouble, blow until your eyes pop, then keep blowing.'

Was he mad? The hell she would leave her British Bulldog at home, but this was not the time to tell him to go whistle. 'Another theory occurred to me.' She hadn't said yes, she hadn't said no. You can't break a promise if you haven't made it. 'Is it possible that Annie was knocked out first, then strangled?'

'This might come as a surprise, but the police undertake investigative work, too, you know. Indeed, strangulation is such a common occurrence among female murders, that the doctor checks the possibility as a matter of course.' Collingwood leaned back on the sofa and stared at the ceiling. 'Annie, I regret, sustained no headwounds prior to death.'

'Could she have been subdued by some other means? Chloroform, for instance?'

'Unlikely.' Contrary to what most people believed, he explained, chloroform took five minutes before it became effective. 'Also, it stinks, so the victim could hardly be caught unaware.' Too strong, he added, and it makes the victim vomit. Too much, it paralyses the lungs, in which case the killer wouldn't needed to have strangled her, she'd already have been dead.

'Chloroform may have overtaken ether as the anaesthetic of choice in the medical profession, but even the experts are unable to judge the dose accurately. Far too many patients have been put under, and never regained consciousness.'

Oh, dear God. No wonder people opted to stay awake during surgery, no matter how bad the pain.

'Also,' he said, 'why bring chloroform, if the killer's sole intention was to knock her out first? Why not go the whole hog, when there was absolutely no chance of the suicide being questioned?'

'The perfect murder.'

'I fear many have been perpetrated in such a manner.' Collingwood sighed. 'What made you ask about her being subdued?'

'Because Annie grew up in the Valleys, and coal mining communities aren't renowned for breeding faint hearts.' Nor, for that matter, were Cornish tin mining communities. 'I can't imagine any woman going down without a fight, never mind a strong, hardened showgirl, yet you said there were fingerprint marks on her throat, rather than signs of a garotte.'

'Annie was definitely facing her killer when she was attacked.' Collingwood stood up and paced the kitchen. 'And to confirm what you're proposing, yes, it's inconceivable that the perpetrator did not sustain injuries as she fought back, even if only bruises.'

'Exactly. Now, Lizzie doesn't have any marks on her legs, neither does Avalon. Half of Oakbourne can testify to that, so can we at least rule them out?'

'We could...' He gave a theatrical pause that any member of the cast would be proud of. 'Unless the victim was sitting down, or on her knees, when she was attacked.'

Damn.

'Tell me about your walk with Hal. Was that your idea, or his?'

'Mine — oh! You think he set it up?'

'I doubt he'd have paid those men to go through that ridiculous charade, rather than just give him a beating. It is, however, a line I've been pursuing. Far more likely, in my opinion, that he would be very much aware that hooligans, homosexuals, opium smokers and the homeless hang around under bridges at night. You said yourself how he'd dressed up. How easy for a showman, and a dandy at that, to provoke them into a fight.'

What's the matter, "Joey"? Cat got your tongue? Or is it that you can't take being on the receiving end, sir? Because that's what this is about, is it not? You chaps hanging around bridges at night — receiving end being the right phrase, I imagine?

'I did wonder what had got into him,' Julia said. 'Calling them cowards, without the balls to fight like a man.'

'Sustaining a minor injury or two is a very good way to cover an existing minor injury or two.'

'While I find a way to check Dodger's shins, as well as Buck's and Eddie Cox's, you might want to see what you can dig up on one Jeremiah Liddell-Gough.' That was Hal's real name, she said, adding how he seemed exceptionally sensitive on the subject. 'And while you're at it, see what you can find about the woman who calls herself Molly Bannister, when the real Molly died when she was ten.'

'Both names duly noted, I appreciate that. I'm happy to look at her legs, as well, if you like, but since this is a serious police matter, I will need to take a closer look at yours, Mrs. McAllister.'

In a lightning flash, he'd pulled her into his arms and was pressing his lips hard against hers. Resistance was futile, since his lips weren't the only thing that were hard, and his arousal instantly stirred hers. As he pulled up her skirt, she pulled down her bodice, thrusting her nipples into his mouth, arching her back on the table. She cried out as her body convulsed around him, moaned as he pressed deeper and deeper, yet even as he ejaculated a voice was saying *this is not a relationship, it is not. This is physical pleasure, purely bodily release* — but if that was all, why was another voice telling Julia that it must stop?

'I forgot to ask,' she said, straightening her clothes, whisking off the tablecloth where the coffee had spilled, picking shards of pie plate off the floor, and thanking God the contents had been demolished or there'd be an even worse mess. 'Has Sergeant Kincaid had any luck, identifying the railway victim?'

Anything to stop him telling her how her hair shone like ripe chestnuts in the sunlight, how no one else put their hands on their hips like a fishwife when they were angry, how he never knew anyone would could eat the way she did and stay slim.

Anything to stop him telling her how much he missed her…

'Nothing so far, and Charlie isn't hopeful,' Collingwood said, retrieving a fork from under the dresser, two knives from under the table, and a cup handle next to the sink. 'Given the slums and scums round the factories and refineries, milestone inspectors aren't exactly uncommon.'

'Milestone inspectors?'

'Tramps, drifters, itinerants…'

For the first time since coming home, Julia smiled.

'What bothers us,' Collingwood continued, buttoning up his trousers, as she swept up the rest of the broken crockery, 'is that the poor bugger was a victim of slave labour.' More common than people might think, he explained. 'Industrialists feel the need to measure themselves against how much they're worth, and what you or I would deem a thousand times plenty is somehow never enough for these men.'

The love of money is the root of all evil. Julia learned that at Sunday school. Indeed, the only decent schooling she received, tin miners' children not expected to better themselves, so what she picked up at Sunday school stuck. And, in this case, never a truer word.

'Needless to say, these tycoons don't get their hands dirty themselves, they delegate. Consequently, holding men, women and, dare I say, children prisoner, and forcing them to work for nothing, is a lucrative trade.'

Suddenly, Julia no longer felt like smiling. If one of this pitiful workforce escaped and there was even a *chance* of the trail leading back, the gang would not hesitate to kill the rest to cover their tracks.

In this age of fluid labour, replacements were not hard to find...

'The missing willow pattern,' Collingwood said, ducking to straighten his tie in the reflection of a wine glass in the dresser. 'I know why it's so important.'

'Do you now.' Her clothes smelled of Hammam Bouquet, her lips were swollen, and already her breasts burned for his touch.

'Not because it's some family heirloom, any more than you're attached to the fountain pen or the mirror. You, Mrs. McAllister, are the least materialistic person I've met, though to be honest, I doubt that even the most ardent hoarders cry over lost gravy boats.'

He drew her gently into his arms and kissed the top of her hair.

This is not a relationship. It is not...

'It bothers you because someone's been snooping through your personal possessions, moving items about, and you and I both know that if you were to ask Molly or Lizzie, they will both flat out deny it. That, my dear Holmes, is what hurts.'

Dammit, he'd hit the nail so squarely on the head it was a wonder the hammer didn't break, and it rankled more than Julia cared to admit that she was too close to have seen it. But he was right. She'd let these women into her home, made them welcome with flowers and food, given them total freedom of the place — only for that trust to be betrayed.

So which of them was the liar?

CHAPTER 18

Leaving the prints pegged up to dry, Julia stepped back to admire her handiwork. Captain Wills stood centre stage in the portrait, his dark blue uniform standing out among the white frocks and sailor suits of his family, right down to the brass buttons, red belt, and sword in its shiny steel scabbard. Such a shame that colour-sensitive plates were still in the, pardon the pun, developing stage, but even in monochrome, he would be well pleased with this.

The reason she'd chosen him, out of all the appointments in the book, as the portrait for which Mr. Whitmore would train his assistant, was that the good captain wasn't going to all this trouble just to stand the frame on the piano and have it dusted twice a week. This, my friends, was a portrait to pass around the mess hall, send copies to relatives and friends, and generally blow his own trumpet. There were other trumpet players in the appointment book, of course. But none whose wives also moved among large army circles, volunteered in several church groups, and was heavily involved in instructional and recreational classes for mothers and girls employed by the factories. Convincing Mrs. Wills of her competency was equally important, and now that Mrs. McAllister had proved herself a skilled photographer in her own right, word would spread.

Shoot the kids,
Hang the family,
Frame them all.

Setting off for the evening performance, Julia's fists clenched in satisfaction. The studio was almost at the point where she wanted it to be. Now, there was just one thing missing...

'No wonder there's no midnight oil in the shops.' The gravel that was Charlie Kincaid's voice was low enough to cut through the drunks, pimps, thieves and vagabonds clogging the Boot Street police station. 'You bought the bloody lot.'

'Only because you'd hogged all the elbow grease.' Collingwood capped his pen and steepled his fingers. 'What are you doing here this time of night, Charlie? Go home, before Clara forgets what you look like.'

'What? And let you have this all to yourself?' The sergeant closed the door behind him, which did nothing to dull the shouts, thuds, curses and yelps, or lessen the stench of sweat, booze, grease, gravy and blood, and, joy of joys, now spewing. 'Tch, tch, shame on you, sir. Posh education like yours, and your mother still never taught you to share.'

'Shame on you, too, sergeant. Stellar military service like yours, and the army still never taught you to take orders.'

'I dunno. Taught me to follow my superior officers, didn't it?' Kincaid leaned his tall, cadaverous frame against the window and packed his pipe with tobacco. 'Come on. Spit it out. What's eating you, John?'

What was eating him was that his beautiful daughter lay in her grave, when she should, by rights, still be alive, and that it was a father's job to protect his only child, and he'd failed her.

Hug me like you used to, Daddy, before I was sick. Hug me tight. I won't break...

What was eating him was that he didn't want to go back to the soulless rooms he'd been forced to rent, having sold his house to cover the costs of having his wife privately confined in a local mental asylum, rather than a free one on the far outskirts of London.

What was eating him was that Julia was slowly but systematically pushing him away, and for the life of him, he didn't know why. By Christ, he missed the citrus scent of her body, the warmth that engulfed him when she snuggled into the crook of his arm, the peace that came from watching her breathe while she slept.

'Canals, Charlie. If you must know, that's what's eating me.'

Forget the Romans, who flooded a small channel between Lincoln and the River Trent, Britain's first proper canal was built to carry coal from the mines in Worsley to the city of Manchester. The duke who owned those collieries had no idea what he'd be unleashing. Virtually overnight, transportation costs fell by three quarters, and it was thanks to fast and consequently unlimited access to coal that the Industrial Revolution exploded. As more and more canals were cut, more and more goods began to be shipped, until four thousand miles of man-made waterways criss-crossed the country, the longest of which was the Grand Union in to London, of which the arm that ran through Oakbourne was a spur.

'How sad, Charlie, that coal, the very lifeblood of industry, is delivered by the same people it turned out of their cottages and forced to become nomads, then demolished those cottages in favour of warehouses, factories and mills.'

'What's sadder is that when the bargees lived in those cottages, carrying freight to set points and back again, they were well-liked and respected.' Kincaid struck a match, and puffed until the tobacco caught. 'These days, they're spat on and despised.'

'Itinerant communities have always been spat on and despised,' Collingwood said. 'Human nature dictates that we don't trust what we don't understand, and the best form of defence is attack.'

'True, but the barge people, poor buggers, didn't have a choice in the matter. Hats off to the way they adapted, though. Creating a new style of culture that had its own unique art and clothes — but even that's coming to an end.' He spread his hands. 'Railways, John. That's the future.'

Collingwood closed his mind to the drunken brawls and fist fights down below, to the piles of reports and statements on his desk, and yet another denial for two extra constables to be assigned to Boot Street, now that the population in this jurisdiction was swelling fast, and crime along with it. But as long as the chief superintendent remained hell-bent on closing this station and merging it with another to glorify his career, there was nothing Collingwood could do, except keep putting in requests. 'Unfortunately, change is moving at a speed too fast for a lot of folk to keep up with,' he said.

In less than a generation, the golden age of canals had been pretty much consigned to ancient history, with railways moving goods so much faster, in a more streamlined manner, and proving infinitely more efficient in terms of the quantities that the trains could cope with. They had changed lives in other ways, too. Foreign travel had become affordable, explorations abounded because of it, and plant and trophy hunters were in seventh heaven, cluttering Britain with everything from rhododendrons to boa constrictors to shrunken heads, toucans and parrots. At home, the lives of the poor had been transformed with day trips and holidays, giving rise to seaside resorts that were heralding a whole new era of entertainment.

'And because so much cargo is on the move at any one time,' Collingwood said, 'precious few checks are made. Especially on the canals, now they're becoming increasingly unimportant by the day.'

'Call me Clairvoyant Kincaid, but I'm sensing a hunch here. This is about the youth on the London line, isn't it?'

'Crooks always find the weak spot.' Collingwood laced his fingers on his desk. 'How better to move slave labourers than by barge? That way, they're delivered right to the factory door.'

Wouldn't that be the ultimate tragedy?

The past and the future meeting in one poignant paradox.

Julia wasn't joking when she said cabaret kept unsociable hours, but lately hers were proving even more antisocial. Still, with one thing short of the studio being perfect, she'd had a call to make after the show, and she couldn't decide whether it was because she'd rectified the situation, or that the Mild West ended in raucous applause that made her practically skip down the street like Avalon Wright.

Molly's voice was back. 'Tomorrow, friends, I'll introduce you to Rushing Water, his sister Running Water and his older brother, Passing ... now, now, you filthy minded lot. I'm talking about his older brother, Passing *Cloud* —'

Julia regretted labelling her a hypochondriac. The poor girl had been spraying her throat almost non-stop, to get back on form, and that summed up the cast, really. The hard work and dedication they each put in. The way Hal was pounding those famously off-key ivories tonight, you wouldn't guess he'd been beaten up less than twenty-four hours ago. He even played up the bruise on the side of his face by painting it red, white and blue, in the form of a Union Jack.

The Great MMM magnificently sawed Lizzie in half, to which Buck called out 'How did you do that?' 'Ah, well, it's the magician's secret,' the river boat gambler replied. 'If I told you,

I'd have to kill you.' 'In that case,' Buck cried, 'don't tell me, tell my wife.'

Was it possible Julia had got it wrong? That she was reading too much into this murder? If Molly picked up men for affairs that lasted purely the time the Mild West was in town, and Lizzie fell in love at the drop of a hat and out of love even faster, why shouldn't Annie Oaktree have had an equally lively love life?

Who's to say she didn't meet a man, whose hobby was strangling women. Travelling shows had a bad reputation before they even pitched camp. Stealing babies, robbing houses, violating women, picking pockets, there was nothing people believed they couldn't do.

Annie Oaktree might well have been skimming from Buck, and he might well have wanted his money back under cover of darkness so nobody twigged. Why should their scam, if that's what they were running, be important?

Equally, why should Avalon's memory — no, let's be straight about this, her *illness* — be connected in any way whatsoever?

Life on the road is unlike any other. Standards are different, expectations are that much lower, while sexual urges are that much higher. If Annie was having an affair with Dodger, surely she'd know he'd never leave Avalon? But if she still had feelings for him — yet was so addicted to that dimpled charm that she couldn't stop — then, yes, she'd be bitter. She might say she felt used. She might call him names to deflect. All that did, with hindsight, was disguise feelings of her own self-loathing.

Hal harboured secrets. The Great MMM certainly did. Such skills as he had could nab him a spot at one of the top London musical halls any old day, and, no one chooses to be poor when they could be rich and famous, especially in the entertainment business. Also, Julia caught him tipping his hat back in anger and indicating, in no uncertain terms, for a dark-haired young woman to leave him alone. Not so handsome when he snarled, was he? Was that because Annie's funeral was tomorrow, and the strain was beginning to tell? Or was the man from Wolverhampton more snake than charmer —?

Running with the same theme, it followed that whether the girls were sticky-fingered and nosey was irrelevant. Julia's money was actually on Lizzie there, being slim enough to move around without making a sound, and rummage through things without (sorry, Molls!) knocking them over. Of course, there might be an even simpler explanation yet. Molly might have done exactly that. Dropped the gravy boat, cleared up the pieces and thrown them away, too ashamed to admit she was clumsy. Ditto the fountain pen, perhaps knocking it on the floor then treading on it, the same with the hand mirror. Who wants to admit they've been snooping?

The bells of St. Oswald's were tolling midnight when Julia finally let herself back in to the studio. Unsurprisingly, the place was in darkness. Not so much as a settlement creak from the floorboards or contracting click of the roof tiles, and ordinarily, such silence would be comforting. These were not ordinary times. The stillness carried a menace that made the base of her skull tingle. This was silly! Hadn't she just proved her suspicions were groundless? Molly would be in the arms of her latest lover. Lizzie would be busy nabbing herself a new husband. No one was waiting behind the door with a cudgel, or wielding a knife taken from the block in the kitchen. All the same, Julia's palms left damp patches on the cotton where she'd smoothed her skirts, because fear wasn't panic or a case of over-reacting. Fear was prudent.

Complacency is what gets people killed…

Late or not, though, there was work still to do. It might not be the most pressing of tasks, but Julia had taken a photo of Mrs. Kincaid's grave, and there was no point in hanging on to the damned thing. In the warm, red light of her darkroom, she poured an emulsion of silver halide crystals in a gelatin base over the glass plate, and smiled. So much better than the old, wet process that Sam had to contend with, when plates had to be developed within ten minutes of taking them!

We can't choose the music life plays for us, JJ. What we can choose is how we dance to the tune.

Oh, Sam. How fast you waltzed to this brand new technology! How you twirled and spun as you abandoned your travelling darkroom, and set up the studio here!

Lost in laughter and memory, Julia gently agitated the plate in the processing bath, then, once the desired level of reduction was achieved — in other words, once the image formed on the glass — halted any further development by washing it in diluted acid, before removing the unwanted residue in a thiosulfate solution. A process otherwise known as fixing. This is the point where the image could now be exposed to light, and Julia could take herself off to bed, safe in the knowledge that Mrs. Kincaid's headstone could rest as peacefully as the woman who lay beneath it. Should she tip the chemicals away now, or wait until morning? While tossing the coin, the bell over the shop door tinkled, and was quickly silenced by hand. Julia turned off the red light and carefully opened the door, in time to see Lizzie lock up behind her, then tiptoe silently up the stairs.

So much for husband number four.

And since the light was off, it seemed the decision about chemicals had been taken for her. Rather than think she was spying on her boarders, Julia slipped off her shoes and padded up the stairs, hugging the wall where the boards didn't creak. The door of the bedroom that used to be Annie's was cracked open. Julia stopped. Should she…? Oh come on, you can't call it nosey, when you might be harbouring a killer under your roof! Peering closer, she watched Lizzie shake ten drops of laudanum into a glass, fill it halfway with water, then knock the whole lot back in one swallow.

In that instant, Julia knew that very same scene would be replayed night after night on the road.

Lizzie — trudging back from the show, her new man, or whatever else she got up to, to a room where she'd never be able to choose her own mattress, scent her own linens, or set out possessions of her own. Her throat would be dry and her jaw would ache from so much false smiling. Her temples would pound from the noise and the strain of folding herself up like a towel. That's when she'd close the door on the world, and reach for the only thing that would see her through.

A shiver ran down Julia's spine. Despite the appearance of order and calm, appearances, as she knew well, can be deceptive. What we pick up from any situation, good or bad, is nothing more than our own personal perspective, and the East Enders who flooded in every summer were proof of that. Like the hop-pickers in Kent, they came to harvest the crops from this aptly-named Garden of London. The money they earned wouldn't keep a dog for a week, yet passing through the rolling farmlands that encircled the industrial core, you'd hear them singing at the tops of their voices — *sippin' cider through a straw-aw-aw* — as raspberries, plums and peas flew into their baskets. Close your eyes, you could almost hear it.

Casey would waltz
With a strawberry blonde
And the band played on…

You'd sing along. You'd clap. You'd wave as you passed by. And not see that the skin on those nimble fingers were shredded from constant contact with sharp thorns on the canes, and forget this cheery band were out picking from dawn til dusk, and at angles they were well aware would cripple their backs before they reached forty. Assuming they lived that long.

Perspective. When push comes to shove, that's all it is. Perspective.

Just as the audience would see Lizzie's dazzling smile and froth of happy, red curls, and not see the strain that loneliness takes. Or the solutions that she took to erase it…

He'd ne'er leave the girl
With the strawberry curls
And the band played on…

The song, so beloved of music halls, almost made Julia twirl down the corridor to her bedroom, as she swung her shoes in time with the beat.

His brain was so loaded
It nearly exploded —

'Jesus Christ!'

In a chair facing the window, its back to her bed, a man sat in the darkness. Silhouetted by moonlight, no mean feat in the smog, she could just make out that, in his left hand, was a virtually empty bottle of whisky. And in his right was a pistol.

All Julia had was a pea in a whistle.

'Good God, Buck, what were you thinking?'

'That William Cody has a lot to answer for,' he said — correction, slurred. Not a muscle had moved. He was still facing the street, knees apart, and she tried not to think about why he'd broken in, or how long he'd sat there, waiting for her to come upstairs. 'These shows he takes round Europe and America? All these spectaculars that cost a fortune to stage, but which rake in three times what he shells out? It's sensationalism, Julia. That's what it is. Sensationalism with a capital S.'

There was no point in telling him that that was the whole purpose. You can't argue with a drunk.

Or a man holding a loaded gun.

'He plays out the great American dream by playing up the great American fear.'

'Ending up drunk and penniless, you mean?' Keep it light. 'Like Calamity Jane, who claims she's never gone to bed sober, or with a dime in her pocket?'

'Indians.' He took a swig of the whisky. If there were two more left in the bottle, Julia would be very much surprised. 'Thanks to him, we've been brainwashed into thinking they were the biggest threat to the American West, but you know the real enemy?'

Thanks to Sam, Julia was well aware that Buffalo Bill's views on the indigenous peoples was the complete opposite. Cody had great respect for the Sioux, the Cheyenne, the Apache, believing they had every right to resist the rape of their land, and fight for their freedom and values. Again, though, it was pointless telling Buck anything. What she needed to do was edge close enough to take the gun from his hand — she didn't like the way he was waving it.

Or the way her stomach was churning.

'The weather, Julia. That was the enemy. Drought, floods, wind, storms. Hail the size of your fist, that can wipe out years of hard work in a heartbeat.'

'I take it you grew up on a farm.'

'What anchors you to *your* childhood, Julia? Tell me the sights and sounds that you miss the most?'

'Seagulls.' It came out before she could stop it. 'Seagulls, pink flowers, and the sea.'

I'd never want to live in a posh place, me. A voice she hadn't heard for more than twenty years filled her head, and the voice was as clear as last week. *For one thing, the ceilings are so high, I'd get nosebleeds painting 'em, and for another, your Ma'd spend half her life cleaning the windows.*

Julia and her father were standing on the clifftop, her small hand in his, and he was telling her how the rich mine owners lived.

That's silly. She remembered giggling, just as she remembered seagulls wheeling over the waves crashing below, shrieking with joy, while bees plundered the clumps of bright pink thrift tickling her bare feet. *We'd have servants to paint the ceilings and polish our panes!*

Not us, lovey. You'd never catch your ole Dad having strangers tramping through his home all day long.

After that, Julia never saw rich folk in the same light. Imagine never knowing privacy! Imagine never being free! For that matter, she never stood on the clifftop with her father again, either. Three days later, his broken body came home in a barrow, and the next time she heard seagulls, they were shrieking in pain.

'Memory and emotion are inseparable, Julia.'

Could Buck read minds, now? Without turning, could he actually see her whole body shake?

'You think of frontier life as all cosy log fires, antlers on the walls, furs on the bed, jugs of moonshine lined up on the dresser. That's not how life is on a farm. Not there, and not here.'

Was this leading up to a confession? If so, was it prior to killing her, himself — or both? *Complacency is what gets people killed…* How could she have been so bloody stupid?

He half-turned his head, and even in the dim light, he looked haunted. 'This is not how I imagined my life would turn out,' he said over his shoulder.

'Buck. Please. Don't do anything stupid.'

'What? Like this?' He put the pistol to his temple.

'*NO!*' She rushed forward, but it was too late.

He pulled the trigger.

Down fell the flag.

Bang!

'I'm sorry.' Buck practically fell out of the chair in his haste to apologise. 'Julia, I am so, so sorry. I didn't mean to scare you.'

'What the hell did you expect? Breaking into my house … sitting next to my bed … in the dark … with a gun…'

'I'm drunk.'

'You weren't, when you broke in.' She snatched the bottle out of his hand. 'Is that my whisky?'

'It's the funeral tomorrow. I was lonely —'

'So on top of being grateful for some stupid practical joke, you think I'm cheap. Get out.'

'No. Not lonely like that. Well — maybe a bit like that. You're an attractive woman —' His face was drawn, his jaw tight, there was no sparkle left in his eyes. 'Right now, I couldn't hit the sea if I fell off a ship, so I wouldn't insult you by trying it on. I just want someone to talk to.'

'Then talk,' she said gently. If this was the only way to coax a confession, so be it. 'But first, I am going to make you the strongest coffee that's ever gone down your throat.'

He wasn't the only one who needed it! Her hands were shaking like the last leaves of autumn.

This is not how I imagined my life would turn out. Waiting for the water to boil, Julia wondered if watching years of planning wiped out by harsh weather had been the trigger for Buck leaving the farm, or whether it was the excuse he'd been looking for. Buffalo Bill wasn't the first man to bring the Wild West to the masses, and he probably would not be the last. By and large, such extravaganzas paid handsome dividends, so perhaps that's what Buck meant? That he never expected so much hard work for so little reward?

Carrying the tray upstairs, soft snores emanated from Lizzie's room as she passed.

They were a bloody sight louder in her room.

CHAPTER 19

'This is really very kind of you,' Buck said.

'Kitting Molls and Lizzie out for the funeral? Hardly.'

After all, Julia was supposed to be a widow, and since no one had noticed her when Sam was alive (being a mere woman and an assistant at that), it stood to reason that no one noticed when she suddenly adopted widow's weeds.

'I'll be dropping more off at the White Lion for Avalon,' Julia said. 'How's the hangover? If it helps, by the way, you look terrible.'

'That, my dear Mrs. McAllister, is because this is not a hangover. Yours truly is suffering from a severe case of whisky flu, and you didn't need to sleep on the sofa.'

'In case you hadn't noticed, rather like Goldilocks, I had three bears in my beds.'

'You should have kicked me out.'

The thought crossed her mind, but he'd needed someone to talk to, he said. Which meant he needed a refuge. A place to relax, unwind and be free. It also meant that, if Buck had killed Annie, he had a conscience…

The White Lion Inn dated from the time of Edward IV, and had clearly been loved and cherished throughout the four hundred years since the first thirst was quenched here. Typical of all coaching inns, it was situated on a busy thoroughfare, in this case the London road, operated excellent stables, served even better food, and offered a very comfortable night's sleep indeed. With industry on the rise, inns like this relied on repeat custom, and word-of-mouth recommendations. Standards couldn't afford to slip.

'What a wonderful, *wonderful* hat!'

Avalon twirled in front of the mirror, and Julia smiled. Even with non-existent husbands, mourning drags on for a year. What self-respecting young widow wouldn't want the widest range of fashion they could lay their hands on, and this was especially true when it came to hats.

Women noticed hats.

Women coveted hats.

Women couldn't resist starting conversations with strangers about hats.

Was it any wonder they became Julia's prime choice of advertisement?

'It's far too good to be lending out, but —' Avalon giggled — 'seeing as how you've pinned it on…'

'Call me a coward, but when it comes to millinery, you girls are on yer own.' Dodger grinned. 'I'll wait downstairs, but for what it's worth, darling —' he planted a smacker of a kiss on his wife's lips, and gave her cheek an affectionate pinch — 'you look absolutely bleedin' gorgeous.'

Julia fluffed up the feathers. 'You're lucky, you know that? True love is hard to find.'

'My mother always said love was a disease that only marriage could cure, but look at us! Four years this summer, and we've never been happier.' Avalon held out her hand to show off her rings. 'Mind you, my Ma still gives me an earful, when I get back. Calls him a cocky little sod, idle little bugger, proper little scrounger, all within earshot, I might add, but you know Dodge. Water off a gander's back. Says Ma's jealous, because she's never known a day of freedom in her life, as much as I love her, Dodger's right.' She turned back to the mirror to preen. 'Tell you what else my Ma says. That the reason we wear black is because once the dead are ripped from their surroundings, the spirit becomes resentful, and that's why they come back to haunt us. By dressing in black, the spirits don't recognise us, which puts paid to any settling of scores, but you know what I think? I reckon the ghosts just want their freedom, too.' Her pretty face clouded as she wrapped Julia's cashmere shawl round her shoulders. 'June loved her freedom, but deep down, she wanted to settle. Do you think she'll be able to settle, Julia? Do you think she'll be at peace in the grave?'

Avalon was asking the wrong person here. 'I'm convinced of it,' Julia said.

Downstairs, Dodger was leaning with one elbow on the bar, and both feet crossed at the ankles. The instant he saw Avalon, he jumped up straight, dimples popped in his cheek, and he came bounding over to take his wife's arm. Julia could understand his mother-in-law's fears. Here was a confident, comfortable, Jack-the-lad type, who was bound to break her daughter's heart. But mother doesn't always know best. When all you know is domestic drudgery, you see life on the road as a drain, not a means of replenishment, and though Julia had put down roots of a sort, there was always an itch at the back of her mind. The itch that whispered "what if...?'

'Where's your tie pin?' Avalon asked, straightening her husband's knot.

'What?' Dodger checked his reflection in the bar mirror. 'Bugger. Must have left it on the bleedin' dressing table. I'll just—'

'No, no, I'll go.' Avalon was skipping up the stairs before she'd even finished her sentence.

'I gather it's your fourth anniversary coming up. Congratulations!'

Dodger's grin widened. 'Every morning, I look in the mirror when I'm shaving me baby soft chin, and think, you're a lucky dog, Rodge. You bloody well are — Oh, thanks, sweetheart, you're an angel.'

'Julia's the angel,' Avalon quipped, 'but it's a funny thing. I could have sworn the mirror was on the wall by the window. Did I really check this hat in the mirror over the bed?'

'No, love, that's that horrible painting of the Virgin Mary holding Jesus' dead body.' He rolled his big, blue eyes. 'What a passion killer, eh?'

'Sorry, darling, that's what I thought, too. But the Virgin Mary is definitely by the window, the *mirror's* over the bed.'

'Nah.'

Laughing, Dodger took the stairs two at a time, and the way the pair of them giggled, you wouldn't think they were off to the funeral of someone they'd lived, and worked closely, with. But, like Julia, showpeople were conditioned to hide their feelings and keep emotions on a tight leash. By God, though, it was exhausting —

It's the reason she'd only put down roots "of sorts". Any day, her past could catch up with her and she'd have to move on, which is why she couldn't afford to make deep emotional connections. There's only room for love, when both parties are committed to the same lifestyle.

John Collingwood couldn't change — and she wouldn't want him to, either.

'If I'm wrong, I'll buy drinks on the house for a week.' Dodger unlocked the door and flung it wide, clearly expecting Avalon to give him a pretend clip round the ear or a playful dig in the ribs. Instead, she burst into tears.

'Hey, hey, hey. None of that, now. It's all right.' He rocked her tight. 'All these rooms look alike, love —'

'I could have *sworn* — I'd have laid my *life* —' she pointed over the bed — 'the mirror was there, it was *there*, when I picked up your tie pin. I know it was, and the painting was *there*.' Wild-eyed, she grabbed Julia's sleeve. 'You saw me. You watched me twirl. Where was the mirror?'

Julia already felt sick. 'Where it is now,' she said thickly.

She could not — dare not — meet Avalon's gaze. Dodger had his hand over his mouth. He also looked about to throw up. She pulled the sash to open the window and let some air in the room.

Deep breaths, deep breaths…

Leaning out, Julia saw warehouses, winches, delivery carts, barges, the whole ugly scene streaked with garlands of smoke from factories filled with workers deafened by noise, and whose lungs were either filled with soot, or boiled raw from the heat from the steam.

Dear God, wasn't that enough despair for one town?

Julia leaned both hands on her desk.

You think life can't get worse.

You watch a woman's mind unravel in front of your eyes. You feel her husband's pain like a nail through your heart. Then, almost immediately, you have to muster enough strength to lay a Welsh girl in the ground, a long, long way from her homeland.

Buck had sent a telegram, informing her parents of the arrangements, and at the same time wiring them funds for the train fare. Their reply was short. *Thank you. Very kind. We will not be attending.* Tossing a handful of earth over the coffin, Julia resolved to take a photo of June's gravestone once it was erected. Whatever the circumstances — whether her parents disapproved of her playing Annie Oaktree, of her itinerant lifestyle, or felt ashamed or betrayed by the path she had taken — no parent should abandon their child. As grief finally took hold, who knows what regret they might feel? A photograph might be some comfort; then again, it might stir up the pain. But without it, they would not have the choice...

Detective Inspector Collingwood attended. In theory, it was in case the killer put in an appearance. Many return to the scene of the crime to re-live the pleasure, he explained to the cast, and, for the same reason, were attracted to the graves of their victims. In practice, he was there to monitor their reaction, in which case he had nothing but disappointment in store.

Leaving the cemetery, Julia passed boys jostling to climb trees so they could swing from ropes tied high in the branches, others played hide-and-seek in the bushes or (don't let the superintendent catch you!) kicked footballs, using the gravestones as goalposts. The wheels on perambulators spun like clockfaces, as nursemaids in crisp, neatly starched uniforms pushed their charges along the gravel driveways. Gardeners dead-headed the first floral casualties of spring — daffodils, tulips and irises — and mulched tender plants to protect them from late frosts.

A peaceful scene, you might be forgiven for thinking.

Unless you'd just discovered that little Georgie's mother had also fallen victim to grief. Visiting the pauper's grave where her son's coffin had been unceremoniously tossed, her foot slipped. Without use of her arms after the accident in the factory, there was nothing to grab at, nothing to cling to, as she plunged twenty feet down. Ten, maybe twelve people had heard her scream, but they knew better than to attempt a rescue. Without soil to act as a buffer between the coffins, carbonic acid formed in the pit, as deadly as it was fast-acting.

The gas was a major peril for gravediggers. Many lost their lives as a result. But a quick death was no consolation for a man who'd lost his wife, his son, his livelihood as well as the sight in one eye and his foot.

Back home, Julia wept. She wept for Georgie's father. She wept for June Margaret Sullivan, whose family had cut all ties with her. She wept for Sam, who'd loved her without condition, and who she'd love unconditionally in return. Most of all, though, she wept for her mother and brother. True, they were safe from the sadistic bastard who took such delight in taking fists, feet, buckles and sticks to defenceless women and children. But these were the two people Julia loved the most in the world, and oh, oh, how she missed them. What she wouldn't give to see them again! Tears dripped on the paperweight on her desk. Another time, and she'd caress the green glass egg in both hands, never ceasing to admire the flower trapped inside. Today, she did not even see it.

How could this morning be such a sickening contrast to a night of unbridled hilarity?

Was it really only a few hours ago when Avalon brought the house down, because instead of dressing in her usual saloon girl costume to banter with Doc Vacation, she strutted on stage dressed as a gunfighter, right down to the big, fake moustache? The audience couldn't get enough. Was that because a spot of cross-dressing always goes down a storm? Or because Avalon wore black tights instead of trousers? Who cared?

As the crowd surged forward — navvies rubbing shoulders with nannies, stockbrokers with stokers — to have Buffalo Buck sign their flyers, Julia was struck by the mob's sense of unity. Rich and poor, young and old, coarse and cultured, they weren't united simply in their love of musical comedy, and a willingness to overlook terrible singing and fat (sorry, Molls) thighs. That same solidarity bound them in opposition to the Temperance Movement, protesting outside against the destructive influence of the Demon Drink, and, watching children pull at their mothers' skirts, insisting they weren't tired and demanding to go back inside, Julia was again filled with respect for the way the cast pulled together in times of crisis. All for one, and one for all. The true spirit that held them together —

Wait!

Wait, wait, wait.

Motive, means and opportunity were the three musketeers of a murder investigation. All for one, and one for all. *All for one, and one for all...* The breath caught in her throat. Suppose —? This was ridiculous. Wild. But just suppose for a minute that, instead of a single individual being responsible for Annie's —

'Mrs. McAllister!'

Deep in thought, Julia hadn't heard the shop bell.

'Mr. Vance.' She forced a smile, but godammit, he was the last person she wanted to talk to right now. Of *all* people, how could she tell him she had no news, good or bad, and prolong the poor bugger's agony? Much less admit that the police weren't even trying?

'I apologise. I made you jump. Only I wanted to talk to you before your employer returns.'

'He'll be gone a while.'

'Even better, you see I have good news!'

'You do?'

'Wonder of wonders, Mrs. McAllister, my son has come home.'

Oh, thank God. The idea of his body bobbing up under a bridge had been too horrid to contemplate, and as far as good news goes, the timing could not have been better. 'I'm so pleased for you, Mr. Vance. Where was he all this time?'

'Well, that's the most remarkable thing. The tale is truly astonishing, and given the hard work and effort that you've put in on his behalf, I thought it only right that you should hear it yourself.'

'Are you match-making, Mr. Vance?'

His spine still made ramrods look slack, his beard was as closely clipped as it had ever been, there wasn't a crease in his silk tie or a speck of dust on his frock coat. But behind the hardness in his eyes was the hint of a twinkle. Why is it that men of means are so utterly repressed? Was it armour, against the brickbats of jealousy? Or holding — what was it? — nine years of grief locked tightly inside, that he'd forgotten how to let go?

'You have a kind heart and a strong spirit, Mrs. McAllister. If you and my boy did rub along, let's say I would not be disappointed. That aside, I believe you should hear his remarkable story with your own ears. Mr. Conan Doyle himself could not pen a stranger tale.'

'I suppose tomorrow —'

'Come now! Please! I live very close by, it will take but a half-hour of your time, and I promise you will not regret this.'

Fresh from a funeral, with bad news piled on bad news, what could Julia say? She'd never taken to Vance, his formality was a fortress, but fear had rendered him vulnerable, excitement even more so. And she was a sucker for "remarkable" stories.

'Let's go, Mr. Vance.'

'Excellent.' He tipped his top hat. 'And please, my dear. Call me Titus.'

CHAPTER 20

Julia's eyelids were heavy, her head swam. Through blurred vision, she was aware of a room she'd never been in before. And yet…

This was a dream. In real life, you don't open your eyes and see willow pattern gravy boats.

She tried to shift, but her limbs wouldn't move. Too little sleep, too much stress, she must have passed out. Fallen into an almost comatose state. *Wake up, girl! You have portraits to take, photos to develop, fake guns to fire. Bang!* Maybe if she sang herself awake?

'I wish I was in Brixton, hurrah, hurrah.'

The sound came out like a mouse with a sore throat. *Wake up, wake up, wake up!*

'The minute I saw the technique in the East Indies, I knew I needed to learn it,' a cultured voice murmured.

Great. Now she was dreaming about Titus Vance. Add in a tax collector, a moneylender and his beery sidekick, and her joy would be complete.

'The trick is to catch your opponent off guard.'

As she struggled to wake, the room swam into focus. Sparsely furnished was an understatement. Two chairs, that was it. Two upright wooden chairs, to be precise. The sort you'd expect to see in a medieval banqueting hall, or round an aristocrat's long dining table.

'After considerable, and I do mean considerable, practice, I am able to time the move to perfection.' Vance took the empty chair facing hers, and panic shot through Julia like fire. *This wasn't a dream* — 'Two seconds exactly to put my forearm across the opponent's throat, at which point everyone, without exception, raises their arms to fight off the attack. That simple, basic instinct allows me to loop my free arm behind their head. Leverage is all mine after that.'

Fire turned to ice. 'You strangled Annie Oaktree.'

'Me? Lower myself to such a vulgar, coarse act? And on a showgirl? A common harlot? Shame on you, Mrs. McAllister, for even suggesting such a thing.'

'I'm glad you find choking more refined,' she said in a voice that belied the terror.

'I assure you, my dear, pushing down on your throat might prove uncomfortable, but it would not put you to sleep. No, no, no. The technique relies on pushing my hand forward, and pressing your chin into my forearm. According to my guru in Java, that restricts the flow of blood to the brain, causing loss of consciousness within a matter of seconds.' His voice was chillingly cheerful. 'Once again, though, timing is critical. One must release one's opponent the instant they go limp.'

'I was not an opponent, Mr. Vance. You tricked me.'

'For which I apologise profusely. I do. However, I think you will agree that the end justified the means. You would not expect a man who collects rare orchids to stuff them under his arm, or ram them into a shopping basket, would you? As care is taken in selecting the right plant, so care must be taken in its transportation. Do, please, call me Titus.'

'Where are we?'

'My home. A delightfully isolated farmhouse, where I would caution against screaming. It will only make your throat sore and waste valuable energy, since no one can possibly hear you.'

He walked across to open the curtains, revealing acres of land as far as the eye could see that was startlingly unproductive for the garden of London. In fact, overgrown and neglected barely began to describe it. Julia had no doubts when he said no one would hear.

'One of the advantages of wealth is that it allows one to purchase exactly the right property, and, providing one pays one's taxes on time, no one questions what becomes of the place.'

'I presume you don't declare rape and murder to the Board of Inland Revenue?'

'Oh, please! That would be the equivalent of pouring acid over those beautiful orchids we discussed. I stoop to neither of those acts.'

'Then why am I roped to a chair, in a house where screams cannot carry?'

Memory flooded back. Vance had come into the shop to say his son had come home, and was keen for the two of them to meet. She'd got into his phaeton. A typically stylish affair, with yellow spokes and axles, royal blue sprung seats and leather hood. They were leaving the outskirts, when he pointed out a heron on the side of the road. She couldn't see it. Turned for a better look. At which point, an arm clamped across her throat, and that was the last thing she remembered.

'Don't tell me. I'm the welcome home present for your son.'

'I don't have a son, Mrs. McAllister.'

'Then who was the boy you were looking for?'

'An invention. A ruse to establish your trust.'

Her stomach lurched. She refused to be sick. 'What about the police? You called at Boot Street twice a day.'

'Did I?' He chuckled. 'Dear me, I can't imagine who planted such a fanciful story in your head. Next, you'll be telling me some tall tale about a railway accident in which a wife I never had died alongside a daughter-in-law I didn't have, either.'

Oh dear God. A tissue of lies from beginning to end. Like a fool, Julia fell for the lot.

'I sincerely appreciate the time and effort you spent looking for this fictitious creature, though. Your diligence and help was a true test of character, which, I am delighted to report, you passed with flying colours.'

She wriggled, squirmed, tussled and tugged. The rope didn't budge. 'Lucky me.'

'Your spirit burns with a hot flame right now. You think that, because you work with the police on the odd occasion, they will come looking for you. I hate to be the bearer of bad tidings —' the hell he was — 'but I assure you, steps are already in hand to ensure that, however much you might want it to happen, that will not be the case.'

'You're wrong. They will find me.' She wished she could believe that, but neither Charlie or John knew where to look.

'Optimism was one of the qualities I selected you for, along with your kindness, generosity, virtue and integrity. You see, the more thoughtful, more decent, more helpful they are, the more of that light goes into me.'

They…?

Julia instantly stopped fighting. 'You do stoop to murder, then?'

'Tch, tch, I fear you are not listening. I have never killed anything in my life, Mrs. McAllister. Indeed, I barely swat a spider or a fly. Nature claims these ladies, not me, for without food, without water, the body cannot survive. The test is how long it takes for them — for you — to resist those forces of nature.'

'I can see why you like this place.' Julia steadied her voice. 'Easy to bury the evidence.'

'Bury? Good heavens, what an outrage! Do you perchance remember Miss Taylor from the library?'

Julia felt a shiver as Kincaid's words came back to her. *A missing librarian.* 'I do.'

She recalled the story in the *Chronicle* now. Two weeks after announcing her engagement, Miss Taylor had disappeared. That was a year, maybe fifteen months, ago.

'She's in the room at the top of the landing. Miss O'Rourke, who worked as a typist in the solicitor's on Cadogan Street, is in the attic. Mrs. Fairclough is in what used to be the pantry, and at some point, I will tell you about the others.' Vance's eyes glinted. 'I did tell you I was something of a collector, Mrs. McAllister.' He smiled. 'Welcome to my collection.'

CHAPTER 21

John Collingwood had only felt like this three times in his life.

The first was when his twelve-year-old daughter — his only child — died. He was sick. Numb. Cold. Sweating. More hollow, more terrified, more helpless than he could ever have imagined.

The second time was when he learned how she had died, that his wife was responsible, that her death was malicious and therefore avoidable, and that he'd be spending the rest of his life with the knowledge that, by rights, Alice should have outlived him, raising children of her own. Instead, he'd never walk her down the aisle. Or kiss his grandchildren. Or see her lovely smile again. She'd been cheated, and there was nothing he could have done to prevent it.

Now, this…

He looked round a bedroom so familiar that each object stabbed him through the heart. The bolsters they'd used in a pillow fight once. The bed on which they made love while rain lashed against the windows, or moonlight flooded the room. The scrapes on the bedpost, from where his police handcuffs were put to more intimate use.

Kincaid had rung him and told him there was no man with a missing son. The desk sergeant was certain that no one had been in twice a day to enquire.

The instant Bert said he'd never heard of Vance, warning flags flew for Kincaid. Titus Vance, it seemed, did not exist.

Kincaid said that, when he telephoned Julia to warn her and there was no answer, he wasn't surprised, considering she'd just left the cemetery. Showpeople, more than most, he reckoned, would know how to throw a wake. In that, though, Sergeant Kincaid was wrong. Showpeople, it turned out, couldn't afford time off to mourn. There were two performances coming up, Buck had explained tightly. The time to raise glasses and memories was after the last adoring fan had trickled out of the tent and the last programme had been signed. At this point, Kincaid had raced to Julia's studio. The door was locked, with the closed sign in place, but his knock brought Molly's head poking out of the upstairs window, quickly followed by a froth of red curls. Julia wasn't home, the girls said.

'Sorry.' The plump one had shrugged. 'No idea where she is, lovey.'

'Me, neither,' trilled the redhead.

Even then, Kincaid felt it was still possible that she'd gone shopping, was delivering a portrait, might even have needed to return a library book. A little strange, perhaps, that she'd gone out still dressed in black from the service, but Julia McAllister wasn't renowned for following convention.

As it happened, Sergeant Kincaid wasn't renowned for being sloppy.

Having got the girls to open up, he set about reassuring himself that he was fretting needlessly. Nothing was out of place in the shop. The money was in the till, always a good sign. In fact, everywhere he checked, normality saluted. On the point of blowing his whistle to summon a uniformed officer to stand guard, he opened the door to Julia's bedroom. The bed was made. The linens were straight. Every item was laid out, neat as any pin on the dressing table, and the wardrobe was freshly scented with lavender sachets.

What stopped him in his tracks wasn't a fringed bucksin shirt under the four-poster. Although why Buck's clothes should be in Julia's bedroom was a line he might want to follow up later. It was the photograph of Sam Whitmore. From the empty space, Kincaid imagined that it normally took pride of place on the mantelpiece. Right now, it lay on the rug, the glass in smithereens from where it had been stamped on so hard that the frame had buckled. This was anger, resentment and jealousy all rolled into one, and it couldn't have been Lizzie's boot, or Molly's that did this. More than anyone, they knew the resemblance between Sam and Buck was merely superficial. Up close, the showman doesn't look a bit like Sam, and for that reason, Buck had no reason to destroy it, either.

Sod whistling for a constable. Kincaid sent straight for his inspector.

'Witnesses saw her stepping into a phaeton,' he told Collingwood. 'But the fact it went thatta way,' he jerked with his thumb, 'don't mean a damn thing.'

Staring at the mangled portrait, trying not to imagine the violence behind the act, Collingwood recalled that, on the previous occasions when he'd been rendered sick, numb and hollow, he had also been immobilised by feelings of guilt, albeit irrational, and frozen by the knowledge that there was nothing in his power that could bring his daughter back. With Julia, it was different.

This wasn't a crime of passion or opportunity. Hell, no. The bastard had stalked her like a wounded stag, and, unless he missed his guess, it was Vance who'd gone snooping through her belongings, not the girls. The hand mirror, the fountain pen, even that stupid sodding gravy boat, he'd taken as sick souvenirs. Smug reminders of how he'd been able to come and go as he pleased, and how nothing of Julia's was sacred or private. The gallows were well familiar with animals like Vance, and police records bulged with statements, bragging about what they did to their victims, and how they prolonged the lives of the creatures they had trapped.

In Collingwood's experience, this ranged between two days and a week.

Where two days would feel like twenty years.

'You were married,' Vance was saying, dragging a cheval mirror across the floor.

Polished rosewood and inlaid with brass, it was very similar to the one Julia used to capture the reflection of her models undressing. Two stripteases for the price of one was exceptionally popular in the saucy picture trade.

'You've known devotion, you've known loss, you've known joy, you've known sorrow. Tell me, what comes to mind, Mrs. McAllister, when you think of love?'

Julia had abandoned any idea of fighting her bonds, especially while he was here. The only thing that had achieved was chafed wrists. There had to be another way.

'Is it rose arbours? Old couples sitting in front of the bandstand? Lovers sneaking kisses under the pergolas?' He stepped back to check the position, then tilted the mirror to the desired angle where she had no choice but to watch her own suffering. Two deaths for the price of one.

How could she have been so bloody stupid? *Complacency is what gets people killed…* How many times had she said that? How many times had she ignored her own advice? She could not — would not — let Vance see her fear, but panic almost made her black out. Knights on white chargers weren't coming to her rescue. That was a fact. Collingwood would see through Vance's ploy, but even the widest manhunt would not find this place. Or at least, not until it was too late.

'Rhetorical question, my dear. Those things constitute romance, whereas love, as you know from your poor, dear, dead husband, does not stem from external sources. Love is generated from within, and it is the giving of self that bestows strength. The giving of goodness and virtue and honesty and light, and you, my dear —' he caressed the rosewood frame like a lover's skin — 'have so very much of yourself to give.'

'The hell I do.' Suddenly she saw a way to cheat Vance of his prize. 'I'm damned if I'm starving to death with you watching,' she spat.

'Language, language…'

'You think you know me.' She pushed and tugged against the restraints. 'You know nothing.' The chair rocked. Pins flew out of her hair. Every ounce of energy went into the fight.

'Careful. We don't want you tipping over, hurting yourself — '

'Too late.' Julia closed her eyes. Swallowed. The side of the skull is always the weakest. '*Wait for me, Papa! I'm coming!*'

With one final push, she forced the chair sideways.

The floor was harder than bone.

CHAPTER 22

Whatever was happening inside Boot Street police station, Detective Inspector John Collingwood was oblivious. Whatever crimes might be taking place within his jurisdiction, he didn't care.

This had nothing to do with his feelings for Julia, which is not to say his stomach didn't churn non-stop in fear. His priority — and this took precedence over everything — was to catch a kidnapper, rescue the victim, and prevent a murder. The same priority that he would assign to every such case, including the body found mangled on the railway line. The only difference between the two was that early investigations into the boy's death indicated a supply chain of slave labour, where the gang would sacrifice any number of lives to save their own skins. To track them to the source required subtlety and silence, since they'd have eyes and ears everywhere. Lone killers don't have a network of informants, but they do have the element of surprise and a bloody good head start.

Subtlety be damned at times like this.

'We're hamstrung when it comes to manpower,' he told Kincaid. 'The chief super won't assign help from other stations on the grounds that, without tangible proof such as a ransom note, we can't be sure this is a kidnap.'

'Bollocks.'

'Politics.' It almost rhymed. 'Four men are in the running for Assistant Chief Constable, and wild goose chases at this stage won't help his bid for promotion.'

'Bodies will?'

'The committee makes its decision next week. The chief super's banking on our not finding the bastard until the appointment's announced, and sod it, Charlie, he's probably right.'

Jack the Ripper may have stopped killing, but he'd never been caught. If Julia ended up another such victim, Collingwood would never forgive himself. His fists clenched. Christ, why did he give the damned key back? He should have stayed. Won her over. Pushed back when she pushed him away, not slunk away nursing his wounds. Worst of all, he should have fucking followed up when she talked about Vance —

Julia, Julia, please, be alive.

'We're on our own, then?'

'We are, Charlie.'

Kincaid took a deep breath, then another. 'I went back through missing persons for the last two years, like you asked. Look for women meeting the same criteria, you said, and seven stood out.' He read from his notes. 'Eileen O'Rourke, twenty-eight, widowed, worked as typist. Mabel Walsh, mother of three, with a fourth on the way. Victoria Fielding, Gladys Fairclough, also married with children, Fanny Griffiths, fifteen, housemaid at the Station Hotel, Nora Armstrong, sixteen, also in service, and Maud Taylor, librarian, newly engaged.'

'That's quite a cross-section.'

'What you mean is, am I clutching at straws?'

'No disrespect, Charlie —'

'Hear me out, sir.' A month passed, he said, before the alarm was raised concerning the disappearance of Mrs. O'Rourke. Luckily, someone remembered overhearing her at the ticket office, telling the clerk that she had a family emergency in London and it was imperative that she caught the next train.

The same witness also recalled a Gladstone bag at her feet. 'Which explained her departure,' he said, 'but not why she never sent for her belongings. A constable was despatched to search her lodgings, but there was no what you'd call personal items, suggesting Mrs. O'Rourke took 'em with her.'

'Or someone else did.' Collingwood heaved open the window, where smoke from the factories mingled with the stink of blood and guts from the butcher's shop across the road. All of it sweeter than the stench of his failure.

'Mabel Walsh's husband couldn't accept that his wife would abandon him and their children, especially in her delicate condition,' Kincaid said. 'But a telephone call was made, anonymously, pointing out that Albert Walsh was known to knock his wife about on a regular basis. The consensus was that Mabel simply had enough, and would go to any lengths to protect her unborn child. A theory borne out when her wedding ring was posted through the letterbox a few nights later.'

Regarding Gladys Fairclough, a smartly-dressed businessman happened to be at the station when the police started asking questions regarding her disappearance. As luck would have it, he remembered her boarding the 8.17 to London with a man whose description didn't match her husband's, and the reason he remembered it was that, so absorbed was this lady, giggling and gazing into the man's eyes, that she didn't notice that she'd knocked the businessman's briefcase out of his hand, spilling his papers over the platform so that he nearly missed the train.

'In other words,' Collingwood said, 'the circumstances surrounding these women's disappearances are completely different, but the pattern is the same.'

'Trawling through witness statements, another theme cropped up. Every testimony came from a well-dressed, well spoken, middle-aged gentleman.'

'Don't suppose he left a name?'

'Oh, yes, very helpful, our witness. Name, address, occupation, the lot. But when I followed through? Load of baloney. Every one of them addresses was false, same with the names.'

Collingwood stared down on the bustle that was Boot Street. At the barrow boys and flower girls, at twirling parasols and doffing derby hats, at leg o'mutton sleeves and rough cloth caps. Like Diamond Jim a.k.a. Texas Jack a.k.a. the Great Mississippi Moonlight Magician, this bastard — *hey presto!* — turned cases where women whose disappearance would normally be high priority into plausible, if unresolved, missing persons cases destined to quickly slide off the active investigation list.

'I'm really sorry, sir.' Kincaid cleared his throat. 'I'd hoped, with all my heart, that them files would throw up a lead or three. Instead, I came up with bugger all.'

Collingwood closed the window. He, too, had wanted pointers, clues and hope to come out of the files. Above all, hope... 'A well-dressed, well spoken, middle-aged man isn't bugger all, Sergeant Kincaid.' He clapped him on the shoulder. 'This is bloody fine police work.' If nothing else, it provided insight into the character of the monster they were dealing with. 'There's a common denominator, too. The station.'

'Jesus hell.' Kincaid flicked back through his notes. 'So bloody clear, I can't believe I missed the connection and — yep. The anonymous call regarding Mabel Walsh's husband was made from the Station Hotel.'

'Get a uniformed constable down there immediately to start asking questions, and post a couple of others around the place in plain clothes. Then get on to the *Chronicle*. Speak to the editor, tell him you have a breaking story about a missing woman, and to make this front page news.'

Now they knew where to start, they could draw this narcissistic bastard out.

'Yes sir!' Kincaid jumped to it, but halfway through the doorway, he turned. 'We'll get him, John.' He shot him a tight smile. 'Don't you worry, son, we'll get 'im.'

He was right. They would.

So why did Collingwood feel they were too late?

CHAPTER 23

'My goodness, you gave me a fright.'

Julia blinked. 'Papa?'

'No, my dear. I fear I am more sprightly than you gave me credit for. Consequently, you will not be joining your father for another nine or ten days, at which point, though, I'm sure the family reunion will be sweet.'

Vance had wedged the chair against the wall facing the door. To prevent a repetition of her suicide attempt, he'd also blocked the chair in with what looked like timbers from a barn roof that had long since collapsed.

'What happened?'

'You tried to thwart my plans and you failed. Simple as that.' His smile was smug.

'Not quite that simple. With my clothes in disarray here, can I assume you took advantage?'

'Mrs. McAllister, I do wish you would rid yourself of the notion that I am some kind of sexual pervert. You fell, you knocked yourself out, you had difficulty breathing, and I did what any gentleman would do under the circumstances. I loosened your clothing.'

Julia thought of another man who'd loosened the buttons of her high, frilly blouse after she'd passed out. A man with a swirling moustache, a goatee beard and shoulder-length hair, who, at first glance, looked like Sam Whitmore but was a decade younger, whose face was round, and whose eyes were darker than obsidian.

My mother always said, if you see an opportunity, son, take it.

And my mother said that when opportunity knocks, pretend to be out.

Idly, she wondered what changes Buck would be making to the next performances, now that Annie Oaktree had dropped out completely. Versatility, of course, was his stock-in-trade. A trait that was equally essential when it came to members of his cast.

Lizzie, not just a contortionist who could tie herself into knots, but a consummate performer to boot.

Me, I'm always putting my foot in my mouth.

The foreman at the factory asked me when I could start work. I said, I'm flexible.

Avalon could throw knives and smiles with captivating precision. She could cartwheel, perform acrobatics, and come up with fresh ideas for the show all while singing *Swankee Doodle Dandy*, and Buck was right. The Mild West did hinge on her, and not because she was ace at sewing buttons, fetching throat sprays and straightening ties. When Avalon was on stage, every eye was on her, and a scene-stealer was exactly what Buck relied on for his performances to flow. Her magnetic presence allowed the rest of the cast to change costumes, swap roles and move props in full view, yet without the audience either noticing or caring.

Molly Bannister, or whatever her real name was, could switch routines at the drop of a Stetson, and had so many jokes that she wouldn't run dry in seven lifetimes.

I ordered steak in the restaurant, they served up fish. I called the manager over and said, just what kind of idiots do you employ here? To which he replied, only the best, madam, only the best.

From the Hot Cross Kid, juggling buns and firing jokes, to Crazy Hearse to General Custard, Dodger's cheeky dimpled grin never wavered. Hal's fingers set the rhythm for whatever mood was needed. Be it drama from a showdown or a lively comic turn, Hal's honky-tonk carried the audience along with showman flair and gusto. And whether he was walking on water, cutting assistants in half, or even making them vanish completely, the Great MMM used charm, every bit as much as skill, to keep the crowd hooked.

Then, of course, there was Buck himself…

'Now that I am satisfied that you cannot further harm yourself, you must excuse me, I have business to attend to.'

'Picking your next victim?'

'Mrs. McAllister!' Vance appeared genuinely shocked. 'Please! You and I have several happy months to look forward to, so many memories ahead. Cross my heart, I would never be unfaithful to you. I simply have a few loose ends to tie up.'

Heart? What would he know about hearts?

He dragged the cheval mirror to its new position. Now she couldn't even see the damned doorway. Just herself. Hair matted with blood from the fall, right eye swelling fast, *but alive* —

'As I outlined earlier, arrangements are already in hand to explain your unexpected departure.'

'I don't suppose you'd care to share those plans?'

'Suffice to say that your employer is about to receive something of a shock, once the police come knocking on his door. The letter you posted from a hotel in Westminster? Tch, don't tell me you've forgotten.' Gloating seemed to be his favourite pastime. 'Typewritten, obviously, though in your distress you omitted to add a signature, but the general gist of it concerns Mr. Whitmore's wicked — *wicked!* — assault on your virtue. It goes on to say how you had to get away. How you could not bear to be in the same place as the monster who violated you. Naturally, you addressed this letter to the police, with whom you have worked so closely in the past, secure in the knowledge that they will believe you.'

'I am fairly confident that Sam Whitmore will not stand trial.'

They'd have to dig him up first.

'I am fairly confident that you are right. But you know, my dear, mud has a nasty habit of sticking. I give the studio three months before it closes. Very sad.'

The door clicked shut behind him, and once the clop-clop-clop of the hooves had faded, there was nothing but silence. Not a whisper of wind in the unfurling leaves. Not a rustle of mice. Not even a moan from the souls of the women tortured to death in this cold, isolated farmhouse.

That they were not physically harmed before their deaths did not make it better.

Vance's thrill came from emotional suffering. From watching them slowly, and painfully, starving to death. Their strength, he argued, was absorbed into him. As though the passing of goodness and integrity was a gift. He claimed he didn't "defile" his collection. That would be to defile himself. Whereas watching them soil themselves doesn't? Not in his eyes. Their shame was their weakness, another reason to taunt them, all the while playing up how no one would come looking for them. No one would come searching. Instead, their children would be crying themselves to sleep, begging Mummy to come home, unable to understand why she had abandoned them. Why she no longer *loved* them. Like a cat with a mouse, he'd remind them over and over how their husbands, fiancés, parents and siblings would be haunted by hearing how the woman they loved, and who they thought loved them back, had run off without so much as a word. Oh, and did he mention it was with another man?

Her ears craned for a sound. Any sound. There was nothing. Not a chirrup of sparrows under the eaves. Not a fly on the window. That too, would be agony for women yearning to hear their children barrelling round the house, squabbling over toys, squealing at bath time, giggling under the bedsheets. Stealing their personal possessions heaped on the misery. These were reminders of a home they would never see again, and of memories that were never destined to be re-lived, and finally, Julia understood the significance of the gravy boat. Not a bland, random or opportunistic theft. Gravy boats were the beating heart of every Sunday roast, conjuring up laughter and reunions that went beyond just the household. Wider family members would sit round the table, friends, too. Rubbing salt into the wound heightened Vance's excitement. How ironic that he couldn't see that they were trophies to remind himself what a big man he was with defenceless women. Women he'd chosen *because* they were sweet and polite, helpful and kind, and who would never understand how one human being could be so cruel. Who would never understand, *why them?*

In that respect, they were lucky.

Julia had already faced a creature who looked like a man, walked like a man, and to all outward purposes behaved like a man, but whose skin covered something that was a long way from human.

Her sigh echoed in the empty room.

June's death had stirred up thirteen years of mud, none of it sweet-smelling, and dredged up heart-wrenching pain in its wake. For one thing, the night terrors returned with a vengeance. She'd see blood. Pools of blood. Arcing, splashing, spreading, staining. They were the last thing she saw before she fell asleep, the first thing she saw when she opened her eyes, and more than once, she'd been jolted awake by her own screams, her nightdress wringing with sweat.

The women in Vance's collection had at least been spared that. In comparison, their torture was short, and, painful as it was to admit, Julia's initial reaction, on coming round after the kidnap, was that she'd deserved this.

She had killed the creature that was a long way from human, and in thirteen years, she hadn't an ounce of regret. Indeed, if she was ever tempted, all she had to do was remember the last time she saw her mother. Cheekbones smashed, jaw broken, her body a pitiful testament to what boots can inflict on human flesh. She didn't say goodbye to her daughter, for the simple reason that she couldn't speak. All she could do was cough blood, while tears tricked down her misshapen face from eyes that were swollen tight shut. God help her, that image would be seared on Julia's retina for the rest of her life, and the same with her brother. Beaten so badly that last time that he would never walk straight again. Assuming he could walk at all.

But what of her stepfather's family? Leaving his body to rot in a pit where it would never be found was the right thing to do, as far as Julia was concerned. On the other hand, he was still somebody's son, somebody's brother. Didn't they deserve a grave to weep over?

Did they hell. To a man, they all knew what was happening. To a man, they turned a blind eye.

So, like Vance, she, too, had paved the way for his disappearance.

Perhaps they were not so different under the skin, after all.

CHAPTER 24

Collingwood stepped out of the solicitor's doorway and whistled the hansom cab forward. Justifying to the chief superintendent why he'd invested a sizeable sum of public money in having the driver wait round the corner for two hours would have been a bloody sight harder, had the trap not been sprung. Justifying to himself why he'd wasted two precious hours of Julia's life would have been damn near impossible, and one thing was sure. He would never tell a living soul that the relief, when Vance turned up at Julia's studio, left his legs weak.

She was still alive —

In what condition, he refused to imagine. In most cases of sexual assault, the victims are dead within a couple of hours. Jack the Ripper could testify to that. In light of the violence with which Vance ground Sam Whitmore's photograph into the rug, Collingwood initially wondered if he'd been so jealous of Julia's employer that he'd try to eliminate the opposition. He quickly dismissed that idea. That was not Vance's way. Cunning, crafty, avoiding confrontation at all costs, he staged the disappearances with astonishing precision. Remembering the items missing from the victim's homes — and how, in at least one instance, a bag had been packed to explain the woman's leaving — Collingwood duly stationed himself outside the studio, hansom at the ready. Vindication came in the Box Brownie camera that Vance came out swinging. Now, it was back to basic police work.

The ostentatiousness of Vance's phaeton took him by surprise. Bright yellow spokes weren't exactly camouflage, but, as the cab clopped behind at a respectable distance, he realised that hiding in plain sight was what this predator did best, and the Industrial Revolution provided the perfect disguise. New money likes nothing more than to flaunt its wealth. Flamboyance and show comes with the territory, and after a while, people stop noticing the details. In the public's eye, it's merely another grandiose gesture designed to rub noses in the gap between the haves and the have nots. Either consciously, or unconsciously, they stop caring.

'Drop me off here, then wait under those trees,' Collingwood told the driver, pointing a hundred yards ahead. 'Keep an ear open for my whistle, you won't miss it.'

The phaeton had turned off the road and was heading towards what looked like a dilapidated farmhouse in the middle of nowhere. To follow in a cab, especially one pulled by a distinctive piebald horse, would only spook him. Collingwood took off his jacket and his armoured derby hat and slung them on the seat. As much as he'd have valued the protection, speed was of the essence here, manoeuvrability more so.

'If I'm not back in an hour,' he added grimly, 'fetch the police and give them this.'

The driver nodded, took the proffered notebook, and, in an act that was presumably meant to reassure his passenger but had the opposite effect, crossed himself.

Creeping through the long grass and overgrown fruit bushes, Collingwood searched for trips and traps that would alert the occupant of the farmhouse. In truth, he suspected Vance was cocky enough in his own planning not to need additional security. All the same, it didn't hurt to check, but while he was zigzagging, weaving, ducking, slithering to ensure he wasn't spotted, the clock was ticking Julia's life away.

Complacency is what gets people killed.

Her voice echoed in his memory. Of all the people Collingwood had met, Julia McAllister was one of the least complacent, and he had a horrible feeling that they'd underestimated the number of Vance's victims. He'd got Charlie to trawl back two years, but Vance was what? Fifty? Fifty-five? The bastard had been doing this for years.

Finally, he reached the farmhouse. The front door was unlocked. Was that a trap? Collingwood eased it open. The hinges didn't groan, and that didn't set his mind at ease. Why, in a ramshackle place like this, would Vance keep the hinges greased? Because he was a perfectionist, of course. The house was a disguise. No one would think of looking inside a dump like this. There was nothing to rob, nothing to raid. It was too far off the beaten track for vagrants to want to doss in. And since he was the only one who used the door, he wouldn't want it grating on his nerves, and — thank you, thank you God — it was the same with the stairs. Perfect condition, despite their age. He could smell the beeswax from here.

Even over the stench of decomposition.

The grip on his truncheon tightened. No amount of police training could have prepared him for this. Prepared anyone…

Every room contained the remains of a woman, tied to a chair facing the open door, in varying stages of mummification and decay. There was no other furniture in the room, save another chair, where Vance clearly liked to sit, reminisce and admire his work.

The rooms were also clean of dust, the floors swept on a regular basis.

The bastard was proud of himself —

After the fifth room, Collingwood forced the anger out of his system. He had to be professional about this. He could not allow emotions to cloud his judgement, but even so. He'd rolled his eyes when the driver made the sign of the cross. Had offhandedly thanked the Lord just now, that his adversary was a stickler. Why not? When his little girl fell victim to such prolonged and hideous suffering, what little belief Collingwood had in God evaporated.

Now, every ounce of that conviction was reinforced.

If there was a God, He could not, in all conscience, stand by.

No divine entity would let this happen.

Julia, Julia, tell me you're all right —

His senses moved to high alert. If she was alive, he'd have expected to hear voices. The only sound was his own blood, pounding through his temples. Collingwood inched up the stairs. There was only one door in this house of horrors that was closed. A closed door meant only one thing.

Intimacy, while Vance tortured his victim.

Taking a deep breath, Collingwood rushed the door. Whatever he was expecting — whatever he'd feared — it was not to find Julia standing over Titus Vance's body.

CHAPTER 25

'Honestly, Inspector, if you wanted a crime scene photographer, you only had to ask.' Despite her quip, Julia's stomach wouldn't stop churning, her chemise stuck to her skin, and her teeth were chattering as Collingwood snatched her into his arms.

'Thank God.' His voice came down a long, black tunnel. 'Oh, thank God, thank God, you've no idea how worried I was.'

'If it's any consolation, I was a tad concerned myself.'

'I should have known a mass murderer was no match for my best crime scene photographer.' He was wiping the blood off her face with his handkerchief, and showering kisses on her head at the same time.

'Let me tell you a little bit about myself, Mr. Vance.'

Trussed like a chicken, Julia had fought her bonds, chafed her wrists, thought Jesus, Mary, Mother of God, there had to be another way — and hey presto, as the Great MMM would say, she suddenly saw it.

By binding his victims, Vance rendered them instantly submissive, never thinking to question his ability to tie knots or their will to survive. Time, she'd decided, to turn that belief on its head, and Julia had the whole cast to thank for her escape. Especially the Great MMM, who'd lifted the lid on how to pull off an illusion.

First, there was Buffalo Buck—

My mother always said, if you see an opportunity, son, take it.

And my mother said that when opportunity knocks, pretend to be out.

There was Dodger to thank, with his bogus falls. Avalon going limp. Hal, who fooled the audience into thinking he was setting the mood, when in reality he kept time for the acts. Ultimately, though, escape hinged on Lizzie's expertise. How to squeeze free of handcuffs and ropes, simply by clenching your fists next to each other, palms facing down.

'See? This creates a gap between the wrists,' she'd explained, demonstrating the technique. 'Gives me enough slack to shimmy free. Has to be palms together, elbows apart, though. Otherwise it doesn't work.'

Advice that Julia followed to the letter.

Rocking her chair so hard that the pins flew out of her hair, she put every ounce of energy into what Vance would assume was a suicide attempt.

Wait for me, Papa!'

Her epic struggle for breath was identical to the stunt Molly pulled when pretending to have a coughing fit on stage.

That's my arty choke.

He'd have no choice but to untie the ropes to stop her from suffocating, only this time, when he trussed her back up, her palms were together behind her back, elbows slightly apart.

By the time he returned, Julia was waiting with the~~the~~ lump of ~~the~~ timber he'd used to jam her chair ~~with~~, and when ~~he opened the bedroom door, Mrs. McAllister was waiting behind it.~~

~~When~~ he came round, ~~it was to find~~ *he* was the one trussed like a chicken. 'You'll pay for this, you little bitch!'

'I very much doubt it,' Julia said equably, 'Now let me tell you a little bit about myself, Mr. Vance.'

The Mild West wasn't so mild after all.

When I was six, my father died, leaving my mother with two small children and a choice between the workhouse or marriage to a domineering bully. Rather unfortunately, she chose the latter, and who knows? Was my stepfather always a monster? Or did having three vulnerable people under his thumb spike his viciousness? Well, I'm sure you know more about that stuff than I do. The point is, for years what that man did to my mother, my brother and me was unspeakable, but we put up with it for each other's sake.'

In her heart, she almost wished that some of the victims in this house had found blessed release from violence at home. Equally, she knew that Vance had chosen them for the simple reason that they did not...

'~~Now~~ I realise you're squirming with anticipation under that rope to find out what happened when it reached the point where I could stand it no longer, so I'll tell you. I lured my stepfather out of the house, shot him with his own revolver, six times, then rolled him into the grave I'd already dug.' Julia paused. She could almost hear the dust motes land in the silence of the farmhouse. 'I was fourteen at the time, and in the thirteen years since his body has stayed hidden, and will indeed remain so. You see my point, Mr. Vance? No? Then perhaps I should make it clear. Being tidy and precise is what makes for a good photographer. That, and attention to detail. For instance, those knots you keep trying to wriggle out of. I should tell you now, you're wasting your time there. I come from Cornwall, and Cornwall is all about the sea. Did you know there are over forty different types of sailors' knots?'

'You think you're clever, but when I get free, what I'll do to you for days — weeks! — will have you begging me to kill you.'

'Such an optimist! I do admire that, but sadly, Mr. Vance, that's not going to happen. When the police find you, there will only be the one wound on your head. This piece of wood you see — and believe me it will be the *very* last thing you see — will hit your skull in exactly the same place I knocked you out,' she tapped her own head, 'where the bone is the thinnest.'

The side of the skull is always the weakest.

'The police will have every sympathy for an anguished kidnap victim, especially one of their own, lashing out in her desperate effort to escape. With just the single wound, it's pretty obvious that this could not possibly be premeditated. Merely an act of desperation. The case won't go to trial, you'll end up in a pauper's grave, and as for the ropes, dear me, I had to tie you up, because I was terrified that you were simply stunned, and needed to restrain you. Now then, Mr. Vance.' Julia weighted the timber in her hand. 'You might want to close your eyes for this.'

~~But Collingwood could never know about her past. He was a detective inspector, and for premeditated murder, you hang.~~ Barely a few minutes passed, she was still shaking, before — of all people — John Collingwood burst into the house.

Thank God! I'd just broken free,when I heard Vance's footsteps on the stairs. I picked up the first thing ~~that came~~ to hand —' Collingwood had difficulty prising the lump of timber from her grasp, Julia's fist was clenched so tight. 'He *is* dead, isn't he?'

'Very.'

'I tied him up tight — I wasn't sure —'

'Julia, I promise you, that monster won't hurt you, or anyone else, again. This little piece of oak has saved the public purse an awful lot of money on a trial.' He rocked her tight. 'You're a heroine, Mrs. McAllister. A grade A, top-notch heroine, and I love you for it, although how the hell you broke free is beyond me.'

'Did you just say love, Mr. Collingwood?'

'Let's get you out of here.'

'Let's answer the question.'

'Let's not, now lean on me, and do as I say.'

'What —?'

'Julia.' There was an edge to his voice as one hand clamped over her eyes and the other round her waist. 'Trust me. Tuck up your skirts so you don't trip, put your arm round me, and for Christ's sake, just follow my lead.'

She was shaking harder than ever as he led her, blindfolded, along the landing, down the stairs and into the light. The stench told her what was so ghastly in there that he didn't want her to see it. The pallor of his skin told her there were several more victims inside, as Vance had bragged. The screech of his police whistle in the silence was sacrilege.

Neither of them had been so relieved to see a piebald horse in their lives, and if the driver wondered what had happened in there to the woman the bloodstained rozzer was holding up, the rozzer's glare cut short any curiosity.

'I won't have to give evidence in court, will I?'

Collingwood had locked the roof trap in the cab for privacy. Even if the driver could hear, though, negotiating delivery carts, buses, broughams, carriages, not to mention skittish horses, boys rolling hoops and an ever-increasing number of motor cars on the approach into Oakbourne kept him otherwise engaged.

'I ... I really don't want to talk about what happened —'

The grey worsted of the jacket that Collingwood had wrapped round her shoulders smelled of Hammam Bouquet gentleman's cologne. Until that point, Julia had assumed reassurance came only in a liquor bottle.

'You won't have to.'

All the evidence they needed lay inside that house, he said. There was no need to drag Julia's name into the investigation, and if she was worried about being seen, that was easy. Why *wouldn't* the police want their crime scene photographer on site?

Back at the studio, Collingwood insisted on coming in with her —

'I'm fine.'

'You're not.'

— and forcing industrial-strength coffee down her throat, along with a ham sandwich that she didn't want and could barely swallow, but which he was adamant would do her good.

'I'll run you a bath, while you eat.'

'There's no need.' Julia was sure the coffee was strong enough to strip paint off metal doors and fire a locomotive far more efficiently than coal. 'Go! Go! Wrap this case up —'

'It's wrapped up. Victims found. Perpetrator dead. Nothing there that can't wait half an hour.'

'The boy on the railway line, then. Follow up on —'

'Case closed there, as well.'

A Mr. and Mrs. Robson sheepishly admitted they'd been forced to tie their son to the bedpost from the age of twelve, which is when they were no longer able to contain his violence.

'Psychiatrists diagnosed the boy as "simple", whatever that may mean,' Collingwood said. 'But the parents felt it was heartless to have him committed to an asylum, when he was fine most of the time. Five days ago, he broke free. Not an entirely unusual occurrence, but he'd always come home when he was hungry. This time, being older, they thought he was having something of an adventure —'

'When all the time he was in the mortuary.'

'Theoretically, I should charge them with unlawful restraint, but Christ, they're about to bury their only child, who'd been a burden to them all their lives. I can't see how prison would punish them more than they're punishing themselves. So, take that bath. I'll still be here when you come out, and in the meantime, I'm going to find out where you keep that special single malt, and pour you half a pint of that.'

'Make it a pint and I'll save you the search.'

CHAPTER 26

Sinking into warm water softened with salts and scented with oil of gardenia, Julia's fears should have subsided. Instead, they had free rein.

Suppose Vance pulled the same trick she had, and was somehow still alive?

Suppose the cab driver told the press that Julia was a victim, and not there to record the scene?

Suppose the police *did* want photos after all?

Suppose, suppose, suppose…

Scrubbing her skin with a loofah, washing every trace of Vance away, Julia knew that the best way to stop her fears from tumbling was the age-old antidote to trauma.

'Before you raid my cupboards —'

Collingwood's eyebrow rose. 'Yes.'

'Take your bloodied clothes off, Inspector, that's an order, and join me, before this water cools down.'

He needed no second telling. His arousal was instant. She had never climaxed so long or so loud. Or felt so feral, so cleansed.

The second time, on the bed, was slower and tender. She wondered what the chief superintendent would make of it, if he discovered how dedicated his inspector was to taking the witness's statement, and how thorough he was in the detail.

'What did you find out about the cast?' she asked, sipping an eighteen-year-old single malt smoother than a silk chemise, and smoky enough to call out the fire brigade.

For the first time that day, Collingwood laughed. 'You do realise that I've been working a kidnap?'

'Did it stop you investigating murder? I thought not.'

Another way to balance out the fear, of course, was to find Annie Oaktree's killer.

Trouble is, I got no money, love, and look at me. Twenty-three's an old maid where I come from in the Valleys, and who'd take on a fairground tramp without a penny to 'er name? No, no, if I'm to start a new life with an 'usband and some nippers, it'll have be somewhere respectable. Suburbs, y'know. Pretend this never 'appened. Which means, see, if I'm to catch myself a solicitor or a bank clerk, I need more money than the rubbish pay this show puts out.

All she'd wanted was a normal family life, and with the show moving on tomorrow, now — more than ever — June Margaret Sullivan deserved justice. Now — more than ever — Julia wanted it for her. Without June, she would never have stepped into the role of Annie Oaktree and learned the tricks of escape, while Vance would have still lured her away.

'I'm not sure what we learned helps.' Collingwood stretched like a cat. 'From what I can gather, the only secret your Honky-Tonk friend is harbouring is shame at being a mine-owner's son.'

That made sense. The youngest son in a family of nine, his whole life had been mapped out for him. Initiative was supposed to have been erased at Eton, at the same time that his musical talents were being directed into predictably genteel channels. He might not be remotely close to inheriting the family empire, but there was kudos in having a son who was a concert pianist. But this is where the vicious circle begins. A large family with only rare (and formal) parental contact has varying impacts on the children. Some harden, some soften, some turn to drink, some turn to the lure of the green baize.

Jeremiah had thrown himself into his art, but artists are perceptive. He'd have compared the hardships of the miners with the fatness of his father's bank account, and there was nothing he could do to even up the balance. Or was there? Usually, boys run away to join the circus for adventure. Not Jeremiah. His motive for hooking up with the Mild West was anything but selfish. Suddenly, as Honky-Tonk Hal, he had a chance to offset the misery of factory life by taking their minds off their struggles with three hours of unadulterated silliness.

'That's not to say there isn't anything else in Mr. Liddell-Gough's background,' Collingwood made clear. 'This is a travelling show. Their sojourn in Oakbourne is short. We can only scratch at their secrets, which might, or might not, explain why there's no dirt on Dodger and Avalon.'

He had a reputation for being a bit of a chancer, but nothing more than that, while if his wife had any previous encounters with naphtha flares, they were not serious enough to roll out any fire hoses.

'Buck's an even darker horse.' Collingwood propped himself up on one elbow. 'I have the full resources of the police at my disposal, yet I can't find his real name, or even where he comes from. God knows what he's hiding there.'

Were there demons chasing him? Debtors? The law? Was it love he was running from, or heartbreak that he could never outrun? Whatever his hopes, dreams and fears, Buffalo Buck kept them firmly hidden beneath a white Stetson and a dazzling smile.

'Molly?' she asked.

'I think we have the answer to her cough.' Collingwood reached for his clothes and grinned. 'That throat spray of hers? Turns out to be a handy little cold remedy, small enough to slip inside a pocket, that she squirts far more often than prescribed.'

'Oh my God, is she ill?'

'Yes and no. Her lungs are damaged, on account of over-using it, which explains the coughing fits. But while the Burroughs Wellcome Company thoughtfully produced a spray to treat seasickness, hay fever, you name it, the main ingredient is cocaine.'

Far easier than injecting herself with the usual seven per cent solution, Julia supposed, and always conveniently at hand. At the same time, it suggested that *seven husbands, none of 'em her own* wasn't the perfect antidote to life on the road after all.

All for one and one for all?

Only on the surface.

Beneath the pasted smiles and bluster lay an abyss of loneliness — the one thing the cast couldn't pull together as a team. A hole so big that Molly couldn't fill it, no matter how many husbands she bedded, or how much cocaine she sprayed. An ache mirrored by Lizzie Pitt, with her whirlwind marriages and laudanum. A feat that even the Great MMM could not pull off.

Our illusionist's ace at making money vanish, not so hot when it comes to making it reappear.

Was it horses? Greyhounds? Cards? How much did he owe, Julia wondered? And who did he owe it to?

Slipping into her chemise while John buttoned up his trousers, she reflected on her detour on the way home from June's funeral. (Was it really only a few short hours ago?)

'Meess McAllister.' The Russian's smile was as fake as the banknotes that he passed. 'What a plessant surprise. Black suits you, too, if I may say so. Brings out the boldness in your eyes.'

'Do you know the one thing that my studio lacks, Mr. Kuznetsov?' Ignoring Malik, glaring in the background, Julia had dragged a chair across the warehouse floor, positioned it opposite the loan shark, tried not to think who might have died in this seat, and leaned her forearms on his desk. 'A back door. Well, no. More accurately, a back entrance, because a door would only lead onto a little plot of land that I don't own.'

'You vant me to lend you more money, when you haffen't repaid a fraction of the last loan.'

'This is the quote from a builder, and this is the contract for the parcel of land — more a garden really — which only requires a signature and the transfer of funds.'

One eyebrow rose lazily. 'This is lot of money, Meess McAllister. A sum, I am sorry to say, that I haff no intention of handing over.'

'According to certain sources, your parents were refugees from Sebastopol. Others put your origins anywhere from Moscow to Odessa to Siberia, coming to England ten, twenty, even forty years ago, if your parents escaped the Crimea.' Julia smiled. 'Which, of course, they didn't.'

A muscle twitched in the moneylender's cheek. 'Iff you haff a point, Meess McAllister, I suggest you reach it quickly.'

'My pleasure, Mr. Kuznetsov.' She paused. 'Kuznetsov. Interesting name, that. I heard it translates as smith, and guess what else I heard? That it's as common a name in the Ukraine as it is here.' She lowered her voice to a whisper. 'And every bit as false.'

'A name is a name. What does it matter?'

'Does being born in Manchester matter?'

Kuznetsov dismissed Malik with a nod that could cut metal, but Julia hadn't given him a chance to respond. She merely drew attention to her connection with the Boot Street police, where she'd learned (she didn't mention that it was through a certain gruff detective sergeant) that not only was this Russian thing an act, but that Kuznetsov was actually a paid informer.

'If word got out, you'd literally be skinned alive by your own people,' she added sweetly. 'And before you have any ideas of my having a nasty accident, a document is lodged at the solicitor's — not the one on this deed, so don't bother following that up — with instructions that, in the event of my death, the story goes straight to the *Chronicle*.'

His dark eyes stared at her for what seemed like eternity. 'Let me see if I have this right, Mees — Meeses. McAllister. You have no intention of repaying me. Neither the debt you borrowed, nor the interest that you owe. Instead, you want *me* to give *you* money?'

Julia stood up and shook her skirts. 'Always a pleasure doing business with you, Mr. Kuznetsov.'

As a result of that meeting, the builder would start knocking holes in the back wall first light tomorrow — because she also knew a thing or two about loneliness. Was only too keenly aware how empty the house would be without Lizzie wrapping her left leg over her right shoulder in the hallway, or Molly asking: 'Knock knock.' 'Who's there?' 'Handsome.' 'Handsome who?' 'Handsome of that whisky over, willya?'

At the beginning, Julia took in her lodgers for the money, happy that they'd only be around for a few days. That way, she couldn't get involved in their lives, even if she'd wanted. At least, not until a girl she'd taken under her own roof was murdered, leaving her no choice, and now, not only was a cold-blooded killer likely to walk free, but that killer was likely someone Annie Oaktree worked with and, if only from a professional standpoint, would have trusted.

Julia's eyes stung as she reached for her stockings.

She'd never forget the riverboat gambler, sawing the lady in half, with Buck asking 'How did you do that?' 'Ah, well, it's the magician's secret. If I told you, I'd have to kill you.' 'In that case, don't tell me, tell my wife.'

Hal up a ladder, unfurling the backdrop of trees. Dodger running in. Pointing to the scenery. 'Quick! We're surrounded by cops(e).' A whistle blows off stage. The riverboat gambler and his saloon girl run in from the other side. Dodger signals *not that way* with his hands. 'Peeler,' he yells. 'Peel 'er?' The gambler shrugs. 'I don't see how that can help, but let's find out.' With one tug, he rips off Avalon's costume down to her spangled bodysuit, to stomping applause from the crowd.

Julia wiped her eyes.

Nothing wrong with that girl's brain —

She heard Annie's voice as if it was right behind her — and for pity's sake! How could she have missed it? In an instant, Julia was throwing off her street clothes and climbing into the cowgirl's buckskin skirt. Dear God, the answer had been staring her in the face all along!

'The trick is to show teeth,' Avalon had said, the first time Julia was set to go on stage. 'That way, the audience won't see the screwed up concentration in your eyes. They won't see your stage fright. All they'll see is your dazzling smile, where smile equals confidence, confidence means they're getting a good show, good show equals value for money, which equals more bums on seats for us tomorrow.

Nothing wrong with that girl's brain —

Annie Oaktree was right. There wasn't a damn thing wrong with that girl's brain.

Julia grabbed the soft brown hat and pulled it low over her eyes. It was another illusion.

CHAPTER 27

Knowing who killed Annie Oaktree was one thing.

Proving it was quite another.

'Look,' Collingwood said, when she told him. 'This has been a rough day, to say the least. You've gone through hell and back, and frankly, I don't know how you're still in one piece, you're just incredible.'

'Oh, come on, John, you know I'm better than that.'

A muscle twitched at the side of his mouth as he placed both hands on her shoulders. 'My point, Modest McAllister, is that, just like at the end of a theatrical performance, you're running on adrenaline. Except instead of wanting more encores, more applause, you're wanting justice.'

'Of course I do! Not only for Annie, but for all the victims at that farmhouse.'

'And you've got it. You've got justice, Julia, in spades.' He leaned in. 'Single-handedly you stopped a monster in his tracks, and saved God knows how many future victims' lives, including your own.'

'Hardly single-handed. You were outside.'

'You had no way of knowing that, which is why you need to slow down, take a step back, and draw a bit of perspective.' With Vance, he pointed out, the evidence was cut and dried, and while yes, it was tempting to rush in and strike while the iron — or in this case, conviction — was hot, deduction wasn't enough. 'To make this case stick, we need either proof or a confession —'

She'd thought she was on her own...

She firmly believed Vance, when he said no one would rescue her…

Truly thought no one was coming…

'How does both sound?' She buttoned up Annie Oaktree's boots for the very last time, and told him — in a voice that belied the churning inside — how, and where, to collect the evidence. 'While you're doing that, Little Miss Poor Shot will be clomping round the stage on a hobby horse, firing guns that read "*Bang!*", and keeping an eye on our killer.'

'Hell, no. If there's even a slim chance of danger, I'm not letting you stand in the firing line, and in any case, you're not an automaton, Julia. You need to eat, nap, let your mind settle. There's nothing so urgent that it can't wait until after the show, or even tomorrow.'

That, though, was where the detective inspector was wrong.

Unless she missed her guess, Annie Oaktree's killer intended to claim another victim tonight.

Hailing a cab, Collingwood wished to God he could knock some sense into Julia McAllister's pig-headed skull.

'You don't mind if I change before I go off, running errands?' he'd quipped.

The blood on his grey worsted had dried to brown stains, and it would take a bucket of bleach to get his shirt back to its original white. But the bee in her cowgirl bonnet would not be evicted.

'I don't give a damn what you do,' she'd snapped, 'providing you collect the evidence, and don't ever again tell *me* what to do. I'll eat when I want, sleep when I want, and if I want to put my head above the bloody parapet, then I will bloody well do it.'

'Not when it's police business, you won't.' Jesus Christ, the woman was infuriating. 'I can't afford civilians buggering up a case on the off-chance that their wildcat theory pans out, and I'm damned if I'm pulling officers away from the farmhouse, simply because you want to play the heroine. In fact —' he was so damned angry with her for even contemplating such a move — 'I've half a mind to lock you up for impeding a police investigation.'

'Do it. See how throwing me in jail helps your stupid pride, when you watch the show pack up and take a killer with it.'

As the cab turned off the London road, rattling over the cobbles past half-timbered Tudor houses, Collingwood buried his head in his hands. Julia had gone through the worst conceivable experience. Duped, kidnapped, terrified to the very limits of human endurance — then, Christ, if that wasn't enough, she'd broken free using skills she'd learned on stage before being forced to kill the beast who'd captured her. And what does he do? He barks and shouts, bosses her about, then throws that same courage and resilience back in her face. He groaned.

'All right, guv?' the cabbie asked through the open window in the roof.

'Fine, thanks.'

Collingwood waved a thumbs up at the driver, and promoted himself to Detective Grade A Bastard.

He'd wanted to tell her that he'd been terrified beyond belief today. That he only wanted to protect her —

'Here we go, guv. Yer said yer wanted me to wait?'

The professional in John Collingwood stopped self-pity in its tracks. He glanced at the building. Took a deep breath. 'I do, and like I said earlier, time is of the essence, my friend. While

I'm inside, I'd be obliged if you'd turn the cab around. We need to return with the same haste.'

He blew out his cheeks. The tableaux in that house of horrors would haunt him for the rest of his life. Each poor woman positioned to face an open door, so Vance could gloat every time he passed. The chairs, the only other furniture in the room, where he could reminisce and no doubt pleasure himself, because death bestowed the ultimate control. In Collingwood's experience, such killers turned out to be unloved, abused, molested children, who projected their anger and resentment on a proxy. Of course, not all unloved, abused, molested kids grew into monsters. Far from it. But Titus Vance mistook kindness for weakness, saw generosity as a flaw, and resented the sweetness and light in his victims to such an extent that he was compelled to steal it. What stopped him from stealing any more was down to one woman, and one woman only.

Collingwood had nearly let her down once today.

He would not do it twice.

CHAPTER 28

'Everything all right, old thing?'

'What happened?'

'That rozzer really had us worried, when he knocked.'

Julia held up her hands. 'I'm fine, honestly.'

The cast had no idea that she'd been abducted. The police were keeping the story from the press until the morning, partly to avoid panic, but mainly to avoid ghouls rushing to the farmhouse to gawp as the bodies were brought out, one by one. The families deserved to be told first, Collingwood had argued, that they might come to terms with knowing they were not abandoned, but tricked in the most callous, wicked way. Julia understood. Processing this sea change of emotions would take time, but more importantly it would take privacy. Best to make light of it, play it down, and thank everyone for their concern.

'We missed you, Snaps, and that's a fact.'

'Ah, but this young lady —' Buck wrapped an affectionate arm around his saloon girl's shoulders. 'Once again, congratulations, Avalon. You saved the day.'

'Pure genius, old girl.'

'The audience had seen the posters,' the Great MMM explained. 'They wanted Annie Oaktree, and they wouldn't be denied. They began to stamp their feet. *An–nie! An–nie!* So what did Avalon do? Ran on stage in a green pioneer woman's frock. *Did someone call for Annie Planetree?* she asked. I said, *but darling, you're not plain. In that case*, she said, swishing her skirts like they do in the can-can, *make it a lime tree.*'

Julia tried to laugh, but the lump in her throat wouldn't let her.

Oh, Avalon…

'Right, then.' The showman snapped his fingers. 'Time for Texas Jack to walk on water. Sure you're ready, Julia?'

'Positive.'

Come what may, she would see this through.

Which is how she came to be standing, five hours later, in a sea of cold chips and crumpled flyers, empty lemonade bottles and trampled jellied eels, her head pounding with Hal's honky-tonk rendition of *Oh Susannah, don't you cry for me, I'm off to Wolver'ampton with me banjo on my knee*.

When she first stepped in as Annie Oaktree, Julia assumed that the perfectionism of rehearsals and the importance of the timing was designed to conjure up excitement in the crowd. In fact, it was the opposite way round. Enthusiasm is contagious. Absolutely. But it was generated here, by the cast themselves, who conveyed that passion to the audience. Passion, not timing, was the foundation stone of the show. Timing was just the grease that kept it turning.

'Our finale needs tweaking.' Buck was taking the cast through the usual post-mortem analysis. 'I think we should end with Diamond Jim and the Hot Cross Kid's exchange in the saloon. Do you remember how it goes?'

The two men nodded.

'Good. Then can you run through it now, please?'

Dodger was still dressed as Marshal Kwyatt Burp, but it was close enough, and luckily the backdrop was still the saloon. Shooting a broad wink at his wife, he swaggered forward. 'Excuse me, mate. I think I'm a moth.'

The card sharp looked up from flipping the deck in his hands. 'I can't help you there, my friend. You need to see a psychiatrist.'

'I do see a psychiatrist.'

'So why are you telling me?'

'Yer light was on.'

'Bravo!' Buck clapped his hands high above his head. 'We'll finish with that in Oxford tomorrow, but right now, it's time to give June Margaret Sullivan the long overdue send-off that she deserves.'

'Wait.' Julia's knees were shaking harder than at any time in her life. 'All of you, I have something...'

What would the Welsh girl think? Sweet Lord, it wasn't just her wake that Julia was about to ruin, but the future of the whole wretched show. She swallowed. With luck — and God knows there wasn't much of that around — June Margaret Sullivan would realise that the best send-off she could have was her killer being brought to justice.

'I have something to tell you.'

I see you've met Avalon, Buck said at the beginning. *I honestly couldn't imagine this show without her.*

From fetching Molly's cough remedy to looking for her husband's tie pin, nothing was too much trouble, but that's not what made her the lynchpin of the Mild West. She was pretty, enthusiastic, a natural improviser, and her magnetic presence stole every show. Yes, she seemed absent-minded at times. The misplaced fan. The wrong address. But when you're moving from town to town, never sleeping in the same room for more than a few nights, who wouldn't be confused? The incident with the war bonnet, though, had set Julia thinking. Hal whooping with delight when it turned up after mysteriously disappearing, ostensibly because Annie had asked Avalon to take it to Julia's studio. Those memory lapses had distracted Julia from following up, but sleight of hand is what the show hinged on.

Annie Oaktree and Buck were stealing as they went along, but Annie was holding out on him. At least, that was Julia's feeling when she searched through June's belongings, and, she reasoned, either Buck killed her because he'd been betrayed, or he (or someone else) wanted something that June Margaret Sullivan had hidden. If so, could she have secreted it in the war bonnet that she was so careful not to be seen trawling over to her lodgings herself? Possibly, except the only thing Julia could find when she searched was eagle feathers and beads.

'She's like a sister to me,' Annie had said of Avalon, 'and I worry about 'er.'

'She does seem a little absent-minded,' Julia pointed out.

'Nothing wrong with that girl's brain, pet.'

Oh, really? Seeing mirrors where there were none? Imagining paintings on the wrong wall? How about almost burning the tent down?

'Suppose Avalon's been doing things, horrible things, that she can't remember?' Julia had asked Collingwood.

'As wild theories go,' he'd replied, 'that one should be released on the Serengeti without delay.'

As it happened, Detective Inspector Collingwood was right.

'It's about Avalon,' she said.

Seven heads turned in perfect unison.

'Oh, no, what did I do this time? I counted out the takings. Padlocked them away. I checked the flares. Lizzie came with me —'

Dodger's blue eyes twinkled. Dimples pitted his cheeks. 'Ah, but did yer remember to feed yer night mares, sweetheart?'

'Avalon didn't need to feed them,' Julia said. 'You did.'

'Yer what, Snaps?'

'Everyone thinks there's something wrong with Avalon's brain.' You could hear a pin drop. 'Everyone, that is, except Annie Oaktree, and because she rumbled you, you strangled her, then tried to pretend she'd hanged herself.'

'Bollocks.' Dodger dismissed the idea with a chuckle. 'I love my wife. Everybody knows how I feel about her, ain't that right, darlin'?'

'Absolutely.' Avalon's face, though, was white. 'Me and Dodge are like this.' She held up two crossed fingers.

'I wish I was wrong, Avalon, I really do, but all this time, he's been conning you into believing you were going insane.'

'What the hell's the matter with you?' Dodger snapped. 'Jealous, are yer, that me an Av's got something precious, while you've got a cold and empty bed at night? Come on, sweetheart. I'm not standing 'ere while some starstruck cow throws accusations in me face —'

'Actually, Mr. Wright, that is exactly what you'll do.' Collingwood stepped out from behind the backdrop. 'And for the record, that starstruck cow happens to be a police crime scene photographer, and I would ask you to show some respect.'

Dodger flashed his Jack-the-lad grin. 'Apologies, Inspector. It's been a bit emotional, one way or another, what with Junie dying, now us moving on. Me temper gets the better of me at times.' He turned to Julia. 'Sorry, Snaps. I know you're under the cosh, too, but you gotta understand. Me and Avalon. We're soulmates, ain't we, sweetheart? Remember that time in West—'

'How do you mean, conned me into thinking I was going insane?'

Julia took Avalon's hands in hers. 'That first time I met you, and you thought you'd lost your fan?'

Avalon nodded.

'It didn't occur to me that someone moved it on purpose, nor those other silly things, but the war bonnet Annie asked you to fetch over? Who told you that she wanted it? Who told you you'd be staying at Vine Cottage?'

'Loada balls! Don't listen, love, it's —'

'Stay where you are, please, sir.' Dodge's shoulder was restrained by a hand that was missing a couple of fingers. 'Carry on, miss.' Behind him, Kincaid nodded his encouragement.

Julia stared into Avalon's big, blue, troubled eyes. 'How often has your husband ever forgotten his tie pin? At the very moment you're seeing paintings on the wall where mirrors ought to hang? And then — when we all traipse upstairs together — they're suddenly in their rightful place, proving your mental frailty, rather conveniently, in front of a witness?'

'Are you saying Dodger staged the switch?'

'As impressive as it sounds —' the Great MMM stepped in — 'it's difficult to see how he could have pulled off a stunt like that. Even I couldn't have done it.'

'But you do,' Julia said. 'You pull off tricks like that ten times a day.'

'With an assistant.'

'Oi, nothing to do with me!' Lizzie exclaimed. 'I've never even been to the White Lion!'

'Me, neither,' said Molly.

'Nor I.' Hal looked worried.

'How about him, though?' Collingwood beckoned forward a youth with ginger hair and freckles.

'I know you.' Avalon's face froze. 'You're the landlord's son.'

'Guess who gave him tuppence to switch the pictures and the mirrors round the second you left with the tie pin, then switch them back again? Right, lad?'

'Hundred per cent, Mr. Collingwood, sir.'

The inspector turned to Dodger. 'Miss Sullivan realised what you were doing. She confronted you, no doubt asking you to stop or she'd tell your wife, and you killed her.'

'I bloody well did not!'

'So if we take your fingerprints, they won't match those on Miss Sullivan's neck?' Kincaid asked cheerfully.

'All right, all right, I killed her, but I didn't mean to, I swear.'

'Heat-of-the-moment?' Kincaid said.

'Exactly.'

'Then you panicked, and made it look like suicide?'

'She was dead … an' … an' … well, she'd always talked about leaving. Junie, bless her, didn't have no family, I thought, where's the harm? The rope was by the bridge. I picked it up without thinking. I'm … I'm really sorry, Inspector. I should 'ave come forward, but I was scared no one'd believe me, and I didn't want to bring bad publicity on Buck.'

'What I don't understand, Sergeant,' Collingwood said, and Julia decided he and Charlie had learned a great deal about the theatre since the Mild West rode into town, 'is if Mr. Wright says it was an accident, how come his hands were clamped round Miss Sullivan's throat for longer than we've been talking here, in order to force the breath out of her lungs?'

'Perhaps he forgot to take them away, sir?'

'Perfectly possible, Sergeant. Though from what I can gather, strangulation is exceptionally tiring, since those wretched victims will try to fight off their attacker — which reminds me. Would you mind rolling up your trouser leg, Mr. Wright? Oh dear, those are some painful-looking bruises on your shins.'

'Then there's the plank, Inspector,' Kincaid said. 'Our Mr. Wright decides to have an assignation, shall we call it, with a young female colleague under a bridge. I understand that, but why did he take a plank with him?'

'Oi!' Dodger wagged his finger. 'There was nothing mucky about it, if you don't mind. I bin faithful to my wife from the day we met, I simply arranged to meet with Junie for a chat, and I certainly didn't take no bloody plank.'

'No?' Kincaid shrugged. 'Then who strapped her to a board, and left her lying like a lump of meat for six, seven, maybe as long as eight hours?'

'Our belief is that you killed Miss Sullivan here, inside this tent.' Collingwood ignored the horrified gasps around him. 'You tied her to one of the bench seats using one of the Hot Cross Kid's lassos, and, close to dawn before anyone was abroad, you wheeled her to the bridge and winched her up using that very same length of rope.' He paused. 'Sergeant Kincaid, would you mind?'

'Not at all, sir. Roger Stanley Wright, you are under arrest for the murder of June Margaret Sullivan —'

'And the attempted murder of your wife,' Julia cut in.

'Are you raving bonkers?' Dodger struggled, but Charlie was used to subduing criminals bigger and stronger than him. 'I admit I was messing about, trying to wind Avalon up, and I see, now, that playing practical jokes and teasing 'er about 'er memory was in poor taste, but I didn't mean no harm. As for Junie, it was an accident, I swear, and you can't prove none of that plank stuff. My brief'll get me off before the case is read in court —'

'I wouldn't bank on that,' Julia said. 'The forensic argument is pretty strong, but add on proof of attempted murder, and I think you'll experience for yourself what hemp feels like, wrapped around your neck. I presume you found the other piece of evidence, Inspector?'

'Apart from the landlord's son, you mean? The unwitting accomplice to proving Mrs. Wright was going mad?' Collingwood pulled a bulging handkerchief out of his pocket, and opened it in the palm of his hand. 'I did.'

Seven heads leaned forward to inspect the contents.

'Five bottles of laudanum, each bought from a different pharmacy by a gentleman claiming his dear wife had trouble sleeping after giving birth. A gentleman, funnily enough, with blue eyes, an East End accent, and dimples in his cheek when he smiled.'

'I can explain —'

'Allow me,' Julia said, explaining to her spellbound audience that Dodger's original intention was to have Avalon committed. Why else go to all that trouble to undermine her mental state? 'The plan was sound enough, until he saw how deeply Avalon was affected by thinking she'd set the fire, when of course it was him. Suddenly Dodger realised there was a quicker, and more permanent, way to be rid of his wife.'

Knowing how crucial timing was to any performance, and with the show packing up tomorrow, what better opportunity than tonight? He would sob. He would howl. He would testify how the fire was the last straw — everybody heard how she couldn't forgive herself, people could have died! Well aware that her mind was getting worse, after the fun and freedom of these past few years, life in an institution was unthinkable for a free spirit like hers.

'Avalon's suicide would be typical of her selfless behaviour,' Julia said. 'The people of Oxford were depending on Buffalo Buck! The show must go on! With her mental state, she was only holding them back, they were better off without her…'

Exploiting her finest qualities was bad enough. What odds that, in the morning, after finding her amid the empty bottles of laudanum, he'd rush off to make lavish funeral arrangements and order a magnificent headstone.

'By which I mean a few drinks in the King's Head, before booking a pauper's grave like little Georgie and his mother.'

Even at the end, Dodger was cheap.

CHAPTER 29

Some wee short hour ayont the twal',
  which rais'd us baith,
  I took the way that pleas'd mysel',
  and sae did Death.

Slumped on the floor of her darkroom — her sanctuary — Julia cradled a glass of cognac in her hands, and reflected on the words of Robert Burns. The moods of Death were indeed fickle. Did he roam the ether, selecting his targets with care — or with malice? Suppose they were random, because he was just so damned busy? Why some and not others, though? Why Georgie? Why his mother? Why the women at the farmhouse?

Why not Julia?

'*Why?*'

Avalon's scream still pierced her ears. Why, she'd wailed, did he hate her so much? What had she done, to make him despise her so badly?

'I loved you,' she howled, as he was taken away. 'I'd have done anything for you —'

And there, Julia thought, was the problem. Avalon didn't care that her husband was lazy or a scrounger, who didn't take care of any of the things he borrowed, or didn't pay his dues as he went along. She was perfectly content to clean up after him, whether the mess was physical or of a personal nature, because making people happy was her purpose in life. She'd paid back the sixpence that he'd borrowed from Julia, not out of duty, fear, or some misplaced compulsion to please him. She did it because she loved him, warts and all, and for a while that was enough for Dodger, too. He needed someone by his side, who would make him look good and shine, on stage and off, and that's where it all fell apart. As Avalon became more and more involved in the running of the show, improvising, developing and improving the acts, Dodger failed to see how brightly her influence reflected on him. Consumed by jealousy and resentment, he only saw her input as stealing his thunder. In his eyes, she'd risen too far above her station, undermining his showmanship and his art, dragging him down, when *he* should have been the star of the show.

Buck might be blinded by that wide-eyed puppy act, but not Dodger. Oh, no. He saw right through her little game. When he first realised she was deliberately sucking the limelight from him, he only planned for her to be out of the way long enough for a new girl to take over. New girls rarely stayed long. Life on the road was too gruelling. After a few months in an asylum, he reasoned that the doctors would see how they'd managed to cure Avalon, she'd be free, and that would be that.

Until that Welsh bitch told him she knew what he was up to. She'd tell Buck, she'd tell Avalon, she'd tell the whole bloody crew, she said, if Dodger didn't pack it in, right there and then. Well, Julia thought, he packed it in all right. Right there and then, he put paid to her loose tongue, probably even thought himself clever, making it look like she'd hanged herself.

The quarter moon shifted slowly across the darkroom window. An owl hooted in the elm tree beyond.

'Oh, Dodger, if you could only see the irony.'

Of all the cast, he had the least talent. The least input. The least diligence. Right from the start, he'd proved workshy. *Hey, Honky-Tonk! Do us a favour and get your lardy arse over here, will ya?* Avalon's mother saw through the act. *Cocky little sod, idle little bugger, proper little scrounger*, she'd say within earshot, which Avalon dismissed as *water off a gander's back. Says Ma's jealous, because she's never known a day of freedom in her life.* Avalon was in love. She didn't see his seething resentment. The fact that he — the scene-stealer, the star! — should have to actually work for his living. The only star Dodger had was Marshal Kywatt Burp's badge.

Annie warned Julia *when you meet him, lovey, you'll see how Roger Wright got his nickname*, which Julia took to mean his cheeky grin and cocky swagger. If she'd listened to Annie, followed up on her words, she'd have realised those were the classic traits of a conman.

'Bereavement would have been far better than betrayal,' Hal confided to Julia, as Buck consoled a distraught Avalon.

'Agreed,' Julia replied, 'but with you, and the rest of her showbusiness family, to support her, I'm confident that she'll come through stronger than ever.'

'This might sound callous to someone not used to our life,' Molly said, 'but to abandon the wake would be to disrespect the dead. You're very welcome to join us.'

'If it's a problem, just think of it as just another show,' added the riverboat gambler.

Julia appreciated the offer more than the cast would know. It was their way of saying that she was part of the family, and it had been a bloody long time since she'd been part of anybody's family. The price for loving had proved too high to pay.

I took the way that pleas'd mysel',
and sae did Death.

Wherever Julia walked, the Reaper's sickle cast a shadow. She'd had enough of Death today.

Warming the cognac in her hands, Julia had no way of knowing whether Buck and Annie were complicit in any of the crimes she'd originally suspected, but she had a feeling those two weren't partners in any sense of the word. Also, whatever demons drove the debonair showman to take his Mild West Show around the country, Julia wouldn't mind betting that that same determination would come into play when taking care of Avalon. Would his admiration turn to love? Too soon to tell. Julia, though, could only hope.

She sipped the cognac, poured another glass.

Ah, yes.

Love…

'About what I said earlier…'

Collingwood had insisted walking Julia home. That wasn't the time to tell him that she'd swapped his stupid police whistle for her Bulldog revolver, and in any case, having a strong arm to lean on came in useful from time to time. Tonight being one of those times.

'… at the farmhouse…'

Did he think she'd forget?

You're a heroine, Mrs. McAllister. A grade A, top-notch heroine, and I love you for it —

'What we have, you and I —'

'What we have, John, is a friendship. Don't spoil it.'

At the gate of the Common, he'd pulled up short, pressing his lips hard on hers. 'This is more than friendship, Julia, and you know it.'

'Is it?' What she wouldn't give to surrender herself to his care, fall asleep in his arms, be cossetted, nurtured, and cherished. 'We're friends with a delightful common interest, but this is not a relationship —'

'If it isn't, I don't know what the hell is.'

'Then let me be blunt.' She pulled away and stepped back. 'You and I do not have a future together.'

She felt for him. Truly. He was broken, bereaved, adrift every bit as much as she was herself, and what she wouldn't give to have him surrender himself to her care, fall asleep in her arms, be cossetted, nurtured, and cherished by her. But a relationship worth its salt hinges on honesty and trust. Sooner or later — make no mistake — her guard would drop. Yes, he'd given his word not to probe into her past, but he'd taken an oath to lay down his life for the law and his country. Regardless of circumstances, he would be duty-bound to arrest her.

And for premeditated murder, you hang.

Whichever way she looked at it, Julia was on her own. But with her debts paid off and 'Sam Whitmore' sighted by her customers, perhaps that was no longer such a bad thing.

A NOTE TO THE READER

Well, Reader —

If you enjoyed *Dead Drop*, I'd very much value your review on **Amazon** and **Goodreads**. And to find out more about what I'm working on next, follow me on **Facebook (Marilyn Todd – Crime Writer)** and **Twitter (@marilyntodd12)**.

Marilyn Todd.

www.marilyntodd.com

Sapere Books is an exciting new publisher of brilliant fiction and popular history.

To find out more about our latest releases and our monthly bargain books visit our website: **saperebooks.com**

Printed in Great Britain
by Amazon